Seth crossed his arms over his chest. "Are you mad at me about something?"

Alana studied his face for a moment before she said, "I suppose I am."

"What?"

"Are you serious?"

He nodded. "Obviously."

Crossing her arms over her chest, she said, "You died then you haunted me." She nodded toward the house. "Then you brought all this with you."

"Ah." She still maintained that feistiness he enjoyed. Seth grinned. "Yeah, sorry about all that."

Alana frowned. "You're not sorry in the least."

"Nope."

"Then why say that you are?"

"I don't know. To see you get fired up?"

She inhaled deeply through her nostrils. "I would've thought that death would've had more of an effect on you, Seth." Alana pushed away from the rock and walked toward the house.

"What do you mean by that?" He walked after her. "And wouldn't you rather death didn't change me?"

Alana stopped so quickly that he nearly walked into her. Face red with anger she pointed a finger at his chest and said, "You needed some adjustments!"

Something about the fire in her eyes and the liquid heat of her tone set off his anger as well. Hell yeah, he needed some adjustments and knew right where to start. Before she knew what hit her, Seth pulled her into his arms.

And made his first adjustment.

What They're Saying…

"The Victorian Lure grabs you right away and doesn't let go until the very last page!... Ms. Purington weaves the story well and leaves the reader hungry for more! I highly recommend this book if you love a great romance or you love a great paranormal...even more so if you love a great paranormal romance!" ~Cathy McElhaney

"I literally could not put this book down. Every twist and turn left me wanting to know more, read more. What starts out as a fictional ghost story, transcends into a truly believable story of love and its ability to weather any storm. The Victorian Lure has been one of the most fulfilling, moving books that I have ever had the pleasure of reading. With an ending I never could have imagined, Sky Purington has proven "Nothing is ever as it appears to be" ~S Siferd- Night Owl Reviews

WONDERFUL story! I read this because I'd read The Victorian Lure and really enjoyed it. In fact, I'll be re-reading this one. It's that sort of book. Brain twister. But I love that. It's extremely sensual and intense. If you're into a dark vs. light sort of read, this is a winner! The Georgian Embrace ~ T.S. Low

The Tudor Revival

Calum's Curse: Ultima Bellum

By

Sky Purington

PREVIOUS RELEASES INCLUDE...

~The MacLomain Series~

The King's Druidess (MacLomain Series- Prelude)
Fate's Monolith (MacLomain Series- Book 1)
Destiny's Denial (MacLomain Series- Book 2)
Sylvan Mist (MacLomain Series- Book 3)

The MacLomain Series Boxed Set

~The MacLomain Series- Early Years~

Highland Defiance. Available Autumn of 2012.

~Forsaken Brethren Series~

Darkest Memory.
Heart of Vesuvius

~Calum's Curse Trilogy~

The Victorian Lure (Calum's Curse: Ardetha Vampyre)
The Georgian Embrace (Calum's Curse: Acerbus Lycan)
The Tudor Revival (Calum's Curse: Ultima Bellum)

This book is dedicated to the memory of my father. I love you, Dad. May we meet again someday.

This is a work of fiction. Names, characters, places, and incidents either are the product of the author's imagination or are used fictitiously, and any resemblance to actual persons living or dead, business establishments, events, or locales, is entirely coincidental.

The Tudor Revival (Calum's Curse: Ultima Bellum)

COPYRIGHT © 2012 by Sky Purington

All rights reserved. No part of this book may be used or reproduced in any manner whatsoever without written permission of the author except in the case of brief quotations embodied in critical articles or reviews.

Cover Art by Tamra Westberry

Published in the United States of America

CHAPTER ONE

THE QUARRIES, VERMONT

"You like to live on the edge." Alana's amber eyes twinkled. "Yet I see a parachute attached to your back."

Eyes glued to her lovely face, Seth nodded. "Yep."

"But didn't you say you had a death wish?"

Wrapping one arm around her waist, he pulled her close until their lips were within inches. Her cinnamon hot breath mingled with his. "Nope. I clearly said it couldn't touch me. Screw death."

Light gold flared to life in her eyes, nearly burning away the molten amber. "Same thing, eh?"

With a slow shake of his head, he released her.

"Live, love, then die." With a wink and chuckle he turned, ran and dove straight off the cliff.

Za-woosh. Air rushed by his face. Cheeks froze. Eyes bulged. Lips thinned. *Thump. Thump*. His heart beat out of control. Adrenalin blasted through his veins. Twirling, moving at an increased rate of speed, he watched the endless cliff walls zoom past.

"Where is it?"

Seth grinned. She'd caught up with him. "Where's what?"

Though they screamed, the rush of air made their words sound far away. Absolutely shining with intensity, a smile lit her face. "The end."

"Who cares?" he responded, spinning mid-air, alive in the rush, the pure adrenaline that he didn't want to end. It'd come soon enough. Always did.

They had fifteen seconds left to deploy their parachutes.

Just enough time.

He again grabbed her around the waist, pulled her close and yelled, "No such thing as the end."

"Oh…" Her voice sounded husky and eager despite the blistering air rushing past them, despite the echoing scream of wind zipping by their ears. "I think you're wrong."

Ten seconds.

"Without doubt."

"You tempt death." She seemed to whisper.

Five seconds.

"Bet your ass!" He winked and released her.

Alana deployed her parachute and her body snapped then floated up.

Grinning, he knew he had a few daring seconds left.

Three.

Two.

One.

Though reluctant to let go of the thrill, he pulled the handle to release his shoot. *Click. Click. Click.* Huh? He yanked again. Nothing. *Sonofabitch.* Seth looked up, then down, and knew that he was out of time. Only one chance left. No worries. With a snap of his wrist he shoved up, then down.

Wooosh.

The parachute deployed.

Two seconds too late.

Relaxing his body, Seth looked up at the blue overhead versus the unforgiving rock beneath.

It'd be fine. It always was.

STOWE, VERMONT

One month later

Alana skidded down the last steep embankment and wiped dirty hands on what had hours before been a brand new pair of expensive light stretch fleece pants. It didn't bother her that they were soiled from a few skirmishes with puddles and a muddy slide into a six-inch stream. Didn't even bother her that she'd ripped one leg running too fast through what seemed a perfectly straight stretch of trees. Nope, what really bothered her was that she couldn't seem to care.

Not since that dreaded day with Seth.

Leaning back against a boulder she shaded her eyes with a shaky hand and stared at the house in front of her. One she'd recently inherited from her grandmother. *Why me? Why did I have to inherit it?* The Tudor Revival style house stared back with its overlapping gables as though its hooded gaze appreciated her about as much as she did it.

Which wasn't at all.

Her grandmom was gone. Why would she want to be here without her?

"Oh, don't look at it like that. It's not gonna bite," he said.

With a heavy groan, she pushed away from the rock and strode for the house.

"Have you contacted my cousins yet?"

Steely determination intact, Alana shook her head and vowed to make a doctor's appointment soon. Or more likely an appointment with a therapist.

After all, she'd been hearing Seth's voice in her head for several days now. Gorgeous, dare-devil, Seth. Could-have-been-her-soulmate, Seth.

Very, very dead, Seth.

"I wish you'd say something. Let me know you can hear me. This sucks."

Alana's chest tightened and she stopped. Crouching, she rested her head on her arms and tried to focus on breathing. *Don't pass out. Not a soul around for miles. Pull yourself together, girl.*

But despite how hard she tried that dreadful day resurfaced and a tear slipped free.

The way they'd bantered. The pure exhilaration she'd felt flirting with him. Their brief interaction had left her far more breathless than the hundreds of feet they fell together. Damn it! She didn't want to feel this way.

"You think this is hard on you? Imagine how it feels to be me. I'm dead!"

Suddenly angry, she roughly wiped away the tear and stood. Sane or insane, dead or alive, the voice in her head drove her nuts. Maybe she should contact his cousins.

"Bet they don't even exist," she muttered under her breath. But she knew they did. Seth had talked about them.

"Ahhh, so you are hearing me. Good. Now start *listening*, Alana. Of course they exist. They were at my funeral." A pause. "But you wouldn't know that, would you?"

Not a day in her life had she believed in the paranormal. Ghosts? Please. But what if she wasn't insane? What if he really was somehow haunting her? *Ugh. This is ridiculous!* She continued striding for the house. Something had to give. She couldn't keep on like this. Every time she thought she heard his voice, she'd be back at that day, watching as his body…

"The Worldwide Paranormal Society. Look em' up. Believe it or not, I've got bigger problems than the fact I'm dead. Much bigger."

Yeah, she heard him in her thoughts but his words didn't match how she actually… thought. Alana almost wished she could hear his voice as it had sounded. But that would just be creepy. And probably confirm for sure that she was a nutcase.

"C'mon Alana. I need you to speak. Tell me what you're thinking. No doubting, that you're crazy. Trust me, you're not. What you're experiencing now is the least of how crazy it gets. Please, I'm begging you, contact my cousins." It almost felt like her head heated for a minute before he continued. "I'm in serious trouble and need your help."

Clenching her sweaty fists, she punched in the code for the front door and entered. Leave it to her grandmom to have this place wired to the hilt with security. A cool, musty waft of air hit her face. Four months in this God forsaken behemoth of a home and she'd yet to give it a good cleaning. Or at least get the musty smell out of it.

She slammed the door shut.

One thing seemed to remain consistent. When she entered the house, Seth's voice stopped. Which in its own way, made her wonder why she hadn't spent every waking moment here since he'd died. She knew damned well why. Because being outside gave her distance. Let her run free. Escape.

Sort of.

Alana ran up the stairs two at a time and headed

for the bathroom. Pulling her just-past-shoulder length red hair out of its pony tail, she stripped down and hopped into the shower. Even as she scrubbed to remove the dirt, she knew she was really trying to scrub away the memories.

Of him. Of her past.

Within minutes she stared at her reflection in the mirror... a mirror that hadn't had a chance to steam over yet. Almost blindly, she secured her wet hair into a pony tail and applied some Cherry *ChapStick*, then pulled on some sweats and a hoodie.

Crash. Bang. Smash.

Alana jumped. What the heck? The sound had clearly come from downstairs. Yet the alarm hadn't sounded. Shoot. Think. Not much in a bathroom to use for defense. Hair scissors seemed the best choice so she quietly slid them from a drawer and cracked open the bathroom door. By nature, she wasn't the type to sit back and let trouble find her. If there was danger, she would seek it out.

Thankfully, the location of the bathroom was angled just off the top of the stairs so she was able to sidle out unseen then peek around the corner. As far as she could see, nobody was down there. *Thump. Thump. Thump.* Her heartbeat increased. A feeling she was well acquainted with. Yet a possible intruder incited a slightly different sensation than the dare-devil stunts she usually chased. She could admit she wasn't totally thrilled with it.

Regardless, she went to danger, not the other way around.

She inched down the stairs, careful to keep to the wall. The middle part of the wooden stairs creaked on chilly days. Nearly at the bottom, she stopped and listened.

Nothing.

The front door was closed. That didn't mean anything. She crept down the hallway to the living room. Everything looked the same. Untouched. Tiptoeing, she continued from room to room, handy scissors at the ready every step of the way. At the last room, more of a connected hallway, she froze. The huge ornate mirror that'd hung on the wall lay smashed to bits on the floor.

Alana slumped with relief. No intruder. Just a too-heavy antique falling off a wall. Tossing the scissors aside she made her way back to the kitchen, grabbed the trash barrel and returned to start the clean-up. Why grandmom had kept such ancient pieces she didn't know, nor did she care. Piece by jagged piece, Alana got to work.

She was picking up a particularly sharp piece when she noticed a word. Or was it? Smoky white, it appeared more like parts of the mirror were more aged and filmy. Peering closer, it definitely seemed like there was a word though. It said, "Read."

By instinct, Alana set it aside and picked up the next piece. This too seemed to have a word. It read, "the." Frowning, she set it aside and tried not to tremble as she picked up the third piece, this one also with a word. It read, "journal."

Read the journal?

What journal? Alana lined the pieces up next to one another. The words had vanished. Just three empty shards of glass. She rolled her eyes. *I'm officially losing it!* Shaking her head, she continued to pick up the pieces. About to grab the last rather large chunk, she stopped. Had the air just chilled?

Goosebumps rose on her skin. The hallway seemed to darken. Almost as if a shadow passed over. For the very first time in her life, she felt a small sliver of… fear?

No. It couldn't be. Alana rolled her shoulders and released a nervous burst of laughter. Seriously, she was just picking up broken glass. Not diving out of a plane. Not skiing off a sheer face of ice. Not diving hundreds of feet off a cliff with a hottie.

No. She was just picking up broken glass in a too-big-for-one-girl Tudor Revival house.

Wiping the sweat off her palms onto her sweats she gave a low whistle and shook her head. Time to get a grip. Without hesitating, she picked up the last shard.

Damn if the words, "Worldwide Paranormal Society," didn't appear in the mirror.

She closed her eyes then opened them. The words remained. Hell. Okay, it was official. She'd lost her mind. Watching Seth fall do his death had done her in. Label her a fruitcake. Past the point of no return. Guess a girl could take only so much in one lifetime.

Air. I need air. Alana tossed aside the glass and stepped out the back door. This blows. I can't believe I've officially snapped. "You suck!" she screamed at no one in particular. Or anyone who'd damn well listen. Even a squirrel would do at this point.

"What's the matter, Alana? House starting to act up?"

Seth. Naturally. Fine. What harm could it do at this point to contact his 'cousins.' Besides, the mirror had told her too! And the voice in her head! Totally justified. A full belly laugh hit her. Who cared, she'd be checking herself into the loony bin first thing in the morning anyways. She whipped out her cell phone and spoke to thin air, "Okay, Seth, you get your way. Don't be disappointed when you realize that you're just a voice in my head."

Good thing she had a kick-ass cell phone provider. It was the only way she'd be able to access the net via her smart phone from this desolate corner of Mt. Mansfield. Oddly enough, she wasn't overly shocked when The Worldwide Paranormal Society had several links. Figures. Now she'd be contacting people who thought she was more insane than she thought herself. Then again, the paranormal peeps were a bunch of head cases anyways. They'd probably jump on her email just so they could claim Seth was their long lost relative. That went with the whole 'spooky' concept anyways, right?

Regardless of her skepticism, something inside her besides Seth prompted her to do it. Maybe it was because some part of her hoped it was him. Maybe because—despite how intense the moment—she remembered exactly what she'd seen before he'd died. The strange light. The look of absolute fearlessness on his face.

Alana clicked through and got a phone number then dialed. Interestingly enough, the area code was out of Maine. Two rings and someone picked up.

"Hello," a man said, a slight lilt to his accent.

"Um, yeah, hi," she answered. Good one, Alana. At least sound halfway bright. "My name is Alana and I'm contacting you because…"

Because why? His dead cousin was in her head? Shoot. She scuffed her foot in the grass and said more surely, "I believe I have something paranormal happening in my house and hope you might be able to help."

That sounded good! Very level headed. Like a woman who totally had her stuff together. Yeah right. In a perfect world. Or at least a month ago.

"Thanks for calling Alana but we're actually taking a break right now. I can recommend a few other investigative teams however."

Oh shoot. Of course they were taking a break. They'd just lost their cousin. Alana bit her lip. *Here I am believing my own insanity!*

"Tell them my name."

This from Seth.

Um… no. Instead she said, "I appreciate that but I'd really like you. I've heard great things and this haunting is intense. I think you'd enjoy it."

"Enjoy it?" he replied.

It was almost as if she could hear the man shift uncomfortably on the other end of the line. No kidding. Who says that? Her obviously! "I mean, I mean…"

"Say it's demonic," Seth said.

Demonic? Isn't that just the icing on the cake. Whatever. "Friends tell me they think the haunting is demonic."

"Ah, lass. Then I understand your concern. I have just the team for you. Have you got a pen?"

Alana frowned. This wasn't going well. "No, I really want you. Are you sure you're not available? Please?"

"No, I'm sorry. But I'd like to help any way I can," the man responded.

"Tell him it's me, Alana. Tell him it's Seth."

With a wave of her hand in the air, she shooed

away his imaginary voice and spoke to the very real voice on the other end of the line. "I don't think you understand, this is a bit of an emergency."

"Have you been physically attacked? Has one of your family members?"

"Uh...no. I mean yes. But no." She rubbed her forehead.

"What makes you think this is demonic?"

Alana shook her head and rolled her eyes. "Well, I don't really know that it is. Just that I'd really like your team to come out." What else to say? "You come highly recommended!" Oh please.

"Now you just sound desperate. Paranormal junkie," Seth said.

"You're a freakin' voice in my head! Shut up!" she yelled at absolutely nobody.

"I'm sorry. I don't think I can help you," said the man over the phone.

"Wait! No!" she yelped into the phone. "I wasn't talking to you!"

"I'm sorry, really," he said.

Knowing damn well he was hanging up she said, "Seth. It's Seth. Please."

Her face burned. Did she really just go there? Oh. My. God.

Dead silence on the other end of the line.

Beep. Beep. Beep. Oh heck. She looked at her cell phone. The battery had died. It had just been full! *You've got to be kidding me!* Classic. Guess these new phones weren't all they were cracked up to be.

"No, it's just me. I used the energy to talk to you while you were on the phone. Drained its juice fast. Glad to know we ghost hunters were right about that." Alana swallowed hard. Great. She decided to respond, if anything to appease her own insanity. "If you really are who you are, why are you haunting me, Seth?" She shook her head and gave a wry grin. "Why not go to the light?"

"Stop being condescending and just talk to me as though I'm still here 'cause I am, Alana. Whether or not you like it."

She squeezed shut her eyes and said, "Fine, you're here. At least to my nutty mind. What do you want?"

A light breeze caressed her face. "I want to live again."

Something about the way he said it, even within her mind, set her teeth on edge, made her skin tingle with awareness. Opening her eyes, she gazed at the brief stretch of lawn and tried to study the slew of deep greens washed across the New England woodland. Alana focused on the simple task of breathing. Even with the mere concept of it being Seth's spirit near her, Alana could admit her knees were slightly weak.

And not because of the fact he might be a ghost.

Nodding absently, she turned and walked away.

Straight back into the house.

***

Screw me!

How many times had he said that to himself since he'd died? What a bunch of bullshit. Seth stared at the door she'd vanished into and knew damned well he wasn't following. No way. Not until his cousins got here.

What if this was the house?

Frustrated, he stalked toward the forest. As usual, he couldn't move beyond the home's yard, or grass area. Turning, he glared at the huge Tudor style home, which was obviously his hell. What fun. He'd spent the last seven years investigating the paranormal. The 'other side' wasn't exactly what he'd expected. Then again, he'd never really overthought it. In fact, he'd never really cared.

Not until two years ago.

Not until the Victorian.

That's where he learned that he was part of Calum's curse. Calum, his ancestor and pain-in-the-ass mentor of sorts. If that's what you wanted to call him. Seth growled and continued to stalk around the lawn… remembering.

It'd been at that Victorian that he and his cousins, Leathan, Devin and Andrea had learned about their role in Calum's curse. A little piece of crap prophecy that Calum had wrapped them up in. In the 1800's Calum had got himself involved in a cult. His punishment for thinking he was better than them and leaving? Three nasty creatures of the night would be sent after his bloodline. Three male descendants to be exact. That meant that Leathan, Devin and Seth were screwed.

But Calum had a plan. He magically caged each beast within the walls of three houses that he had built. The problem? Each of those creatures could someday be unleashed if the stone they were trapped by was found. And that stone needed to match the descendant's magical aura. And naturally, when the first stone was found, all descendants would become warlocks and possess kick-ass powers.

Seth ground his non-existent teeth and snarled. Wasn't he supposed to have been a warlock? Immune to this crap? That was the thing. The minute the Victorian's mystery was unraveled by his cousin Leathan, all three men came into their 'gift.' Their evilness. Warlocks all. Leathan had reluctantly accepted the new gift. Devin, rebelled. Seth? He loved it!

But it hadn't saved him from dying.

So he had a few bones to pick.

Figuratively speaking.

Seth had spent a great deal of his life defying death. Living on the edge and staring death in the eye was his thing. So what happened that day when they'd jumped off the cliff?

When all else failed he'd implemented his magic. A last resort of course. Alana wasn't supposed to see that. But he knew she had. He still remembered looking up at the blue sky, at her stunned face, even more beautiful caught in shock. Her amber eyes had flared almost a goldish white, a stunned shade of fear he'd never seen in anyone's eyes before.

Still.

He smacked down.

She landed with the soft thump beside him, a small squeak of anguish broke from her mouth as she struggled to free herself from the parachute and get it off his body.

His body.

Now that's when it got really weird.

There's nothing quite like the sensation of looking down at your own body. His first thought? *I'm not as mangled as I thought I would be.* Maybe his magic had preserved him a bit. In fact, he didn't look like he'd fallen hundreds of feet to his death and smattered like a bug on cold, hard rock. Nope, in fact, he appeared rather intact. No brain matter splattered across the ground. His tongue wasn't hanging out of his mouth. His body wasn't bent at odd angles. As far as he could tell, it was a clean death.

But it was death.

Once all of the initial assessments had past, Seth couldn't deny he'd felt a twinge of…panic? He'd shaken his head and blinked. Panic? What the hell? Something told him if he could break into a sweat and get a dry mouth, it'd have happened at that exact moment.

He looked down at his own dead body.

That sucked.

Hard.

Seth continued to stalk around the Tudor style house. He really wanted to follow Alana inside. But he was scared. He looked to the darkening sky and rolled his eyes. Time to officially admit it… he was petrified. You couldn't pay him enough to go into that house. Dare-devil Seth had finally come up against something he didn't want to face head on.

At least not without his cousins.

Or without Calum… and Adlin.

Calum would make his presence known soon enough. He always did. But Adlin, now Adlin had just sort of become part of the picture too. Adlin was a wizard who was originally born in fifth century Ireland but had ruled over the MacLomain Clan in the thirteenth century. He was also someone who adored Calum's parents in eighteenth century America and was determined to help them all through this.

Besides, he seemed to keep the ghostly Calum in check.

But where the hell were they now?

Grumbling, Seth stalked the grounds and watched as night fell and lights turned on inside the house. Despite himself, anger started to be replaced with curiosity as it had every night since he died. Drifting closer, he tracked her until she ended up in her bedroom on the second floor.

He might be dead but he was still a man.

Or at least he hoped.

Interesting how she always kept the curtain open in one window. Even tonight. Even after all the craziness. He knew… hoped, that deep down inside she really believed. Believed that he was real and watching…caring? Sure, why not. Shit, for some reason his soul had stuck by her side, at least in the yard. It had to be because she was there when he died.

Alana.

He'd met and slept with a lot of girls but she was… something else. Not the usual super-sexy type he favored, she had her own sort of allure. Kind of soft and challenging all at once. He had stood about 6'4 and the top of her head had barely crested his upper chest. Those long, thick dark brown lashes of hers had always complimented the mad frenzy of freckles over her upper cheeks but been at odds with the pure fire of her hair. Her gently sloped cherub cheeks perched on high cheekbones combined with her full lips gave her a quality that while not classically beautiful appealed to those nature oriented. He struck her a prickly leaf in the middle of a thousand placid leaves. A shooting star in the midst of a thousand bored, motionless stars. She had a way of shining through with the light in her eyes and the pure animation that kept her face telling a thousand stories.

He knew he could do better.

The Tudor Revival

He was Seth.

But for now, he'd watch. Had no choice.

Alana stood staring blindly into her bedroom mirror...as though she didn't really, truly look at herself. This was the same thing she did every night. As if she didn't care, and he supposed she really didn't. She whipped off her hoodie revealing a prim white bra holding back a delicious set of c-cup breasts, then slid off her sweats, revealing an equally functional set of cotton panties which in his opinion, covered a set of curvy hips he'd be willing to sample.

Then she executed what'd become his favorite part of every night. God forbid it differ in spite of the day's events.

She pulled a 'waste of time elastic' from her hair.

Seth gawked. As he did every night.

All of those deep red glorious locks sprang free. He could tell they'd been wet but it didn't matter. The way they fell around her face, each little wave stroking either her chin, or chest bone or even the errant strand that whipped up toward the corner of her lips. He especially loved those. The way they'd catch and she'd haphazardly pull them away, as though they were a minor irritation.

What he wouldn't do to catch one of those hairs in his lips.

If he still had them.

Curvy little body full steam ahead, she crawled into bed and did what she did every night... pulled free a small cross, held it tight with one hand and put it over her chest. He didn't get this about her but didn't overly analyze it as he was always too focused on her creamy white breasts heaving as she said a prayer.

He knew it was wrong to watch such an intimate moment. But he could never quite look away.

A loud keen started. Seth drifted away from the window. As he did every night. And every single night it pissed him off. Why the hell did he move away? Why didn't he stick around to see what that sound meant? Why didn't he stick around to see if she was okay?

But he didn't. Instead he lowered and fell away.

He always fell away.

CHAPTER TWO

Beeeeep. Beeeeep.

Alana jolted up in bed. What the hell?

The alarm system was screaming. The one that said someone was at the front door. Blinking, she tried to acclimate herself. Dim light flooded into the room. She glanced at the clock. Six A.M.. Who was here this early? She'd never had a visitor.

Scrambling from the bed, she fumbled into her clothes and threw on a loose robe for good measure. Alana tucked her bedside .38 caliber under her arm and bee-lined downstairs. Flicking a single switch, the whole house was lit. If she didn't like who she saw outside the glass window, the button would be pushed connecting to 911. In this case…thank you grandmom.

She probably should have done that yesterday before stalking around the house like wonder-woman with scissors.

Pausing on the landing, she peered outside. All she saw was a pick-up truck and a man and woman standing at the door. Still. She beeped the intercom from there. "Who are you?"

The man looked up, almost as though he knew where she stood, hidden in the shadows of the second floor. "The Worldwide Paranormal Society. You called me earlier."

Tying the robe tighter around her she nodded to herself. "How do I know that?"

He didn't miss a beat. "Seth. He's my cousin."

Alana's breath escaped her. Seth's cousin? For real? Alana didn't question her sanity anymore. She set aside the gun, flew down the stairs and opened the front door. Frozen, they all just stared at each other. The man was tall, easily 6'3 with dark auburn hair and intense smoky pale green eyes. Very good looking. The woman was a few inches taller than her. She was beautiful, even with a long scar running down her cheek.

"You're here for Seth?" It seemed so easy to ask that. In fact her question had come out in what seemed a rush of thankful air.

His easy eyes and the woman's warm smile made it easier. It was the woman who responded. "Yes. I'm Isabel, this is Seth's cousin, Devin."

Alana could only nod and back into the house, welcoming them in. It was real. *This* was real. She knew it the moment she'd opened the door. Or had she known it all along? No matter, it was real.

Devin reminded her a little of Seth. The way he walked into the house as though he owned the space already. As though he held no fear. He scanned the house briefly before his attention turned to her. "Where is he?"

Shaking her head, she tried to talk but knew her mouth only gaped. *Ugh!*

Isabel talked to her but signed with her hands as well. "He's worried. Forgive. It's okay. Do you sign?"

Alana tried to acclimate. Sign? What?

"She's deaf, lass. Do you sign?"

She jumped at Devin's barked response and shook her head no.

Isabel's hand fell on hers and she said, "It's okay.

I read lips and can speak as well. Don't mind him right now, please."

Only then did Alana realize that Isabel's incantations were very slightly off. She smiled, nodded and shut the door. Holy hell. I'm in way over my head. Or I'm way too shallow. How do I deal with these people?

Within seconds, Devin turned and flew back outside, leaving the door wide open. She and Isabel followed. If she wasn't mistaken, Devin sniffed the air then proceeded to romp around the lawn like a beast. Hell! What had she missed?

Before she could pursue him Isabel grabbed her arm and shook it. "He's trying to find, Seth. It's alright."

She stared at the woman. "Alright? Are you out of your mind? None of this is alright!"

Why she freaked out on a perfect stranger in the pre-dawn hours Alana would never know but this was totally not okay. Seriously, what was the matter with these people?

Devin was halfway across the lawn when he stopped short. He cocked his head to the side as though he'd heard something, then she heard his strangled voice say, "You sonofabitch. You're here. Hell, I've missed you. We've all missed you."

What? Alana felt Isabel's hand fall away. She watched Devin's body shake slightly. Was he crying? Another car was screaming up the goat-path she called a driveway. Spinning, she watched a BMW skid into the driveway. Before it came to a full stop, one door was open and the driver leapt out. She watched in disbelief as another guy, 6'3 too, flew by her and strode up next to Devin.

The new guy said, "It's Leathan. I'm here Seth. Shit lad. So glad we found you. So glad we could!"

A tall, black-haired woman walked up and stood on the other side of her. "I'm Dakota, Leathan's wife. He's Seth's other cousin."

Alana knew she stared, up and up at the woman. Tall and something out of a paranormal sex novel, this woman ruled all. She looked at Isabel again. Just as fierce, just as beautiful, in a different way. This was completely insane. Things always made sense in her life. Four perfect strangers showing up first thing in the morning speaking to a man who didn't exist on her front lawn….

Pure insanity.

But she could handle this. She could handle anything. Head held high she nodded to both women, turned and headed for the house.

Regrettably, darkness swallowed her first.

***

"Does she know the full story? Someone should tell her. Why hasn't he?"

Alana stayed still and continued to listen. It's what she'd done from a young age and instinct told her to do so now. She still found it hard to believe that she'd passed out. That was a first.

"I don't know. Would she understand the dynamics?" Isabel said.

"Not sure it matters at this point," Leathan said.

Interesting how she already knew their voices. Isabel's was old fashioned southern American but missing some sounds due to deafness. Devin's had a distinct Irish lilt. Dakota's was local with a bit of a British bite to it. Leathan's was Scottish.

"How do you know she's not listening right

now," Isabel said.

Alana smiled to herself. Smart woman.

"Doesn't matter," Leathan said. "If she is, she should wake up and join the conversation. We've got a cousin trapped on the other side and we need to get him back."

Get him back? Huh?

"If I were her, I'd stayed zonked. Damn, she's just been loaded down with four people she doesn't know that believe Seth's still out there. That he still exists. Baby steps, fellas."

Alana narrowed her eyes mentally at Dakota's voice. That woman was trying to bait her. Hmph. Yeah, she got it. Still. Bunch of bull! All of this!

"I get why he won't come in this house, but he needs to," Devin said.

"We're here now. He will. It won't get him," Leathan said.

"What won't get him?" Alana said softly and slowly opened her eyes.

"Ah, so she's awake," Devin said, a rather warm smile on his face despite the odd circumstances.

Alana took in her surroundings. Obviously someone carried her into her living room. The sun was out and the shades were wide open. Sitting up on the couch, she scrunched her nose. This room was pretty shabby in blinding daylight. Stinky too. "You took the sheets off the furniture. Thanks."

Leathan winked. "Don't spend much time at home, do you lass?"

"Not really." He was pretty damned hot too. With cool streaks of blond in his hair and those intense deep chocolate brown eyes... yep, she understood Dakota's attraction.

"We're really sorry to crash in on you like this," Isabel said kindly. "And for making you pass out."

Alana felt a mad blush crawl over her face and knew her freckles probably jumped out to smack them in the face. With a heavy sigh she replied, "No worries. Thanks for getting me in here. All my years of extreme sports and this…" She gestured at them, the house and outside with a loose wave, "makes me hit the ground. Unreal."

"Honey, you haven't got a thing to be sorry about. Everything going on here and everything we're about to tell you is far beyond any death defying stunts you've pulled," Dakota assured.

Alana wasn't sure if that made her feel better or not. She eyed them. They eyed her. Not particularly shy by nature she suddenly felt uneasy. "So what can I do for you all?"

That hadn't come out right. She'd meant to ask how she could help.

"Tell us about the contact you've made with Seth," Leathan said.

"Please," Dakota added.

"He's been." She stopped and frowned. *A voice in my head?* Her mouth turned dry and she pinched the bridge of her nose. *Someone I thought I could care about? Shoot, she was thirsty.* Alana licked her lips and was about to continue when she stopped short.

A strange woman had just walked into the room. Pale with red-rimmed eyes, she held out a glass of water. "Drink."

Alana hated that her hand shook slightly as she took the cup. She didn't show weakness. Not a day in her life. Heck though, she was thirsty. She took deep

The Tudor Revival

gulps of the cold water and nodded in thanks.

"I'm Andrea, Seth's sister. I arrived while you were passed out."

Oh. Oh! Seth's sister. Pretending to be busy relishing her water, Alana studied Andrea as she sat next to Devin. Short and petite, she was really pretty. She didn't look much like Seth, maybe a little around the mouth.

That sexy, perfect mouth of his. Alana closed her eyes and breathed deeply.

"I'm sorry… that you had to be there that day…"

Alana met Andrea's eyes and nodded. She was too. But damn, the heartache they all had to be feeling. Rubbing her lips together she figured she ought to say something. "He was a really good guy. I'm so sorry for your loss."

That didn't sound very sincere. She took another deep swig of water.

An uncomfortable moment of silence stretched before Andrea softly asked, "Please. Tell us what he's said."

Okay. She could do this… had to do this. Alana locked eyes with Andrea and replied, "He's scared."

An audible gasp emitted from everyone in the room. Had they not expected that response? I mean really, Seth had died! Maybe she should add what else she was sure he was feeling. "And pissed."

This brought a bunch of "yeps" and "of course's" and "I'm sure's," from everyone. What was wrong with them? The fact Seth was pissed made more sense than him being scared? Then again, she knew Seth well enough to understand. She swigged down the last of the water. With a sharp shake of her head, she stood and said, "I'm sorry. I need some air."

Once outside, Alana strode for the rock. The big slate of raw Mt. Mansfield left-over perched at the far corner of her property. It allowed her to turn her back to the mountain and watch the house with a wary eye. It sort of sat half-protected by trees and half in the yard.

"They're only here to help."

And there stood the only problem with the rock. Seth. He seemed to frequent it as much as her. Alana ran her fingers over the engraving in the rock and shook her head. Yeah, she supposed she should be scared she was talking to a ghost, but she wasn't. He didn't seem like a ghost... just a voice in her head. "So you're real. Obviously."

"You should know." She heard the smile in his voice before he continued. "They're my family and my best friends. You really need to talk to them."

Crossing her arms over her chest she leaned back against the rock and stared at the house. "I'm uncomfortable with all of this."

"But you're not afraid."

"No." She sighed. "Not anymore."

"You were though?"

"Obviously!" Alana scuffed her foot. Nothing quite like talking to thin air.

"You didn't need to be afraid, Alana. Well, maybe a little."

She frowned but didn't respond.

"Okay, maybe a lot. Suck ass situation," Seth conceded.

"Ya think?" She rolled her eyes and sighed again.

"You'd rather be skydiving right now, eh?"

A small smiled tugged the corners of her lips but she said nothing.

"Me too," he said. "But we're not."

Shaking her head she replied, "Nope."

"Getting used to talking to someone you can't see?"

Alana shook her head again. "Nope."

"I like you. You know that?"

Ignoring the thrill that shot down her spine she was about to respond but he did first.

"You keep a level head. Makes sense. You're a thrill-seeker."

Right. Thrill-seeker. Very true. What had she hoped he'd say? Not that. Andrea was heading her way so she said nothing else. The girl probably already thought she was ten shades of crazy.

"Hey," Andrea said. "You okay?"

"Sure," Alana responded. For some reason, Andrea put her at ease. "Just trying to get used to all of this."

"I know." Andrea leaned back against the rock beside her. "Very cool house."

"You think?"

"Sure." Andrea cocked her head. "But definitely creepy."

Alana laughed. "Uh…yeah!"

The home was classically beautiful as far as houses went. Larger than most Tudor Revival's, it boasted over thirty rooms. The decorative woodwork between the patterned stonework was exceptional. Well over a hundred thin windows gave the home elegant eyes. Eyes that overlooked a backyard rich with a thick English garden now in its decline and beautiful old pine and oak trees. Her grandmom had loved this house and its surroundings and years of love shadowed the property.

"It's really enchanting. Like something out of a spooky fairytale," Andrea said. Almost as if she was having the same thoughts.

"He's okay." Alana wasn't sure why she said it but felt Andrea needed to hear it.

"I know." Andrea swallowed hard. "Is he here right now?"

"Yes. Tell her yes," Seth said.

Alana met Andrea's nearly teary gaze, unsure.

"Tell her," he repeated.

Nodding, Alana whispered, "Yes, he is."

A tear rolled free from one of Andrea's eyes but she said nothing, just turned her head back toward the house.

"Tell her it's okay. Tell her I'm okay," Seth said.

"He wants you to know he's okay," she repeated.

"Why can't I hear him?" Andrea whispered.

"I'm not sure. Tell her I think it's because you were with me when I died that you can hear me," Seth said.

Alana cleared her throat. "Seriously?"

"Yeah. Tell her."

"He thinks it's because I was with him when he..." her throat suddenly felt thick, "died."

Andrea's posture stiffened but she continued staring straight ahead. "Has he gone into the house?"

Brows together, Alana waited for Seth's response. This was weird.

"No," he responded. "I can't. She knows that."

Alana said, "No. He can't. You know that."

"Why?" Andrea asked.

"Awe hell," Seth said. "Don't make me say it."

Gooseflesh rose on Alana's skin but she repeated

his message.

"So he's afraid the third creature is trapped in this house?" Andrea asked.

Third creature? What the hell? But she repeated the message.

"Damn straight I am. What do you think?" Seth replied.

Alana repeated his message.

"We're here now, Seth. And besides that, we don't even know if this is the house."

Silence from Seth. Alana knew she had to say something. Now. Right this very moment. "What's the journal?"

Andrea's head turned slowly, her eyes locked with Alana's. "What?"

"No shit. What?" Seth's voice seconded.

"In the glass," Alana said softly. "Broken glass… it said something about reading a journal."

"What broken glass?" Andrea said.

She shook her head and pushed away from the stone. "An old mirror. It was probably nothing."

Andrea said almost adamantly, "It all means something." Before she knew what was happening, Andrea grabbed her arm and pulled Alana after her. Stumbling forward, she was amazed by the smaller woman's strength. What the heck? Yeah, she could stop her but obviously Andrea was pretty intent. She led her into the house and nodded at a chair. "Please. Sit. Listen to us."

No doubt about it, Seth and his sibling shared the same assertiveness.

Leathan quirked a brow at Andrea. "What's up?"

Andrea plunked down in a chair and glanced around, upset. "This is the third house."

"How do you know?" Devin asked.

"Alana's been told to read the journal."

"Wow! Really?" Dakota said, round eyes turned to Alana. "Who told you?"

"Probably Calum or Adlin," Andrea said.

"Who?" Alana asked.

"Ghosts," Isabel provided. "Both meddlesome."

"Seth hasn't told you much, has he?" Devin said.

"Obviously not," Leathan said.

"Will someone tell me something…anything? I guess I need to understand… or move out," Alana muttered.

"I don't think moving out is going to help you much. There's a pretty good chance that you're supposed to be here," Andrea said gently.

Oh wonderful. "Then tell me, please. What's going on?"

It was Leathan who decided to fill her in. Obviously, he was usually in charge. He just had that way about him. By the time he'd told her about Calum's curse, the creatures of the night haunting three houses and the fact that he, Devin and Seth had become warlocks because of the curse, Alana's jaw hung open. And she didn't care.

"You can't be serious," she whispered. Seth, a warlock? A slow smile erupted. "This is some kind of joke, isn't it?" Alana glanced around, for the first time noticing the cameras and equipment. "Some sort of paranormal reality show?"

They all stared at her.

"Seriously, I think you're supposed to get permission from the homeowner first."

Andrea sighed. "Stop it, Alana. This isn't a joke. You know Seth's been talking to you. Yes, we're asking you to believe a far-fetched story, but it's all true. We've already tackled the creatures from the Victorian and Georgian. Leathan and Dakota hooked up in the Victorian and had to battle a vampire. Isabel and Devin, the Georgian, to fight a werewolf. In both houses, Calum and Adlin assisted. Sort of off and on. So they're the good guys. Well, Calum's questionable. He's the whole reason this curse exists and his descendants are being hunted down like animals. But there's not much we can do about it except get through this together."

Alana kept eyes locked with Andrea. She was telling the truth. Or at least believed her lies. Well, there was only one way she could think to handle this. "I need proof."

Devin snorted. "More than Seth talking to you?"

Dakota grinned. "I see why he'd be attracted to her. Both dare-devils but her practical nature must intrigue his act-without-thinking way of looking at life."

Everyone looked at Dakota and shook their head.

She shrugged and winked. "Say you weren't all thinking the same thing."

Leathan turned his attention back to Alana. "Fine. I'll show you footage from both houses."

"And I'll go make coffee." Devin glanced at Alana. "You do have coffee, aye?"

Nodding absently, she watched as Leathan set up a laptop in front of her. Over the next hour he showed her footage from the other houses. Things she never would have believed existed. Mind-blowing, freak-you-the-hell-out sort of stuff. If what she was seeing was doctored, they'd done a phenomenal job with it. She'd accepted a cup of coffee from Devin quite a while ago and took an absent sip of the cooled brew. Honestly, she was pretty surprised that her hands weren't shaking, that her whole body wasn't!

Eventually, Leathan clicked off the computer. Speechless, still processing everything, Alana sat back and gazed unseeing at the blank screen. No idea how much time might've passed, she jumped a little when Devin set a platter of munchies on the coffee table and said, "Hope you don't mind. Thought everyone could use a bite."

Releasing a heavy sigh, she nodded. "Of course. No problem."

"I know it's a lot to take in," Isabel said softly.

"Sure is." Alana glanced around at the living room. It suddenly looked far more sinister than it had earlier today. "So what sort of creature is trapped in this house?"

"Good question," Leathan said. He stood and began to pace. "Something nastier than the rest."

"Without doubt," Devin agreed and chomped a kernel of popcorn.

"I just don't get any of this," Andrea added. "Seth died. How is he supposed to fight a creature if he's already dead?"

"Good point," Dakota said. "Maybe he skipped his curse by default somehow?"

"No." Leathan stopped and eyed Alana. "I don't think so."

"No," Devin agreed. "Nothing about this bloody curse has been easy. Can't imagine that'd change now. I mean seriously, Seth's dead. It's already harder than the rest."

"Exactly."

Alana sat forward, back ramrod straight. Who

had said that?

Everyone swung around and looked at the mirror over the mantle.

"Calum!" They said.

Alana blinked, put a hand over her mouth and tried not to pass out...or scream. A man's face, though hazy, looked back through the mirror. Blurry and whitish like the words she'd previously seen in the broken glass, he seemed to look directly at her. "Indeed my wonderful offspring, I'm back again."

"Why are you in the mirror?" Devin asked and swigged some soda.

Wow, nothing like being super casual about this. But as she gazed around, it occurred to her that no one was particularly freaked by his appearance.

Calum grunted and said, "That's the thing about this creature. It actually sees me better when I manifest in a room. Let's just say, they were right about mirrors being windows from which those in the afterlife can peer through. But usually only in certain cases."

Leathan sighed. "Could you be more direct, Calum."

"Oh lad, you know that's not my style." Calum chuckled. It appeared as though he flicked a top hat. "First thing you all should be focused on is Seth."

"Precisely."

Alana frowned. Who had said that?

"Here. Over here."

Everyone turned to a smaller mirror perched on a corner table and said, "Adlin!"

"Aye, how are you all?"

Alana narrowed her eyes at what looked to be an old man with white hair. Though his appearance was clearer than Calum's it was still hard to make out.

"Been better," Leathan said. "Seth's dead."

"Mmm, you don't say?" Adlin cocked his head. "Are you quite sure?"

Dead silence.

Alana tried to swallow but had no luck.

"We went to his funeral. Alana saw him die. Aye, he's dead," Devin said softly.

"I see," Adlin responded.

"Oh, don't be cryptic, old man," Calum said. "Tell them."

"Tell us what? Out with it! " Leathan said, arms akimbo as though he couldn't decide which ghostly face he wanted to throttle first.

A cool breeze made the hair on her arms stand up. Alana shivered. Calum and Adlin vanished from the mirrors.

Devin held out a device and said, "The temps gone from sixty-five degrees to fifty-eight. Fifty-five."

A dark shadow slid over the room. The air thinned as though she stood at a high elevation. Alana shriveled back in very real fear.

"Forty degrees," Devin gasped.

Leathan shook his head, stood and staggered. "Out of the house. Now!"

All gasped, staggered and stumbled out the front door. The fifty degree air hit Alana's face like a warm Caribbean day. It felt truly wonderful. It was a strange sensation, being gripped by absolute fear while feeling complete and utter safety.

"What happened in there? Talk to me, Alana," Seth said.

"Nothing. Everything," she said, still trying to

catch her breath.

"Huh?" Dakota asked.

"She's talking to Seth," Andrea provided.

Everyone turned her way. Alana shook her head. Nuts. She proceeded to tell him what had happened. Thankfully, all remained silent... seemed to understand. Still, it was weird talking to thin air around a group of people.

"So what the hell did Adlin mean?" Seth asked.

Shaking her head, Alana replied, "I don't know. Adlin seemed to imply." She looked around at everyone and shrugged. "That you might not be dead?"

Everyone nodded. Seth's shrill response made her stagger back. "What?!"

"Are you okay?" Isabel held her arm.

Alana nodded. "Yeah. Seth's just... upset."

"I love how you can hear him. That's pretty cool," Dakota said. "In that I know he's listening, I've got a question. Seth, are you positive you died? You know how my story went."

"I'm speaking to you through a complete stranger, Dakota. Good chance I'm dead, sweatheart," Seth said.

Alana rolled her eyes at absolutely no one. "Yes, he's sure."

"What are we missing, then?" Andrea asked.

"Something, that's for sure," Devin said.

"Where was I buried?" Seth asked.

Alana repeated the question.

"Boston. His hometown," Leathan responded.

"Did they actually see my body in the casket?"

"I'm not going to ask them that," Alana responded.

"Ask us what?" Devin said. "If it came from Seth, say it, lassie."

Oh fine. "He wants to know if you actually saw his body in the casket."

Devin's brows slammed together. "Well…no. We were told his body was in rough shape."

Alana grimaced and shook her head. "No, despite the fall, he didn't look too bad."

"That's sort of odd," Isabel said. "He fell hundreds of feet, right?"

"He did but…"

"But what?" Leathan asked.

"I don't know. There was this light right before…"

She heard Seth sigh. "I should've probably told you."

"Told me what?"

"He was using his magic," Devin said.

Of course. His magic. That made perfect sense. "That's right. He's a warlock."

Alana knew she sounded disbelieving but she couldn't help it. The concept was crazy. About as crazy as all of this.

"So you know what I am now. I'm sorry. It's the truth. I did use magic. But it didn't seem to work," Seth said.

"Strange that his magic didn't work," Dakota said. "Or at least the unusual luck he's always had."

"We need to know what Adlin knows. As always, there's more to this story," Leathan said.

"They need to get my body," Seth said.

"He wants his body," Alana murmured.

Isabel frowned. "But he's been buried."

"Or so we thought," Andrea said.

"Right," Leathan said. "Or so we thought."

"Before seeing the words in the mirror and hearing Seth have there been any other unusual things happening in the house?"

Alana shook her head. "No. Nothing."

"Well, not that I want to but we've got to go back into that house. We've got to find out what Adlin knows," Leathan said.

"Great," Devin said. "Think our magic will be as strong without Seth?"

"We can only hope," Leathan said. "Why don't you ladies stay outside while we get this sorted out. The creature is obviously acting up because we're here."

"He's right," Devin said. "We need to make contact with Adlin. Something tells me that once we do, we'll be able to at least exist in the house through this."

Alana felt more than uneasy. "Why don't we just leave? Do we have to stay here to figure all this out?"

"Regrettably, yes." Andrea gazed up at the house. "If Calum is here, then this house is the last in the curse. It has to be dealt with so that we can put this to rest…or not."

With a curt nod, Leathan said, "Come on, Devin. Let's go in."

"Coming," Devin responded.

Dakota and Isabel frowned but nodded.

Worry made Andrea's features appear drawn. "Be careful. This one's not like the others. I have a really bad feeling."

"It'll be alright, cuz." Leathan squeezed her shoulder then gave Dakota a quick hug. Devin did the same. Apparently nobody was going to get overly sentimental. As they walked into the front door, Alana watched the other women. Each and every one had a stern expression. Each and every one looked ready to go to battle.

Minutes passed. Everyone remained silent. Isabel paced.

"They need me in there with them," Seth said.

A shiver of warning rippled through her body. "What is it? What haunts this place?" She whispered.

Almost as if he breathed against her ear and she could feel the heat of his warm breath on her neck he said, "Death."

Just as the sun crested over the top of the Revival, a loud boom sounded from within. The ground shook. A few tiles fell loose from the roof and crashed down. Light flared brightly from the windows.

And the front door burst open.

CHAPTER THREE

Seth stared, dumbfounded, at his body.

Shaking his head, he again tried to talk to Alana. No luck. Now that they were all standing there looking down at his living body, not a soul could hear him. If he could shake his head he would. He was alive! Kind of. Not really. Who knew?

Adlin apparently.

They all stood, except Seth of course, in another cave not all that far from the one he'd free fallen into. Like him, they eyed his body in the simple wooden coffin. Not one of them had completely dry eyes... except maybe Alana. Then again, she was still in shock and he didn't much blame her. There's nothing quite like seeing your home turn into the house of horrors, literally.

After Devin and Seth came flying out the door with wild eyes and hair standing at odd angles, they'd hightailed it for their cars. Somehow this time, Seth had been able to follow. It was the first time he'd left this property since he'd 'died' and truth told, it felt good as hell.

"I can't believe he's still alive!" Andrea said. "H...how?"

Seth looked at Adlin's ghost again and agreed wholeheartedly. Right, how?

Adlin shrugged. "I saved him. He saved him too."

"How the?" Leathan said.

"Not that I'm complaining but seriously, how?" Devin added.

Adlin looked at Andrea and arched a brow. "You've read Sky Purington's, The MacLomain Series. You tell them."

Her eyebrows lowered for a moment before they shot up. "Noooooo! The old Viking magic?"

Adlin nodded. "Yep."

"I totally forgot about that," she murmured.

Seth looked from person to person. What were they talking about?

Leathan nodded. "I read the series after Andrea. How could I have forgotten?"

"Care to fill us in," Devin said.

"It's old magic that Adlin's descendants used in medieval Scotland. One wizard can save another by walking through the place in between heaven and hell. Seth must have with Adlin."

I did? Seth had no recollection of that.

"Exactly," Adlin said and looked directly at Seth.

Or at least Seth thought he did.

Adlin continued. "With magic I've kept his muscles supple and strong and as you can clearly see, his body well kept. I could not have maintained his current state much longer."

Holy creepy but Seth could admit he was grateful.

"But how did you get his body here?" Leathan asked. "He's already been buried!"

"Was he?" Adlin asked. "Did you ever actually see his body?"

Devin flinched. "No. Closed casket for obvious reasons."

"Aye, obvious reasons indeed," Adlin snickered. "I stole it!"

Everyone looked between Adlin and Seth's body,

amazed.

Alana sort of floated around the crowd clearly unwilling to look at his body. Seth moved closer to her. "I won't bite, you know."

She sucked in a little gasp and shook her head.

It seemed she could hear him again. Okay, he supposed he got it… her sudden fear of him. This was a lot to take in.

"So why is his spirit not connected with his body?" Devin asked.

Adlin's eyes twinkled and he nodded at Alana. "I'd guess because of her."

Alana frowned and said weakly, "Me?"

"You were with him when he "died." You're connected to the house that trapped the creature he's meant to fight. Makes perfect sense," Adlin replied.

"Maybe to you," Alana muttered. "Sorry, I don't know what to say. Still trying to…" She glanced briefly at his body, "get a grasp on all of this."

Adlin nodded. "No doubt, lassie. No doubt."

Seth had to admit she was handling it well. Then again, she was about as crazy as he when it came to living on the edge so maybe she was just trying to treat this like another extreme sport. Really extreme!

"So how do we get his spirit back into his body?" Dakota asked.

"Good question," Devin seconded.

"Simple enough," Adlin said. "He's got to crawl in."

Dead silence.

Seth crept closer to his body. Crawl in. Huh? Seriously?

"Is his spirit here right now?" Isabel asked Alana.

She nodded slightly, her wide eyes now officially

locked on his body.

"Of course he is," Adlin agreed and smiled.

Leathan frowned. "Bet he's wondering how the hell to crawl into his body."

Halleluiah brother, Seth thought.

"Aye, he needs to focus on his body. He needs to go right down into it and position his viewpoint as though he's looking through his body's eyes," Adlin said.

"That's just trippy," Dakota said.

But Seth wasn't worried. As though jumping into the cave mouth that'd gotten him into all this, he catapulted down into his body… and hit the floor.

Adlin chuckled.

"What's so funny?" Leathan asked, a deep frown brought his brows together.

Adlin shook his head and said, "He's trying now. I would suggest silence."

Silence? Seth was fuming. He'd rather they all yell at the meddlesome wizard even if he was supposedly the reason Seth was "alive."

Frustrated and determined, Seth swung up and around and once more focused on his body. Moving slowly this time he angled down toward his face, his closed eyes most specifically. If he could remain there, just beneath his lids, he knew he'd have it. But how to stay right there? Closing his mental eye, or at least what he'd been looking through so far, Seth focused on what it'd felt like to be in his body. The weight of his arms hanging off of his shoulders and the length of his legs. Funny, until this moment he'd never realized how heavy his body was.

With the focus of sitting behind his eyelids and wearing a heavy suit, he concentrated.

Focus… just continue to focus.

Snap. Pop. Woooooosh.

Seth struggled for breath. Was an elephant sitting on his chest? This felt horrible! Though he wanted to panic, he didn't. He never had. Why start now?

Breathing downright hurt… but he breathed. Somehow he breathed. He could sense it more than anything. No air rushed into his lungs. Or did it? Something stung. Something tasted horrible. Something smelled like absolute crap.

As though a spear broke through his chest, he arched.

And opened his eyes.

His real eyes. He knew it without doubt. It felt like the skin came unglued when he did. The elephant on his chest grew heavier. The dank, terrible smell of rot grew stronger. In fact, he felt disgusting. What was this?

Adlin's voice filtered through his misery. "It's rebirth, the first weight of life, Seth. It will pass."

Life? Hell no. Life didn't feel this way. At least not how he remembered it. With a great deal of effort he moved his tongue, just enough to scrape it over his molars. Not a good idea. Nasty.

"What's happening?"

Leathan's voice sounded like a thunder drum and Seth flinched. He heard a round of gasps.

"He's in his body now. Silence," Adlin said softly.

Uh…yeah! Silence would be wonderful. The wind high above the cave sounded like a tornado mere feet away. The trickle of water on the cave walls, a rushing river intent to wash him away. And the smell, what was that?"

Oddly enough, he sensed movement in the room and it didn't hurt his ears nearly as much as the sound over everyone's heartbeat. Peering up into the bright light, he saw her.

Her.

Alana looked down at him with… trepidation? Confusion? Fear?

Seth didn't like her looking at him like that. Like an angel with an attitude. Better yet, an angel that didn't particularly want to save him. One who wished she could turn and never look at him again.

That pissed him off.

Blood boiled and rushed through his head, then right down through his core and limbs. Without hesitation, he reached up. Or at least thought he did. Surprisingly enough, he felt her hand in his. Soft, cool, smooth, she touched him. Alana's face was clear now in his vision and her expression startled.

For several moments all he could do was stare up into those amber liquid pools. Her soul was in her eyes. And he liked what he saw.

"Seth?" Andrea whispered.

Blinking, he turned his gaze to his sister who stood on the other side. Tears welled in her eyes. This drove home the fact that he'd been dead. Kind of. Awe hell. With renewed determination he breathed deeply. Ouch! But the elephant had become a dog and the raunchy smell of death had nearly diminished.

"You can do it, lad," Devin said softly from somewhere near his feet.

"Aye," Leathan agreed.

"Few more breathes," Dakota whispered.

"It'll get better," Isabel said just as softly.

His eyes returned to Alana. She stood a silent

sentinel, as though she wasn't sure whether she supported his spirit melding with his body. Regardless, her small hand squeezed his.

He squeezed back.

The amber in her eyes flared as they had when they first jumped together.

It was time to jump again.

Using all the warlock power he'd come into Seth focused on being part of this world, part of his body. The dog became a cat on his body. The cat vanished. The smell vanished. He felt light. Blinking again, he lifted his other hand and took Andrea's. Running his tongue over his teeth one more time, he spoke. "Get me out of here."

As if they'd been waiting all along, Devin and Leathan moved Alana and Andrea aside and swooped in. Even though they each put an arm under his shoulders, Seth engaged his abs and sat up. The minute he did coughs raked him. But Devin and Leathan held on through it. Eventually, they subsided, as did all the feelings he'd felt when he first entered his body.

"You okay?"

He cocked his head slightly toward Leathan's voice and nodded.

"Missed you, lad," Devin said with a smile in his voice.

Seth worked at a grin then croaked, "Where's Alana?"

"Here," she said softly and appeared in front of him, Andrea on one side, Dakota on the other.

Alana's face somehow gave him strength. No, her eyes, now a super-pale amber, as though her soul had somehow thinned for him… waited for him?

"Right here," she repeated and reached out to take his hand again.

"Your hand is so soft," he said, so low he barely heard his own words.

"Your hand feels like sandpaper," she responded with a wink.

A smile hurt his face. "You're still you, eh?"

She squeezed slightly. "Well, what did you expect?"

"Not this." Another rough round of coughs broke from his chest and he released her hand. Once he caught his breath he lurched up and said to his cousins, "Get me out of this fucking coffin."

Devin and Leathan didn't hesitate but dragged him out and let him lean back against the coffin. Thankfully, they kept holding on. After a minute or so, he shook his head.

They let go.

Damn it felt good to stand on his own two feet. He'd missed this! Bracing his hands against the coffin, Seth hung his head and tried to gather his thoughts, tried to discreetly get used to the uncomfortable feeling of being back in his body. In a million years, he would've never imagined being separated from his body. He always figured he'd escape it.

But what had he really escaped?

"Death, laddie. Death."

His eyes snapped to Adlin but the ghost was nowhere to be found.

"Are you okay?" Andrea asked.

Seth looked at his sister and nodded. "I'm good. Just a little off right now."

She wiped away a tear. "I'll bet. I'm so glad to

have you back."

His cousins said nothing but he knew they'd mourned too. What a long road. Or had it been? "How long was I gone?"

"About a month," Leathan responded.

"That's it?"

Devin nodded.

"Felt like an eternity," Seth said.

"I'll bet," Leathan said.

"It must've been a heck of a ride, lad," Devin said softly. "Even for you."

Seth snorted. "You've no idea."

"Nope, we don't," Leathan said. "But when you're ready, you'll bloody well share."

A strange sensation rolled through him. It almost felt as though he didn't want to share. That though he'd hated it when he'd been wherever he'd been it hadn't really been so bad. Odd. Maybe he just felt that way because of the immediate and very negative feeling of being back in his body.

"Are you sure you're okay?" Alana asked, her voice whisper soft.

He looked down into her eyes, slightly disoriented by standing taller than her again. "Yeah, I'll be all right."

But would he? This was seriously messed up.

"You want to get out of here?" Dakota asked.

With a slow nod, Seth gazed around at the cave. "Yes."

"Hell right," Leathan agreed.

"Let's go," Devin said.

Both nodded avidly but neither left his side. He knew that they were waiting to hold him up if he couldn't successfully walk. Though the thought aggravated him he understood it. But he'd always been strong and daring and heck if he needed help now. One step in front of the other, he walked. And it worked. Seemed extremely odd but it worked. Amazing how good the human body felt after you got past the disturbing part of entering it. A certain sort of energy had started to enter his body.

As he headed for the mouth of the cave, his slow walk became a steady stride. His tight muscles loosened and life started to flow rapidly through his veins. Somehow he was stronger because of his experience. He knew it without question. The minute he stepped out into the muted sunlight, canvassed by trees, it felt like he'd stepped into heaven. Though the air was cool, it felt like bliss rushing into his lungs. The forest seemed slightly ominous, but the stark beauty of its energy made him stop short.

The others came up behind him and stopped as well.

"Gorgeous, isn't it?"

He nodded when Isabel asked. "Never quite saw it like this."

"What's he talking about?" Andrea asked.

"It's sort of like how I felt when I lost my hearing. My other senses sharpened. Even though he has no disabilities, I think that death itself was one and now his senses are more in-tune than ever."

"Wow," Devin said.

"That's intense," Leathan agreed.

"Seriously?" Dakota said.

"He's standing right here. Why don't you ask him," Alana said.

Silence.

"She's right." Seth turned and eyed them all,

gaze softening on Alana. "Just ask me. Don't speculate. I don't deal well with anything less than direct. You know that."

He was surprised to see them all look crushed. Andrea shook her head sharply. "No, don't look at us like that, Seth. Don't look at us like we're somehow wrong for wondering why you're acting the way you are. You died. We were devastated. This is a lot for everybody to handle."

Had to love his sister, he knew her well. "I think Isabel's right."

That's all he was willing to give right now. He swung and stalked into the woods. Everything smelled and looked different. About thirty steps away he swung back abruptly. They all remained where they'd stood. "This is what you feel like when you turn, eh Devin?"

Devin didn't flinch. "Probably. But my senses are that of a wolf so I can't be sure."

Seth sighed. "Of course you can be sure. We deal in magic, bro."

Leathan stepped up. "What he's trying to say is he's scared shitless. We lost you. Don't spit nails at us because you're confused. We're on your side."

Blinking, he staggered back a step. Nobody moved an inch save Alana. She was by his side in an instant. "What the hell, Seth."

Not weakened in the least from the tough love his cousins dished out, he focused on her. "I'm fine. No worries."

"Are you? Really?" she whispered. "You're white as a ghost."

Ghost. Good way of looking at it… of looking at him. "I'm fine. Really."

Her small hand landed on his forearm. "I think you need to rest."

"Probably," he muttered, ignoring the stunned look on everyone's face. True enough, he never relented to anything, never mind a pint-sized redhead.

"Where do we go from here?" she asked.

His eyes locked with hers. Good question.

A blush crawled over her cheeks and her freckles seemed to grow larger. "I mean, where do we all go."

Funny how her skin glowed now just like it did before she jumped off a cliff. He'd never get tired of that. Tired of that? He shook his head in confusion. Tired of what? Death really had messed with him for thinking long-term thoughts about any girl!

Turning away, he responded, "Your house. There's no other place for me to go."

Damn. That had sounded intimate. As he strode in a random direction he shot over his shoulder, "I've got to face whatever's in that house then we can all move on with our lives."

He'd made it a few more steps before Leathan said, "Um, Seth?"

Screw their sentiment or good intentions, this creature needed to be dealt with. He continued walking.

"Car is in the other direction, laddie."

Seth frowned and stopped at Devin's voice. Awe hell. He turned and strode in their direction. "Fine, let's go."

Everyone started walking. Nobody said a word. Good. He didn't need a lecture. He didn't need to be asked questions. And he certainly didn't need to talk about the creature he was about to face.

Within a half hour in all of which no one spoke,

he stood in front of the house. A house he'd only been able to drift around. A house he'd been unwilling to enter. At least in the state he'd...been in. He'd been petrified. And as much as he hated to admit it, the feeling hadn't entirely vanished.

Leathan stood on one side, Devin the other.

"With Calum's help we were able to make the house a little safer," Leathan said.

"And just how did you do that again?" Seth asked.

"With this." Devin held up an old journal.

Seth's eyes widened. "Calum's journal for this house?"

"Aye," Leathan said. "No need to search this time. It was literally handed to us."

"Calum's really starting to loosen up, eh?" Seth said.

"Seems so," Devin replied.

"Or this creature's so bad he had no choice," Dakota said.

Leathan nodded. "Very true, lassie."

Seth stopped at the front door, thoroughly irritated by the blatant fear he felt. "So how's that journal supposed to help?"

"Not sure. Calum didn't say. Just that it'd help protect us inside the house and that we all needed to be here," Leathan said.

He rolled his eyes. "Super." Not allowing himself time to overthink or let the fear take root too deep, Seth put his hand on the doorknob and entered.

It felt odd to finally enter the house he'd only hovered around. While the interior was obviously done in true Tudor style, the house looked nearly unlived in. Besides the living room, the furnishings elsewhere were covered with sheets. He frowned. Alana had been here long enough that it shouldn't look this neglected. Seth was about to say as much but she hadn't entered with the rest of them. "Where's Alana?"

Andrea nodded towards outside. "I think she headed for that rock again."

Without hesitation he headed for the door. This haunting could wait. "Be right back."

Though Devin and Leathan looked a little shocked neither argued with him.

What was with her and that rock? Strangely enough, he felt almost betrayed that she'd go there without him. It had sort of become their spot. But there she was leaning against it, eyes closed, face tipped to the sun. How many times had he watched her do that? And just as he'd felt when he watched her before, he marveled at the sheer smoothness of her ivory skin illuminated in sunlight.

Seth didn't say a word but leaned back against the rock next to her. It felt warm against his skin. The air felt clean going into his lungs. In fact, his body felt clean, even his teeth. For a moment, he felt at peace. As though the giant house in front of him didn't trap a beast set to destroy him. It was as if he was exactly where he was supposed to be with exactly who he was supposed to be with. He too leaned back his head, closed his eyes and let the sun warm his face.

A minute or so passed before she softly asked, "What was it like being...wherever you were?"

"Lonely," he answered honestly.

"I'll bet."

"Thank you."

"For what?"

"For being there. Hearing me."

"I didn't do it on purpose so you don't have to thank me."

He tilted his head forward and opened his eyes to find hers studying his face. "What's with you? Can't you take a compliment?"

She didn't bat a lash. "Sure. If it's deserved."

Seth crossed his arms over his chest. "Are you mad at me about something?"

Alana studied his face for a moment before she said, "I suppose I am."

"What?"

"Are you serious?"

He nodded. "Obviously."

Crossing her arms over her chest as he had, she said, "You died then you haunted me then," She nodded toward the house, "brought all this with you."

"Ah." She still maintained that feistiness he enjoyed. Seth grinned. "Yeah, sorry about all that."

Alana frowned. "You're not sorry in the least."

"Nope."

"Then why say that you are?"

"Dunno. To see you get fired up?"

She inhaled deeply through her nostrils. "I would've thought that death would've had more of an effect on you, Seth." Alana pushed away from the rock and walked toward the house.

"What do you mean by that?" He walked after her. "And wouldn't you rather death didn't change me?"

Alana stopped so quickly that he nearly walked right into her. Face red with anger she pointed a finger at his chest and said, "You needed some adjustments!"

Something about the fire in her eyes and the liquid heat of her tone set off his anger as well. Hell yeah, he needed some adjustments and knew right where to start. Before she knew what hit her, Seth pulled her into his arms.

And made his first adjustment.

CHAPTER FOUR

Stunned, Alana never expected what hit her.
Or had she?

The minute Seth's lips came down on hers she was free falling. The sensation was better than the best rush she'd felt. And she'd felt a lot of rushes. Yet he had a way of taking her past the edge of the cliff and beyond that heart-thumping near panic feeling that daredevils sought. Opening her mouth, she kissed him with as much enthusiasm as he did her. Blood rushed through her body so fast, her knees buckled.

But he held her up.

And he kept kissing her as though he wanted to suck the life out of her. It almost felt like he did, her senses were so far gone in pure feeling. At some point he pulled back slowly because it sure as heck wasn't her.

"I'm sorry," he said softly.

Her eyes opened slowly. Seth stared at her, his lips still dangerously close, the expression on his face one she'd never seen before. Damn, he was so good looking...and so close and strong and tall. For several moments all she could do was stare at his lips. Moistened and as gorgeous as the rest of his face, Alana felt lost. She never thought she'd look at this face again. His jet black hair glistened in the sun and his cutting, far-too-intelligent blue eyes never left hers.

She shouldn't be standing here with him right now. He died! He was dead… but not.

And God had she missed him.

Confident that her legs were no longer jelly, Alana untangled herself from him. There was no doubt he was sorry, but what for exactly? The kiss? Or everything else? She shook her head, turned and headed for the house. It would be a lie to say that she was truly mad at him. If anything, she felt bad for what he'd gone through. However, since the moment she'd met Seth, their relationship had been too fast, too furious, too over-the-top.

That's why she'd never let it go beyond friendship.

Seth said nothing more but followed her into the house. Alana would've thought she'd be terrified walking back into this place but knowing Seth and his team were here made it a little more tolerable. Besides, what choice did she have?

She'd promised her grandmom.

Despite the paranormal activity, Alana was once more acutely aware of the state of this place. Though she hated to admit it, she'd always been sort of happy Seth didn't come in when a ghost. He had to be wondering why the house looked so unkempt.

"In here!" Andrea said.

At least the living room had plenty of room to sit. It was huge. With two full sofas facing one another and boundless armchairs, this room like nearly all the others was built to host many. For a split second she considered hiring a cleaning crew to come and spruce this place up. Truth told, on her sanest day she wouldn't have strangers come in this house. Besides, of course, the ones who were already here.

A few laptops were set up here and there. More equipment had been added. "Why the camera facing out the window?" she asked.

"Victorian," Devin muttered and studied his laptop.

Huh?

"Nevermind him," Dakota said. "He just didn't like the Victorian that brought Leathan and I together. Come sit." She patted the spot on the couch next to her.

About the last thing Alana wanted to do was sit but she did. Seth, however, stalked around the room like a caged beast before he eventually left.

"Don't mind him," Dakota said. "Never could sit still."

Yeah, she got that, same with her. Regardless, Alana nodded.

"How are you doing, sugar?" Isabel asked and sat on her other side.

Alana would be lying if she said she didn't find the women somewhat comforting. They had a way about them. "Okay I guess."

"Okay is better than bad," Andrea said and winked. She sat across from them next to Devin.

"Yep, it is," Dakota agreed. "If I was in your shoes…no, I'm sorry, when I was in your shoes, I was going nuts. You're handling all of this really well, Alana."

"I agree," Isabel said.

"Aye lass," Leathan said. He was buried behind another laptop in the far corner.

"According to what I've seen so far, I really don't have much choice, do I?" Alana hadn't meant to sound so crass. Still, her emotions were pretty borderline right now.

"Nope, girl, you don't," Dakota said, eyes direct

and attitude no-nonsense.

Alana liked that. "I need to understand what the hell is going on now. What's in this house? How is Seth going to fight it? Why am I part of this?"

"That's what we're trying to figure out, lass," Devin said. "As soon as Seth finishes romping around we'll start reading the journal. That should shed some light."

As soon as Seth finishes romping around? It was only then that it occurred to Alana that while the women were fairly calm, Devin and Leathan's posture seemed stiff. How often did they wait for their cousin to relax? Or was this just a matter of them being compassionate because of his ordeal?

"I'm finished," Seth grumbled. He plopped down on the other side of Devin and slid the laptop his way. Scowl on his face, he proceeded to click away on the computer, his eyes flickering rapidly over various things. "Camera's caught nothing of what happened to you in this house with the creature. Why do you suppose that is?" Before anyone could answer he continued, "Nevermind. What I figure is this creature doesn't sit still any longer than I do. Makes sense."

"You're tired and hungry," Andrea said. "I'm going to go fix you something to eat."

Seth didn't respond but continued to eye the computer screen. He tapped the backside of his fingernail on the screen. "What's this?"

"That's it. Whatever it is," Devin replied.

"The shadow that passed over the room when you all ran out is the creature I'm supposed to fight?"

"Yep," Leathan said, his eyes still glued to his laptop.

"You all look scared shitless," Seth muttered and

clicked a button, studying the screen more closely.

"We were having the bloody life sucked out of us," Devin said. "No doubt we were scared shitless."

Alana shivered and tried not to think about it. As though he sensed it, Seth's eyes shot to her and narrowed. What? Did he expect that she would've merely shrugged this off? Guy would have to be out of his mind.

"What was it like for you?" Seth asked.

A brief flicker of interest flashed over everyone's faces as they looked from Seth to Alana. Okay. Fine. She'd tell him. "It sucked. Hard."

"That tells me everything I need to know," he muttered dismissively and refocused on the screen.

"Excuse me?" What a jackass.

Seth's eyes slowly rose to hers. "It sucked…hard? That's all you can say? I was a friggin' ghost outside your house for weeks haunting you and all you can say about what happened in here with my greatest enemy was that is sucked hard?"

Oh no he didn't just say that! She felt her face get red. "Yeah, Seth. It sucked. From the second you died in front of my eyes in that cave, to the insanity you made me feel talking in my ear the past several weeks to the totally evil thing in this house that's after you. It felt like it wanted to eat my soul and digest it slowly. It was that bad!" Alana leaned forward and narrowed her eyes in challenge. "You need more details asshole?"

Isabel gasped. Dakota snorted. Leathan and Devin made sounds that could have been muffled chuckles. The air nearly crackled with energy between her and Seth as the second's ticked away.

"It's been my experience through all of this that

anger gets us nowhere fast," Isabel said, her gentle voice breaking the uncomfortable tension between them. "Perhaps it's time to take a look at that journal."

"Agreed." Devin smiled warmly at Isabel.

Alana frowned at the floor. Seth really could rile her up. She'd forgotten about that. It had been their swift downfall to begin with. Literally.

Leathan sat next to Dakota. Luckily, the sofas were so large they could easily sit six people each. He eyed the room briefly before he pulled a brown leather encased book out of his pocket. "Here it is."

The tension had fizzled and everyone's attention became solely focused on the journal.

"It's like the first one," Andrea whispered.

"Aye," Leathan responded.

When Alana looked at him with curiosity he responded, "The first journal had nothing on its pages. Or at least not anything anyone could see save Devin, Seth and me."

"That's unbelievable," she responded.

"I thought so too at the time, but it's true," Andrea said. "Using magic, Calum somehow managed to write it for their eyes only."

Alana didn't know what to make of that. What to make of any of this really. Could everything her grandmom had ranted about for years be true? Lord, she hoped not. But shoot, she'd already seen and experienced so much in this house, nothing seemed overly far-fetched at this point.

"It's something else," Dakota said. "But they know better than to keep it from us now, eh boys?"

All three nodded and grumbled.

Leathan began reading what Calum had written

in his journal.

"May 13th, 1870

We've started construction on the new house. I must admit that I'm tired. So tired. I feel so old. My thirty-seven years feel like two-hundred. It's no wonder considering I started this nightmare nearly that long ago and traveled over three hundred years through time to build the houses to trap these beasts. Now, after building the Georgian, I find myself obsessed anew with the thought of my beloved Anna. Is she, as it seemed there, that aware of me? Does she follow me from the afterlife? While I hope, I also dread the thought. She has always deserved better than me."

Leathan sat back and pinched the bridge of his nose. "He's a mess."

"What did you expect?" Andrea asked. "You saw what happened in the Georgian." She glanced at Devin then Isabel. "I'm sorry. I mean your house."

Isabel shook her head. "It was your house before ours and did you no favors. Speak how you like about it. Or should I say how it was."

"What exactly happened in the Georgian," Alana asked.

"You mean what didn't happen," Seth muttered.

"Dimensions," Leathan responded and frowned at Seth before turning kind eyes Alana's way. "Bloody house covered a span of three hundred years but made sure it brought Devin and Isabel together."

"Ah." She lightly nipped the inside of her cheek in contemplation. "And what did the Victorian do again?"

"Pretty much the same shit," Seth grunted.

Andrea gave him a bag of chips and a soda.

"Brother, I'm glad to have you back, more than you know, but could you stop swearing? Seriously. Driving me crazy."

Seth shrugged a shoulder and continued to study the laptop. "Sure sis."

But he'd said it like he could really care less. Alana crossed one leg over the other and sat back. Seth was officially a lost cause. Yeah, he'd been dead, not fun, but he was out of his mind right now. Best to listen to the rest of them. They seemed far saner.

"If we're going to stay here very long, someone's going to need to run to the grocery store." Andrea smiled at Alana. "It's enough that we crashed your house. We don't intend to eat all your food."

"No worries." Alana sighed. "You'd be welcome to whatever I have. Pretty much live on granola bars, chips and soda."

"Mmm hmm, saw that." Andrea's expression grew worried. "A decent meal would do you good."

"Maybe after we learn more about this house," Leathan reminded. "Remember how easily we became distracted in the Victorian, lass."

"He's right," Seth said. He tore open the bag of chips, cracked open the soda and started munching like he hadn't eaten in centuries.

The way Alana figured, it probably felt like centuries. His body had to be depleted. Then again, technically, his body should be a broken husk. But that obviously wasn't the case.

Leathan continued reading from the journal.

"May 15th, 1870

The foundation for the house is underway and I

can't help but think fondly of Isabel and the Georgian."

Leathan paused and looked at Isabel. Startled, Alana glanced at her as well. Isabel's expression seemed slightly nostalgic. "Go on, Leathan."

So he did.

Calum wrote, "I'm glad that Isabel ended up with it. Such a lovely home. Much like this house will be when finished. It is my hope of course, that its walls will be strong enough. That the spell I lay upon it will be strong enough. So many types of creatures my former clan could've sent after my family and they chose this one last. I sometimes wonder why they didn't send it first. Surely it's far more powerful than the others."

Alana coughed. Leathan stopped reading. They all looked at her except for Seth. His dour expression remained on the computer screen.

"You okay hun?" Dakota asked.

Yeah. Nope. What exactly was in this house? The tickle persisted.

"Here, drink." Andrea handed her Seth's soda.

Grateful, she drank a few sips, acutely aware that his lips had been there minutes before hers…which was about the last thing that should be on her mind! The feeling passed and she nodded at Leathan. "Sorry about that. Go on."

Nodding, he read, "The stone needs to be well hidden. But where? I had the other two well- planned but this time I'm aimless. Lost. Where should I hide something from one of death's minions, a reaper itself?"

Seth's head snapped up. He narrowed his eyes. Nausea welled up in the pit of Alana's stomach. A reaper? Like the grim reaper? Oh dear God. They existed and there was more than one?

"Damn it all to hell," Seth barked and stood. It took mere moments of romping around the room before he stopped abruptly and a strange, devilish twinkle entered his eyes. "What's it gonna do to me? I've already died, sort of. I've been defying death my whole life." He turned slowly and exclaimed to thin air, "Bring it!"

"Seth!" Andrea stood and frowned. "Could you be any more of a moron? Seriously. What are you thinking?"

"Lad doesn't do much thinking." This time Adlin spoke from the large mirror over the mantle, his ghostly image wavering. His heavy frown confronted Seth. "Hate to say it but you need to learn respect. Some creatures respond better to it."

"Respect! The gall!" This from Calum who peeked out from the glassy reflection of the coffee table. "Death deserves no respect."

"I tend to agree," Seth seconded.

"I never did label you the brightest of the three," Adlin said sarcastically. "Death deserves more respect than anything that's out there, save God himself. And most times, the two go hand in hand."

Calum and Seth snorted. Andrea plunked down on the sofa and appeared completely defeated. Alana bit her lower lip. Her grandmom had repeated those words to her many times as a child.

"I beg to differ, old man," Calum said. "This creature wants my descendant dead."

Adlin huffed. "They all did, fool. This one's no different in that respect."

Calum's spirit wavered in the glass. "I beg your pardon. This fool's managed to save two lads so far. The reaper won't get who it's come for."

"How do I fight it? What do I do?" Seth asked.

A tapping sound came from beneath the coffee table as though Calum clicked a fingernail on it. "You keep reading that journal."

"And locate the bloody stone," Adlin added before they vanished.

"They seem a little less comical this haunting," Devin said.

"So far," Seth growled. "Give them time."

Leathan ignored them and kept reading from Calum's journal.

"May 19th, 1870

It's a rather nice spring here in Vermont. So far everything is going smoothly. Luring this creature is going to take a little something... or should I say someone extra and I think I've found the perfect person. She's young but Isabel was the same age. It needs her more for her supernatural abilities than anything."

Leathan stopped reading and frowned. "Why the hell didn't Calum mention this to us when he made his ghostly appearances? Why all the mystery?"

Before anyone could answer he continued reading from Calum's passage. "She's amazing and beautiful and different. It's as though we've always known one another. I'm not entirely sure what to make of Grace outside of the fact that I need her for this project and—"

"Stop," Alana said and he did. "What did you say this woman's name was?"

"Grace."

A strange feeling began to uncurl in her belly. What were the odds?

"Why?" Seth asked.

"Nothing. Sorry, continue," Alana said.

Leathan nodded and kept reading. "And I feel she's somehow connected to this property. It will take time to figure out why she's connected but for the first time since I left Anna behind… I find myself attracted to a woman. How terrible of me. But I can't seem to help it. She's alluring with her long black hair and sultry golden eyes."

Alana jumped up. "Sorry. I've gotta go to the bathroom. Be back."

Before anyone could say a word she bounded up the stairs. No running to the rock this time. Halfway down the hallway with its wooden beams and old world feel, she stopped and leaned back against the wall. There's no way it was connected. Impossible, right? Biting her lower lip, she dropped her head and tried to remember everything. All the stories told.

"Well aren't you something," Seth said as he sauntered down the hallway.

"Of all people, they sent you to check on me?" She rolled her eyes and said, "And here you ventured, deeper into the abyss of your worst nightmare."

"Okay, enough." He leaned against the wall opposite her. "Sorry I was a jerk down there. I don't want to fight with you. Got enough to worry about." A charming smile erupted. "Besides, you're the girl who lured me here, right?"

Alana almost rolled her eyes again but saw a glimmer of something in his eyes that gave her pause. A certain something that hadn't been there in the old dare-devil Seth. Was that caution? Concern? What she mostly wondered though… was the same glimmer reflected in her eyes?

"I just needed some space," she said softly.

"Let me tell you something about space," he said. "In the end, once you leave your body, you'll have plenty of it. While you're still here on Earth, take a little less of it. Enjoy the people around you. Or at least," he swallowed hard, "don't run from them as fast."

Speechless, she stared at him. It was as though he'd somehow read her mind. Running was what she'd always done best. Straight off a cliff, out of a plane, anywhere she could find that gave her lots of space extra fast. "I can't," she murmured, "this."

His brows came together and he frowned. "This what?"

Alana leaned her head back against the wall. "Grandmom used to tell me I was special. That I was different. That if I aimed high, I could conquer the world."

"Sure, what good grandparent wouldn't say that."

Alana wet her dry lips. "She was different too."

Seth's blue eyes appeared black and intense in the dim light of the hallway. "Are you trying to get to something, Alana?"

With a slow blink she shook her head and said, "I remember the first day I moved into this house." She looked down. "This very carpet appeared brand new. Everything was freshly polished." Alana inhaled deeply, remembering. "The whole house smelled of lemon oil."

Seth remained silent as if he understood she needed this moment.

"Grandmom would take my hand and walk me down this hallway. The sunlight would stream through the windows. I remember struggling to see a dust mote but none could be found. This house was spotless... even of dust it seemed."

"A kid sees things different. Dust probably wasn't on your mind," Seth said.

His kind tone pulled her from her brief reverie and she once more locked eyes with him. "The lack of dust has been on my mind for a very long time. Every old house should have dust motes floating in the sun. Even newer houses should, don't you think? I mean dust is dust. Human skin, hair, something."

Seth shrugged. "Our memories from childhood don't include dirt, Alana. What's up? Why are you obsessing?"

"Because of her," she whispered.

"Who?"

Alana nodded to the picture on the wall beside him. "My grandmom."

Seth turned and froze. Within seconds everyone was heading down the hallway as if he'd called them with his mind. Had he?

Devin was the first to speak, "Holy hell."

Leathan said, "That's got to be her. Strange, I don't remember seeing this earlier."

Seth at last tore his eyes from the woman in the painting and looked at Alana. "That's your Grandmom. Really?"

Alana looked at the three foot tall painting hung across from her and nodded. Her Grandmom stared back, her long black hair flowing around her shoulders and her golden eyes sultry and far too direct. "Her name was Grace."

"Wow!" Dakota said. Whipping out a small black box she looked at Alana and said, "This is an EMF detector. It helps to detect the Electro Magnetic Field around an object. Do you mind if I run it around the picture?"

Alana gestured at the portrait. "No, it's fine. Go for it."

Strange crowd she was in but she understood. This is what they did. They investigated the paranormal. Little did they know just how supernatural her Grandmom really was. Or so she said. But now... it seemed more likely than ever. Ugh. Why hadn't she believed her! Deep down Alana knew she must've known. And denied it.

Seth continued to stare at the portrait, his eyes searching before they slowly swung her way. No one noticed. They were too busy studying the woman whom Calum must've spoken of in his journal. With a sleek casualness, he came to her, his gaze curious and a slight too cunning. Hand against the wall by her head he leaned in close and whispered, "You keep secrets."

Alana ground her jaw but kept her eyes locked with his. "I love my family."

His eyes grew darker, more mysterious. "Me too."

"Then why look at me like that. As if I lie."

"Because you do. About something."

"I think all of our truths will come out in this house," she countered softly.

Seth cocked his head. "I hope so."

"She's gorgeous!" Dakota chirped and stuck her head into their private alcove. "Seth, stop being so intense. Alana, have you got any more pictures of her?"

Her eyes dropped from Seth's and fell easily to his wide chest which was far too close right now. "Somewhere. Sure."

"Well, I'd say we need to see them because this is definitely the woman Calum is talking about," Leathan said. "Very interesting that she's your grandmother."

"For sure," Andrea said.

They had no idea. Not one of them. The world tilted. Her hand rose to Seth's chest. He didn't budge an inch. He felt so hard beneath her palm. Suddenly, the feel of him became a lifeline to this world. Alana breathed deeply through her nostrils and released the air through her mouth. This, them… him, felt like too much.

"Shhh, come here." Before she could dart away Seth's arms were around her. So much taller, his chest became a pillow. A hard pillow but a place for her cheek none-the-less. Had to hand it to him, he had a strange way of driving her to insanity then being the one to catch her when she fell. Not that she was falling. Her legs still worked. Alana wasn't running though. Seth felt safe. In the midst of all the insanity, he was a lifeline… a crazy, intense, out-of-control-himself lifeline. Regardless, some air would do her good.

"I have to get out of here," she mumbled.

His body moved as though he nodded his head. "Good idea."

Before she could respond he grabbed her hand and pulled her after him. Right down the stairs and out the door they went. The late day ushered in coolness and sunlight zig-zagged through the trees.

There was barely a chance to admire the scenery he moved so fast. Seth, by his very stride, relished being outdoors again. That alone, brought a small smile to her face. What could he be thinking? There was little they could do anywhere without equipment.

Seth spun and she nearly walked into him. "See, that's where you're wrong."

"So you can read minds," she murmured.

"When I want to." He winked. "But there are things we can do out here that'll get your blood rushing."

"I don't," she started to say.

"Yeah you do." He pulled her after him. Strangely enough they didn't go any further than her rock before he turned and said, "Climb it, then climb that."

Squinting, she looked up the rock to the Pine tree beyond. "You're out of your mind."

Seth shrugged. "Yeah, so? Always have been. Go for it."

Her brows lowered. He was serious. But even as she doubted him her eyes were scouting a way up the rock then further onward. Hell, it could be done. Why hadn't she seen it before?

"Because I was too busy talking in your ear," he said.

Alana glanced at him only to find him leaning sideways against the rock with a shit-eating grin on his face. "You did talk too much."

Seth nodded slightly then looked up. "You first or me?"

That familiar bubbling sensation started beneath her skin. A challenge. With a wink she responded, "Me."

His strong hand cupped her behind and helped hoist her up the rock. Only about twenty feet tall, she found footholds easily in the craggy rock. At the top, she didn't hesitate but ran and jumped, grabbing the lowest limb on the nearby pine. Like she'd let him beat her! Determined, eager, angry almost, she hoisted up then stood, then jumped for another. Who cared if the bark bit into her skin or the branches scraped her face, it felt like bliss.

The sharp bite of pine stung her nostrils in the cooling air. The needles poked her bare skin. Still, she climbed. Higher and higher. The rush of knowing that so many feet lay between her and the ground started to burn through her subconscious and the familiar rush of living on the edge made her breathe faster.

"Slow female."

Seth was right behind her, then trying to sidle up past her on the opposite side. Hell no! With a grunt and thrust she started to fly. Before she knew it she was out of branches and scooping a hand along the sharp spines at the top.

Seth swung onto the branch opposite her within seconds, his blue eyes alive. "Not bad."

"Not bad? Hmph." But Alana wasn't aggravated in the least. No. She was totally stoked. The climb had felt amazing!

Seth threw back his head and laughed. "Great to be alive!"

It did feel great to be alive! Gazing around, she grinned. They were high. Higher than the house and most of the surrounding trees. Seth sat nonchalantly, looking as sexy and comfortable lounging on a tree branch as he did a sofa.

She couldn't help but grin. "You're pretty proud

The Tudor Revival

of yourself, eh?"

"Damn straight." Grinning, he stretched his arms over his head and held onto the branch with his muscular thighs.

Doing the same, Alana couldn't help but love life. This was life! The fresh air, height, freedom…him.

Seth leaned forward and propped his arms on the branch like some sort of sexy fairy. "So tell me more about your Grandmom. About this house."

Alana did the same, swinging her legs, inhibitions non-existent. "Not much to tell. She was old. So was this house. Never knew my mom."

"Ah." Casually, he picked at a piece of bark. "So it's that same old story."

His bluntness didn't faze her in the least. Seth wasn't known for tact. "Guess so."

Starting on another piece of bark he asked, "How do you suppose Calum knew your Grandmom? Time frame doesn't work out."

She'd already been thinking about that. "Who knows. Magic?"

Seth's finger stilled on the bark and his clear blue eyes rose to hers. "Really?"

"Oh, don't be an ass." Alana leaned forward like a cat stretching out, purely enjoying the freedom around her. "Your attempt at manipulation is obvious."

Grinning he responded, "Is it?"

"Yes."

"Then I won't do it again."

"So you admit it."

"Admit what?"

Alana grinned. "That you're trying to work me

into putty until you get the answers you want."

Seth brushed away the air with a hand. "Naw. That'd be tactless."

"Yep."

"You like the way you feel right now, Alana?"

"You know I do."

So fast she barely saw it he leaned over and grabbed her wrist, his eyes deadly serious. "Then fess up."

Alana wasn't surprised in the least by his behavior. Seth always lured his victims by pushing them to the edge. The only problem as far as she was concerned? She wasn't nearly close enough to the edge. With a wide grin she said, "You really want my confession?"

An equally wide smile split his face. "Yep."

"Then come get it!"

Before he had a chance to respond she flipped around the branch and began to free fall. She'd measured the distance between every branch going up and knew right where every single one was going down. Seems he did too because she heard the woosh of sound coming down hard behind her. Alana timed it just right and swung off the last branch, slid down the side of the rock and landed hard on her feet. Within seconds, Seth thumped down behind her.

There were a lot of things she wanted to say to him. Mostly that she'd won. As was to be expected, his family was lined up in front of them, every last one of them wearing a look of blatant exasperation. Alana spit a pine needled out of her mouth and said, "Everything's okay."

The women chuckled. The men frowned.

"Really, everything's fine. We just needed some

time alone," Seth assured, a grin obvious in his voice.

Leathan pointed at the house with his thumb. "We got a bad spirit in there and you're climbing trees, lad. Bloody hell!"

"That's right, hubby," Dakota said to Leathan with a pointed look. "We've got a bad spirit in there and they're climbing trees. Kind of like us at the Victorian playing in the snow and taking too long to get wood from the basement."

"I'm with Leathan, time's limited. Gotta move on this," Devin said.

"Sort of like us vanishing into the woods and avoiding everyone at every opportunity when things got rough at the Georgian, right Devin?" Isabel asked.

Devin and Leathan wore mad frowns when they said, "Right!"

Seth stretched and grinned. "Sucks to be on the other end of the haunting, eh?"

"You're facing death bro!"

"Are you outta your mind!"

"Stop!" Andrea said and shook her head. "The three of you are crazy. Seriously crazy."

"Agreed." Seth grabbed Alana's hand and pulled her toward the house. "At least we're all crazy together."

Alana stumbled after him, a small grin on her face. Despite the fact that Seth generally irritated the hell out of her, she'd give him ten points for being fun. He had an unintentional way of keeping her mind occupied and very excited. An excited mind was a happy mind in her book.

"It's death, lad. Death wants you."

Seth didn't slow his pace at Leathan's declaration but only pulled her faster. "Fine, if death wants me, it'll fight me." At the front door he stopped short and turned, his come-hither eyes magnetizing yet pushing her away. "You," he said softly. "You stop here. Go away. Climb a tree, jump off a cliff." He paused for several seconds before he said, "Not time for you to face death."

Affronted but used to him, she said, "Then why the drama? Why the tree? You're a mess. You did all that for me…kinda." Alana stopped and moved closer. Her throat felt thick and underused. "But you did it for you too."

"No," he said calmly. "It got you out of the house. Away."

"No," she responded. "That's where you're wrong." Inch by inch, she ran her hand up his arm until she grasped his forearm. "It got me closer to this house. And you."

As though he'd been slapped, Seth pulled away and entered the house. Alana watched him go. Knew somehow if she followed there'd be no going back. How did she know that? Halfway into the foyer he turned and said, "You're still standing there. Make up your mind, Alana."

Seth turned and walked into the living room. Alana stood on the threshold. What had she really expected? That he'd carry her over? That he'd want her to fight alongside him? Nope. Not Seth's style. So she stood there for a minute or so knowing damn well his family was behind her waiting. No matter what any of them thought Alana knew she had to walk back in. She knew that this was her fight too.

After all, Calum, the man who had built this house, had fallen irrevocably in love with her Grandmom.

CHAPTER FIVE

Seth scowled his way through the entire meal until he just couldn't help himself and smiled at Devin. "Hell of a meal, cuz."

Devin chuckled. "Amazing what you can do with potato chips, cheese and some salsa."

Leathan winked at Alana. "Don't mind them. You look good considering your diet."

"No doubt," Seth said through a munchful, eying Alana with appreciation. The girl looked absolutely miserable, but hot none-the-less. After a swig of soda he asked, "How the hell do you stay so slim living on potato chips?"

Her amber eyes flared to life. "Keep burning the carbs."

One thing was for sure, he loved teasing her. Seth'd never been more proud than he was the moment she'd entered the house earlier. For that matter, he'd never been so proud than when she'd scaled that pine out back at the speed of light. Watching her cute little ass shimmy up that tree had been the highlight of his year. Chick had some mad moves. Best thing? She had absolutely no idea how smoking hot she was. Half her allure he supposed.

"I'll go buy some food after this," Devin assured. "We eat a lot."

Alana merely nodded and munched. Something about her kept Seth looking again and again. Maybe it was the way she fired up against him. If he pushed a little too hard, she pushed back harder. Her eyes would flare, her lips would thin and she'd give him that look that said, "Oh yeah, buddy? You think you've whipped me?"

Seth contemplated her mouth. Her lips were a little too full for her face and her straight teeth a little too white for her skin tone but somehow it pieced together well. He liked it. His favorite part was always the animation that drove her face from calm to moody to wild. The way her lips pulled back slightly and she breathed too hard when she got worked up. He honestly couldn't help wonder again and again what she'd be like in bed. A fucking wildcat he imagined. Again and again.

Grinning at his own thoughts, Seth asked with a very direct look her way, "So where are we sleeping tonight?"

"Wouldn't you like to know," she cut back.

Oh, he liked that. And damn if she didn't know it. Or did she? Girls didn't typically make him behave this way. Usually, he'd tower over them, slip them a sexy grin, and saunter his way through the rest of their brief relationship. Typically, he got them into bed before he dove off a cliff with them.

Time to focus. "So where's the journal?" he asked.

"Here," Leathan said and opened it. "Everyone good with me continuing to read over supper?"

"Aye," Devin said.

Seth and the women nodded.

Leathan read.

"May 30th, 1870

I'm becoming obsessed with her. This house needs to be built. A creature needs to be trapped but there's only her, Grace. Why does she become more beautiful? What is the draw? This isn't right. The attraction is so strong. I watch her walk around the property as the men build. Unlike Isabel, she does not dictate. Instead, she is a silent matriarch to whom the men seem to respond. The house has only just begun but I believe she has a picture already in her mind of how it should look. Every angle, every slope, is being created in her eye. Is Grace the very creature I hope to trap? Who else can she be? So precise. So perfect. So very much my enemy."

Seth had watched Alana the whole time Leathan read. He'd watched her lips go slack, her eyes wander aimlessly. What was it between her and her grandmother? What did she know? He wanted to take her hand, squeeze it, and reassure her somehow. The inclination annoyed the hell out of him.

Leathan continued to read.

"June 5th, 1870

The house is going to be amazing and I think I have a solid grasp on my feelings for Grace now. She is but a woman and I but a man. Isn't that what they all say? Well, it is true. I hold tight to my feelings about my beloved Anna. After what happened in the Georgian I know that she's watching me more closely than ever from the afterlife. That what exists between here and there is but a sheath of reality."

Leathan turned the page and stopped.

"What?" Andrea asked.

"It's blank," he responded.

"I don't believe you."

"It is. Not lying."

Devin leaned over and started to flip through the rest of the journal, shaking his head. "It's empty," he assured.

Seth grabbed the journal and flipped through it

again. "He's right."

"How is that possible?" Isabel asked.

"Good question," Dakota said.

"This makes no sense," Seth said. "She helped him build this house. Her granddaughter lives in it." Frowning, he continued to study the book.

"Which makes no sense," Andrea murmured. She glanced at Alana, "Sorry, but you know what I mean. How can you be her granddaughter? You must be a great-great granddaughter."

Seth set down the book. He'd been onto that before he led her outside. What had made him lose his train of thought? Clear as day he'd known that the math didn't add up but once he got her outside and seen the stress leave her pretty face. Once he'd seen the color return to her cheeks and fire light her eyes again, nothing else had mattered, least of all rationale. He knew better! It was almost as if he'd been bewitched.

Alana was busy running a potato chip through an errant chunk of salsa and not responding.

Andrea asked again. "Alana, who is Grace to you?"

"My Grandm—"

"No," Seth said. "She wasn't. You're lying. Don't try to deny it. Dealing with lying people is one of my strongpoints." Alana pursed her lips. "As a warlock." Her body nearly deflated.

Her hands began to shake but she shoved them in her pockets and stood. "I've gotta go the bathroom," she mumbled and strode from the room.

No doubt, she liked to avoid uncomfortable situations via the "bathroom." But why was this making her so uncomfortable. Seth immediately followed her into the foyer. Alana turned back, obviously about to say something but the words died on her lips.

"What, are you surprised to see me?"

Seth whipped around and blinked. "Calum?"

Calum waved him away and walked into the foyer. "Of course. And you are Seth. Not surprising in the least."

Seth leaned against the banister. Huh?

"Holy crap." Alana stared into the living room.

Seth looked that way. It wasn't the same! His cousins were gone. And Calum! He wasn't peeking out of a mirror but whole and wandering around as if he was judging….

"What the hell!" Seth said.

Calum pretty much ignored him but still managed to murmur, "What the hell what?"

"You! This!" Seth exclaimed. Alana seemed as confused as him. He took her hand. Okay, it felt real enough. The look of panic and horror on her face probably matched his. He kept his voice low when he asked her, "Are you seeing what I am?"

"It's so clean," she murmured in wonder, her eyes scanning everything. "And new! Like when I was a kid."

"Oh, heck," he replied and turned to Calum. "Do you know who I am?"

Calum whipped off his top hat and spun. "Of course, lad. You're Seth, my descendant."

Seth was all about excitement but he'd had enough of it for at least another day. Dying had pretty much covered everything. Now, here he stood, face-to-face with Calum who was very much alive. All he could think of was how envious he'd been of Devin when he'd traveled back in time. Now, knowing damn well he'd done the same, Seth wanted none of it. At least not yet.

"Where is everyone?" Alana whispered.

"They're not here," Seth responded. And of course he knew what to say because above all else, he was a warlock now. And everything he'd learned about his new gift told him to take slow moves. That he knew the truth. But still, take slow moves. After all, he didn't know exactly where he was.

"You've just arrived in the past. The date is one year after the last journal log that Leathan read. "It's June 6th, 1871," Calum said matter-of-factly as he walked over to join them.

Seth stared at the man who had haunted them for so long. A guy who'd caused this whole mess. A guy that looked a lot like him! "Stop."

Calum did, his expression compliant.

"I don't understand," Alana said.

"I'm sorry, my dear," Calum said, an instant wide grin on his face as he took her hand. "I'm Calum. Not the ghost but the living, breathing man in the year 1871. I apologize for the inconvenience."

Stunned, she looked him up and down but kept her composure. "I'm sure you are."

Seth wondered if she even understood.

Calum turned and strolled up the stairs. "Grace will be back soon."

Alana stormed by him and caught up with Calum within two seconds. Step by step, she followed his stride up the stairs. "Rude! You!" She grabbed his arm. "Stop!"

"Make it quick," Calum said, coming to an abrupt halt.

Watching with amusement, Seth wondered if she'd actually push Calum down the stairs.

"What the hell are you talking about, 1871? And stop being so presumptuous about all of this. I'm scared. Talk to me."

Both Calum and Seth stared mutely at her.

Calum cleared his throat first. "I'm sorry." Discombobulated, he took her hand and had her sit on the stair next to him. "You seem to understand some of this."

"Of course I do!" Alana growled and looked between Seth and Calum. "I'm rolled back in time, eh?" She gulped but continued. "That's fine. Whatever. But I'll tell you this, the least you can do is explain things."

Seth knew his mouth hung open. What a woman!

Calum nodded. "Aye, you're not where you were before." He looked at her with admiration. "And you're taking this rather well I must say."

"I've no choice, do I?"

Calum looked over her carefully. "No you don't."

"Well then," Alana stared down at Seth. "I need to know how this house is coming along. More importantly... I need to know where Grace is."

"Here! Who wants to know?"

Seth's attention swung to the woman who strode into the foyer. If his mouth had been gaping before it'd officially hit the floor at this point. The woman in the portrait! Grace. Damn, was she fine. With the same determined stride as Alana, she stopped short, her intelligent eyes moving swiftly over him and landing on Alana. A flicker of recognition flashed in her eyes. "Alana?"

"Indeed," Calum remarked. "Isn't it something. She's all grown up."

"Yes she is," Grace murmured and stopped at the base of the stairs. "And why is that?"

"Mommy!"

Eyes watering, Alana spun and stared up the stairs. A little girl barreled past her and flew into Grace's arms. You're home!"

Seth couldn't help but stare. This was stupid crazy. Damn if the little girl didn't look like a little version of…

"My sweet Alana," Grace scooped up the little red-headed girl.

For the first time in his life, Seth was completely caught off guard. When he looked at Alana, he could tell she was too. Her face was white as chalk and her lower lip trembled. Wide liquid gold eyes stared at the scene unfolding in the foyer.

"How?" she whispered.

Grace set down the little girl. "Go run outside. I'll come play soon."

Nodding, little Alana bounced off out the door, for the most part oblivious to the strangers in her house. Then again, how old was she? Four?

As graceful in action as she was in name, Grace smiled warmly at Seth then turned her attention to Alana. The adult Alana. "Forgive my rudeness. I've been away for a few days." Her affectionate eyes moved to Calum. "She really has no idea, does she?"

"I told you she wouldn't, my dear. I am very good at what I do."

"Without doubt you are."

Alana seemed to suddenly get a grip. "What the hell is going on?"

Seth didn't miss the nostalgic way that Alana's eyes remained glued to Grace's face or the way she clenched her fists tightly within her pockets.

Grace's expression was nothing less than affectionate. It was obvious that she knew exactly who Alana was. Undoubtedly, she gazed at Alana as fondly as she had the little girl who just ran out the front door. "You know me as your Grandmom, do you not? At least an older version of me."

Alana's eyes remained locked on Grace. "Mmm hmm."

"Well, the truth is sweetheart, I'm your mother. Always have been."

Sonofabitch! Alana's face went through about six emotions in one second flat. She shook her head.

"It is the truth," Calum declared. He ran a hand through his hair and shrugged. "We had to do it this way."

Seth got a hold of his senses. "Had to do what this way?"

Alana and Grace continued to stare at one another. Calum answered, "Play with Alana's memory a bit. It was the only way to get her back to this house."

"Let me explain," Grace began.

"Please do," Alana said.

Seth had to admit, she was taking this like a trooper. Had some part of her suspected? Of course, must have.

Grace slowly sat, angled on the bottom step. Seth knew she wanted to go to Alana, take her hand, even hug her, but knew better. "You see, we in our own way, are part of the very curse laid on this house. Well, at least I am and through me… you…

somehow."

Alana shook her head. "Vague. I need more. Much more."

Grace's brow arched. "You keep a cool head, my child. I'm impressed."

"You didn't exactly raise me to think inside the box," Alana countered.

"No, I didn't. With good purpose."

"Hope so."

Seth didn't miss the sarcasm. Neither did everyone else. Alana's face was getting red, her freckles more pronounced.

Grace folded her hands on her lap, expression reserved. "I do not know why I was drawn here. I do not know why I need to be part of this project. I am eternally grateful to Calum that he's allowed me to help as I have." Her gaze flickered briefly to Calum before returning to Alana. "With Calum's help, I was able to make you forget your childhood here and the next hundred and ten years or so. I aged far slower than normal, as did you. It might have had to do with my craft or it might have had to do with this very house."

"Your craft," Alana whispered. "You did have a craft, didn't you?"

Grace looked down at her folded hands before her level gaze returned calmly to Alana. "I do. As do you."

Damn. Was Alana like him? Seth kept his mouth shut and listened. No easy task for him.

Alana swallowed and said, "This is too much."

"I agree," Grace responded. "You always did try to fly free from it. I never could keep you from trying one stunt after another." She smiled softly. "In fact,

I'm quite sure you're outside right now trying to scale the nearest tree. You'll be up it in an instant."

"She is a feisty—"Calum said but stopped when Grace shook her head.

"You," Grace looked at Alana with her heart in her eyes, "are a spirited and wonderful person."

Hands out of her pocket, Alana's white-knuckled fists closed over the edge of the stair. "There's been a lot of deceit here. You get that right?" Her face turned redder. "You told me my mom had died. You were everything. You were my grandmother."

"Yes," Grace whispered. "I'm so sorry."

Alana stared blankly at the door where her younger self had left. "That little girl will be lied to her whole life. Everything she thinks is real will not be."

"There was no other way, lass," Calum said.

Oops. Calum should have kept his mouth shut. Alana's attention swung his way. "Actually, there was. You, or her," she nodded at Grace, "could have told me the truth. I could have been raised understanding all of this." Before Calum could respond, she stood and shook her head. "No, don't even. I need to get out of here. This completely stinks."

Alana stormed out the front door. Seth crossed his arms over his chest and eyed Calum. "Wow, you know how to piss em' off in any century, eh?"

"Well, now." Calum stood and perched his top hat on his head. "I get the job done, aye?"

Seth shrugged. "Yet to be seen, in this house anyways."

"Enough," Grace said fervently, her beautiful eyes landing on Calum. "She's hurting and I do not blame her."

Calum's expression softened. "Oh, I do know. Please don't misconstrue my blatant talk for lack of compassion."

Grace eyed him with a mix of sharp wisdom and downright desire. "It is, as always, your timing, Calum." Her eyes turned to Seth. "Go after her. Please."

Seth snorted. What? Why? He had a ton of questions for Calum. And her for that matter.

"She's right, lad. Go after her," Calum agreed. "You're the only one she has here that makes sense."

"No. I have questions for you and I want answers."

"He's handsome but stupid," Grace remarked.

"Excuse me?" Seth said.

"He's young," Calum explained. "In years and magic."

"I do not care," Grace said.

"Alright, here's the thing," Seth began.

Grace shook her head sharply, "No. You go. Talk to my daughter. Calum and I will answer all of your questions when you return."

Seth grumbled. Alana was a big girl. It seemed to him she was handling all of this just fine. Regardless, the look he was getting from Calum and Grace was damning. They were serious. "Tell me one thing and I'll go."

Calum said blandly, "And that is?"

"Does she have magic too? Is she a warlock like me?"

"No," Grace said so softly he barely heard her. "She is a necromancer."

Seth frowned. "What?"

"Necromancer, lad," Calum said, his blue eyes turning dark. "She can communicate with and summon the dead. She can control them if she wants. Her magic is much darker and stronger than yours."

His mouth turned dry. Of all the things he'd expected to hear, this wasn't it. Alana…a necromancer? He shook his head. "That's impossible. She's so…nice."

"Necromancers aren't necessarily evil. Most are quite kind," Grace murmured.

"Does she know?" Seth asked.

Grace shook her head.

All he could picture was Alana lying in bed with a cross on her chest. Wow, if she only knew. "I think I better go after her."

"Good idea," Calum said.

When Seth stepped out of the house it was into a whole new world. Though still late spring, early summer, the lay of the land was different. There were even more trees. Morning light flickered through the forest. The first place he checked was her rock. Nope. Not there. This time she'd left the property. Where would she go right now?

"Hello mister!"

Seth looked up. Little Alana swung on the branch her older self had sat on with him hours earlier. Her red hair glistened in the sun as she waved down. A small smile erupted and he waved back. It was strange seeing her as a child. It had to be even stranger for her. Pulling off his sweatshirt, he jogged into the woods. Chances were she was running. Hard and fast.

Using his magic, he tracked her the best he could. Though he tried to talk to her through his mind she didn't respond. Eventually, he ended up trekking up the mountain. Alana was going for height. More height than a tree could offer. About twenty minutes later, he found her. She sat, legs bent, head on her knees on a sharp slope, sort of a sheer face of rock that slanted at about a seventy degree angle. Yeah, it was dangerous, but she'd found far trickier spots.

Seth plunked down next to her within a few minutes.

They said nothing for a little bit. Good view. It overlooked a wide span of tree tops.

Knowing damn well she wouldn't talk first he said, "It could be worse."

Alana said nothing, just tucked her chin on her crossed arms.

"At least everything is being explained up front. You should've seen what my cousins went through."

Still, she said nothing.

"Listen, I know this sucks. Totally agree. But it's happening. You need to face it."

Her head tilted slightly and her bloodshot eyes narrowed. "Screw you."

Seth crossed his legs and leaned back on his hands. Okay, maybe he hadn't approached this correctly. "Okay. How about this. You're not alone. I'm right here with you. We'll get through this together."

Good for him! And they all said he was unfeeling and self-serving.

Alana rolled her eyes and turned her gaze back to the horizon. "You're not part of what I have to deal with Seth. Stop pretending. You and your cousins have your own issues. You deal with them. I'll deal with mine."

The Tudor Revival

"Seems they're interrelated," he responded dryly.

"So? Doesn't mean we have to work as a team." She sighed. "You are all about you, Seth, and the next big adventure. I don't need that. Don't want it. Stop feeling the need to help me out. Go deal with your own bag of screwed up crap."

Seth felt his blood heating. "I'm all about the next big adventure? What about you? You're not happy unless you find a rush. You need to live on the edge just as much as me. Who the hell are you to point fingers at me when you're just as guilty?"

Jaw grinding, her amber eyes shot to his. "Guess we know now why I'm such a freak. I was born over a hundred and thirty years ago."

"Oh, stop it. So what. Life's a bitch. Get over it." Seth laid back and propped his head on his hands. "You've got magic. You're a necromancer. Embrace it. Stop playing the helpless victim. This shit rocks."

"I'm a what?"

"Necromancer. You can summon the dead. Pretty cool."

He had a split second to admire a fluffy cloud high above before a strong set of fingers closed around his ball sac and squeezed. Ouch! His instantaneous reaction wasn't nearly fast enough. Alana had somehow straddled him while continuing to squeeze harshly where no woman should squeeze harshly. It didn't matter that their bodies had slid down the slope a few feet, she glared and said, "Oh, I'll embrace it, you jerk."

Seth ground his teeth, furious. "Get off me."

Alana squeezed tighter. "Make me."

Seth knew what she wanted. He'd seen it before with Dakota at the Victorian. She wanted 'out' of this situation. Before Alana knew what hit her he had her flipped on the rock. Locked beneath his body, her legs lay open on either side of his hips. For the first time, Alana was right where she belonged. He was pissed off. Elbows on the rock by her shoulders he said, "You seriously think I was gonna push you down the side of this rock? Easy hundred foot drop. As if you didn't know."

Closing her eyes, she breathed deeply. Her chest rose and fell rapidly. For all the fury he'd moments before felt, it took less than a second for the feeling to turn sharply to lust. Suddenly, the reality of being back in his body and having a woman pinned beneath him made him dizzy with need. Hell. The human form was incredible. All the sensations he'd come to take for granted swamped him.

Though her eyes remained closed, Alana's breathing switched pace. She felt it too.

Using his thighs to spread her legs a bit further apart, he leaned down and whispered, "I don't want to fight anymore."

CHAPTER SIX

Alana slowly opened her eyes. All she wanted to do was fight.

Seth's eyes matched the blue sky behind him. How many times had she imagined this? Hoped for this? But fought it. His gorgeous face hovered over hers. His wide shoulders blocked the rising sun. Strange how every sensation in her body seemed overly acute...every fine hair on her body, every pore in her skin. She'd swear steam burned off the sun between the rock and the sky, concaving them in sensuality.

No lie, she had wanted him to shove her off him. She'd wanted to fall backward until all of this went away. Surprisingly, she wasn't all that shocked to discover she could summon the dead. It fit in with all the stories her grandmom had told her. And there was the fact that she could hear Seth when he was 'dead."

But right now, pinned beneath him, she felt a whole new rush hovering just out of reach.

She'd managed to keep Seth at bay for months.

No more.

Rather than crashing down, his lips found hers with tenderness. Slow and easy, he worked his tongue into her mouth. Alana met him just as gently, wrapping her tongue with his in an easy motion. So fluid and seductive, she fell into his slow, lapping pattern. A sharp wind blew in from the east but she didn't feel it. Protected by his strong body, it was all heat and kindling and the sparks of a brand new fire.

"Alana," he murmured, his mouth left hers to trail to the soft area just behind her ear, then further down the overly tender portion of her neck. She raised her hands over her head when he pulled her shirt free. Laving and worshiping, he suckled her nipple through the thin material of her bra.

With a deep throated groan, she pulled his shirt over his head. Muscles rippled and flexed down every part of his shoulders, arms and chest. He was an athlete. Not an inch of flab to be found. Alana wrapped one leg over his ass and ground against his obvious erection. His hands molded and pressed against her breast, his steaming hot breath teased the skin of her upper stomach.

Seth's breathing increased as he ground into her. She'd never been so wet. Never wanted something so much. Nearly frantic, he pulled off her shoes, tugged down her pants and panties. Though she heard the zip of his fly and the tear of a miraculous condom wrapper, she couldn't focus enough to see anything. Digging her nails into the rock, she gasped when he caught her under the knees, came down on her and pushed desperately.

Alana bit her lip and flinched.

Though Seth stopped halfway, it was too late. His warm breath rasped next to her ear. "How long has it been?"

Leaning her head against his she responded, "Too long."

Lowering her legs carefully, his lips found hers again. His kiss was long and languid and thorough. Gentle hands skimmed her body, flaming her skin. In contrast with the cool wind, it felt surreal and incredible. A steady throb returned to her groin and she moaned. Seth pulled back slightly then continued to push into her body. The sting was gone. In its place, a wonderful fullness, one that had her grasping his shoulders.

When Seth's lips pulled away, his eyes locked with hers and he whispered, "Just relax. I won't hurt you." His eyes turned gentle, kind. "I promise."

Alana believed him. Releasing the tight grasp on his shoulders, she braced her feet on the cold rock. He didn't make her wait long. After a brief pull back, he slowly thrust forward. She gulped. He did it again. This time something ignited deep inside. The muscles in his shoulders tensed. In fact, all of his muscles, including those in his face, seemed tightly restrained. Closing her eyes again, she let the feeling of him sliding in and out become her world. At first it was incredibly slow and paced. It was as if he was giving her time to get used to it.

All at once, as though an elastic snapped, he pushed forward hard.

Her eyes shot open and she moaned. Pure pleasure!

Instinctively, she wrapped her legs around him and brought him closer. Somehow, he touched something in her that felt amazing. He suddenly felt amazing. The wind blew louder, whistling off the sheer rock face, only adding to the thrill of the ride. And it was a ride. One that he was taking on her... with her. Alana kept her cheek against his, blown away by pure sensation. His body moved faster, his skin became hotter. It didn't take her long to figure out the pace and to move with him. Seth. Oh my God, Seth. More. More. More.

His lips skimmed her cheek until his tongue

flicked against her parted lips. When she gasped for air, his mouth hovered over hers, as though he wanted to breathe in her rapid pants, her need for him to bring her off the edge of something just out of reach.

As though he knew just what she needed, his sharp thrusts slowed, his movements almost teasing. Alana wrapped her legs higher, tighter. His lips lowered and smiled against hers before he murmured, "Time to jump."

With his words he pressed in deep, a low, deep primeval sound bubbling up through his chest. When he thrust forward even further and deeper, his body jerking, Alana fell off the edge. Vibrations started in her core, spanned out to her outermost extremities before they shot back to her groin, her belly, her breasts and then harshly exploded in what was easily the most intense rush of her life. Uncoiling rapidly, every muscle in her body started to shake then burst with feeling. Pure, mind-blowing, awesome feeling.

Holding onto him became impossible. Her limbs fell limp, pure jelly beneath his long, hard, quivering body.

"What the....hell.....unbelievable," he said hoarsely, his body suddenly heavy on hers. As though he was lifting the world, he pushed himself off of her and fell heavily beside her. Cold air rushed over her body but she didn't care. It all felt wonderful, perfect, beyond anything this life had offered her so far. Or any other man for that matter.

Neither of them said anything for a long time. Alana was incapable. Caught somewhere between euphoria and bliss, her tongue didn't seem to work. They might've laid on that sheer sheet of rock for twenty minutes or two hours for all she knew. One thing was for certain, it was the best experience of her life.

But all good things must come to an end.

Eventually, Seth got up and dressed. Alana made sure she got an eyeful. The man really was well made. Not only muscled on top, the firm globes of his butt led to great thighs and solid calves. She only got a side glimpse of his penis but it was well worth the view. Though flaccid, it didn't seem overly affected by the cold weather. Seth was thicker than most and, she blinked in admiration, pretty damn long.

A crooked grin and a devilish twinkle in his eye turned her way as he zipped up his jeans. "Might've been a long time but you're no shrew, eh?"

Not embarrassed in the least that he'd read her thoughts she offered up a come-hither motion with her forefinger. "Gimme my clothes."

Braced on the slope of rock he shrugged, his eyes roaming appreciatively over her naked body. A body that she left sprawled out for his full evaluation. Alana hadn't been bashful a day in her life. Why start now? Yet a predatory glimmer had entered his now dark eyes. When had they turned so black? Was that the warlock?

Something hungry and dominant seized him. Before she knew what hit her, he was on his knees, his hands grasping her trembling thighs. "You're brave, aren't you?"

Though Alana shook her head, she didn't fight him when his large hands grasped her backside and brought her center against his too eager lips. The next thing she knew, his lips were manipulating her almost as well, if not better, than his cock had. Wow! Biting her lower lips, she ran her hands through his thick, black hair and allowed him to control her position. Undulating, mesmerizing, Seth's tongue was soon taking her back up that cliff, tempting her to jump.

Her body starting to roil, thrust, want more. The feeling was becoming almost too intense and she tried to push away but he locked her in place, forced to keep feeling…and feeling…and feeling… until suddenly the blue sky above was full of a thousand little stars. The rock beneath vanished. Her body shot up with a startling jolt. Though Seth's strong arms held her she felt like she was flying away. It was if she'd seriously fell off the sheer rock and was falling and falling and falling.

"So good," he murmured against her belly. When had he arrived there?

Her hands were now twisted in his hair, her skin covered in a sheen of sweat. Carefully, she unraveled her fingers and ran her hands over her super sensitive breasts. His eyes followed, digesting every centimeter they traveled. "I need my clothes," she said half-heartedly.

"I don't think you do."

When his fully clothed body covered her nude one, she shivered beneath the delicious contact. Seth didn't kiss her just sort of stared at her face. His gaze roved her lips, cheeks, eyebrows, until it landed on her eyes. "I didn't expect this."

Alana didn't know what to make of the statement so she said, "It probably shouldn't have happened."

A startled expression flickered on his face before he lifted away and said, "But it did."

That's not what he'd intended to say. But who was she to call him on it. She wanted out of this uncomfortable moment. "Clothes. Please."

In no time, she was dressed and standing. Though sore in new areas she felt revitalized. There was still a lot to think about and Seth had conveniently managed to make her forget that her world had been turned upside down.

"You want to be alone."

"No." Why had she said that? "Come. Climb with me."

Seth nodded. "Okay. You sure?"

Hell no! "Yeah. Come on"

Alana didn't make her way back to the path sidling the mountain but continued up the sheer rock face. The grade became steeper until she was nearly vertical. One nook at a precious time, she studied the wall and found a place for a hand, then a foot. All the while she felt the ache in her groin from sex and the ache in her heart from being deceived by Grace. It was an odd combination of feeling and emotion. But as she moved, her focus became the objective, moving to the top of the mountain.

Eventually, the rock face ended and she swung onto the ledge. Seth sat beside her.

"It's a small mountain," she muttered.

"Still more to climb."

"Sure. Always is I suppose."

"So why have you always been so confident you'd make it, Alana?"

Leave it to Seth to skip all the moments in between. He was referring to the fact that she was taking all of this better than most would. Stealing a few moments on this mountain was her way of acclimating to all of this. Standing, she said, "Let's go."

Not waiting, she started up the forest path. The rest would be good old fashioned hiking to the top. Boring but predictable. Not such a bad thing right now. Grace was her mom? How could that be? Alana searched her childhood memories. She tried to relate to the little girl who'd run into the foyer. How could that have ever been her? Her mom and dad had died. Her Grandmom had raised her. That's just how it was. That's how it'd always been. Right?

Reality really started to hit her as she strode the path. Alana just had sex on a mountain with Seth of all people to escape the hellish truth she'd been told. Sure, Seth was incredible, totally hot, but he was Seth. She knew damned well that he was the sort of guy that once he'd had it, he'd move on.

Which was totally fine. He needed to move on.

"You've got a lot on your mind," he said, his steady footfall behind her.

"Wouldn't you?" she snapped and veered off the path.

Seth didn't follow. He went his own way. Good. Alana tromped through leaves and over stumps. The incline grew steeper but she used saplings and bushes as leverage. How could she have completely forgotten? Why couldn't she, despite how hard she tried, find the answers within her mind? Yes, she remembered growing up in the Tudor house. Her Grandmom had always been good to her. She'd been an eccentric old woman with a kind heart. The thought that she was over one hundred and thirty years old blew her mind. The thought that she herself was over one hundred years old made her nauseous. Twenty minutes later, deep in thought, Alana knew she'd chosen poorly. Normally, she'd never go this

The Tudor Revival

route. But today, in her current mood, why not?

Leaning against a small tree at the top, Seth leaned over and shook his head.

Alana didn't give him the satisfaction of a glare but kept pulling herself upward. The leaves were slick with moisture and the branches weak. Despite that, she knew how to judge the ground for hidden rocks. Though it took her twice as long, she arrived next to Seth in one piece and kept moving.

Surprisingly enough, Seth kept silent. Good for him. Smart man. Sort of.

The top wasn't her goal. Tourists roamed around up there. Instead, she opted for a nice, clean sheet of rock just beneath the top. The view was spectacular and the pure feeling of lack of security worked for her. Pulling off her shoes and socks, she plunked down and swung her feet thousands of feet above Stowe.

Seth sat beside her and said, "Nice view."

"Could be better."

"You're grouchy after sex, eh?"

"Nope. Just grouchy after sex that follows my world being turned upside down."

Seth grinned, obviously proud of himself. "I'd think you'd be feeling more relaxed now. You got off a few—"

Alana shook her head and frowned.

"Ah, well." Seth's grin vanished. "I'll go, give you some breathing room." But he didn't move.

Alana clucked her tongue. While she didn't want him here some part of her was glad he was. Now that's cliché! Leaning back on her palms, she shook her head and pretended she wasn't acutely aware of how close he sat. "Why are we here? And I mean the house, not the mountain."

"I'm here because I descend from Calum. You're here because you descend from Grace."

"That easy then?" she asked.

"Could be."

Her gaze lingered on his profile. He was such a good looking guy. The sort she knew damn well every woman drooled over. After all, she had. Flashes of his body pushing into hers flickered in her mind but she shoved aside the visuals. If she didn't, she'd be straddling him again in no time. "You might be good at all of this by now but I'm new to it."

Seth shook his head and arched one dark brow. "Are you really, Alana? Somehow I doubt that."

"What do you mean?"

"What's up with holding a cross over your chest every night before you sleep?"

Air clogged in her throat. Pushing past it she said, "You spied."

"I was dead. Of course I spied."

"So that excused you from common decency?"

Blazing blue eyes turned her way. "Um, yeah!"

What a loser. "How do you figure?"

His eyes narrowed. "You have no idea what it feels like to be without a body. To lose everything that made you you. The only thing that grounded me to this life was you. So did I stalk you, watch you, hell yeah."

Alana swallowed hard and pulled her eyes from his. "You still had a conscience."

"Did I?"

Her eyes swung to his. "You know you did. I heard it."

"Can you hear it now?"

Jaw grinding, Alana looked to the horizon. The sun sat overhead and left them in shadows. "You were a voice in my head. The thought of you in whatever form spying on me doesn't sit well."

"Then I'm sorry. Had no choice. You drew me in. It was as if I had no choice."

"Why not just lead the conversation with that, Seth? Might have made me less edgy."

"Less edgy?" He growled. "Unlikely."

Alana tilted back her head and gazed at the sky. "I really don't like you."

"Could've fooled me."

"Here's the thing." Her eyes pinned his. "I might've screwed you but I'm not smitten. You've got nothing on me. You're good looking and you were where I needed you when I needed you."

Seth eyed her for several moments before a slow grin crawled onto his face. "Fine. Whatever works."

Alana wanted to shove him right off the cliff. What a complete jackass. Seriously, what sort of girl fell for a guy like him? A complete idiot without doubt. Looking back, she'd had it all figured out before they'd jumped into that quarry. Seth was an easy one to peg. Nothing overly fazed him for long, least of all a female.

She swung away from the cliff and stood. "You know what Seth?"

"What's that?" he said, still staring out at the horizon.

"You and I are both unlikable characters in any good story."

Alana didn't wait for his answer but began her descent. People had never been her thing in life. Nature and all it had to offer were. Now she had a little more to face. Time to focus on that. Grandmom wasn't Grandmom, she was mom. The year was 1871. Alana laughed as she barreled down the mountain. That's right, it was present day. Tourism didn't exist on this mountain right now. Regardless, it wouldn't have mattered. Her focus had little to do with what year it was and more to do with the people who were part of it.

She swallowed a wry grin. It was 1871 and the year didn't matter. She'd traveled back in time and the year didn't matter! Ripe. Damn Seth to hell. Somehow, she blamed every last inch of her predicament on him.

If he followed her, she paid no mind. But he didn't follow her. She knew it with every ounce of her being. When she made it back to the house she went straight to her rock. It was there that she looked at the house for the first time. It was then that she fell back in awe.

It was beautiful!

How had she never seen that? Alana shook her head. She hadn't seen it because it hadn't been like this for her. At least not how she could recall when in the future. The windows were brightly shined, the stonework glistening. The gardens were well groomed. No house had ever looked better. This one was in its prime.

"Don't you remember gardening?"

Alana frowned and closed her eyes. "I'm not ready to talk to you yet."

"I know," Grace said gently. "Trust me though, you won't ever be ready to talk to me so we might as well start here, now."

With a deep breathe through her nostrils, Alana

once more gazed at the house and shook her head. "It shouldn't be this easy for you."

"Easy? Do you really think it is?"

Alana felt closed in and angry while she simultaneously wanted to hug her most favorite person on Earth. No stranger feeling existed. But frustration and blatant betrayal won out. "I'm not ready for a family reunion."

"It's inevitable, dear."

"Maybe." Alana eyed her...mother, who stood calmly beside her. "When I'm ready, if I'm ready. And who knows." She gestured toward the house. "Could be I won't be here long enough."

"It could be you won't," Grace agreed. "However, you and I both know that you're here for a reason, as am I."

No. She wanted none of this. Never did. Alana walked away. As she did so it occurred to her that this was something she did too often. Walk away. But it felt right. And it avoided pointless confrontation. Dealing with Grace was something she wasn't quite ready for.

Halfway across the yard she realized that her house really wasn't hers anymore. How moronic! She could do one of two things. Turn back and re-bond with her 'mom,' and beg a room or continue on and pretend like she belonged here. Because, truth told, some part of her did. Alana sighed as she strode in the front door. Calum was nowhere to be seen. Okay, she supposed. Yet, somehow, she'd wanted to confront him and tell him how she felt about this. A man she barely knew! Alana trudged up the stairs. She'd tried to tell Seth but look where that'd landed her.

On a rock with her legs spread.

Without giving it thought she stormed into her bedroom and plunked down on the bed. It didn't look at all familiar. Why would it? Clearly a room fashioned for a little girl, it wasn't a part of her. Alana put her head in her hands. Stupid. It was a part of her. All of this!

"Don't be sad. I have to leave for a short while but I'll be back."

Alana slowly looked up and met... herself in the eye. A much younger version of herself stared back, wide eyed. It was strange to look at oneself as a child. Funny, she couldn't remember being this age. She nearly snorted but stopped herself. Of course she couldn't remember being this age. She'd been brainwashed. But obviously, at one time, she'd been young and innocent.

With a warm smile she said to the child, "Well, I look forward to seeing you again."

Young Alana grinned, a bright light entering her eyes, before she skipped out of the room. How strange to see herself so happy. Laying back she flung her arms over her head and stared at the ceiling. The truth of the matter was that she hadn't been all that unhappy at all before Seth had died. Mostly because of him.

Mostly because of their friendship.

One she had probably just tossed out the window.

Alana sighed. What a day. She'd traveled back in time, slept with Seth and learned that she was a...necromancer? Numb, Alana watched a small spider make its determined way up the wall. Somehow, she could relate with the insect. It, like her, had the drive to move on, not give up.

At least she hoped.

"What are you doing?"

"I'd think it's obvious, taking some time alone." Her eyes slid to Seth who stood in the doorway, his tall frame leaning casually.

"Ahhh." His brows lowered. "You do realize we've traveled back in time. I for one don't want to be stuck here."

Seth was so nonchalant with his tone it was as though they'd never shared such an intimate moment on the mountain. But she felt the soreness between her thighs and felt her heartbeat increase at the mere sound of his voice. "Have you talked to Calum?"

"No." Seth crossed his arms over his chest. "I wanted to talk to you first."

"We've been doing plenty of talking," she replied softly.

"Not really." A frown tugged at the corners of his lips. "Seems we've done more arguing than anything." He strode to the window and peered out, an evasive maneuver that told her how uncomfortable he really was. "I'm sorry if I ever made you feel...I don't know...bad. This whole situation stinks and like you I'm just trying to figure everything out. I'd like to think that we're still friends. I don't want to lose that."

Alana's eyes lingered on him even as he continued to stare outside. She didn't want to fight either. Nor did she want to dislike him. As was Seth's way, he managed to irritate her one minute and infatuate her the next. It would be easier if they got along. Maybe she needed to just take him in stride. Though he could so easily be offending, she knew he could be caring too. How much his cousins cared about him spoke volumes. Did it bother her that they didn't seem to know who she was? Sure. But Seth was Seth. It wouldn't have fit his personality to tell his family about her. No matter how much time they'd spent together.

"I suppose we're friends," she murmured and sat up slowly, tucking her legs beneath her. "But just friends."

His clear blue eyes turned her way and he hesitated several moments before he said, "If that's what you'd prefer."

"It is," she replied automatically. "I tend to think if we're anything more we won't be able to muddle through this mess."

"You're probably right." Seth's eyes lingered on hers and the words hung heavy in the air.

Alana cleared her throat. "Where do we start?"

Though the words were directed at their situation of being flung back in time, they both knew her question covered the new version of their 'friendship.'

Nodding at the door, he said, "We should probably tour the house. Get a layout of the land so to speak."

Glancing around the room, she was able to better appreciate it. She didn't doubt for a second that their truce made that possible. Seth was all she really had in this whole disaster. Or at the least the only one she was willing to trust. If they were able to set aside their tumultuous feelings for one another and work together, all of this might be manageable. As a team, they might better figure out a way home.

"I don't remember this room at all. The toys, the bed, nothing," she said flatly. "You would think that I'd at least have a sense of déjà vu despite the magic."

"If Calum and your mom…Grace, wanted you protected, my thought is they wouldn't allow for any loopholes." Seth walked over and held out his hand. "C'mon, let's go explore."

While she hesitated a fraction of a second, she still placed her hand in his and allowed him to pull her off the bed. She'd be lying if she said his touch didn't send a shiver of excitement down her spine. Pulling away her hand, Alana led them out the door and down the hallway.

Everything was so clean, beautiful and quaint. It was hard to believe that this house would be used to trap death itself. The feeling of peace within these walls was intense. "Save the layout, none of this looks familiar."

Seth followed her from room to room. "I wonder how long Calum and Grace have been here."

"Not long I'd say." She sniffed. "Smells like fresh cut wood."

"It does." Again, he stopped at the window on the same side of the house and stared out.

"Why do you keep looking outside?" She asked. "Everything okay?"

He nodded. "Yep. Guess I just feel uneasy in here. I've been outside this house floating around and now I'm walking around in it. Knowing that the reaper is coming and that this is its cage is unnerving."

Alana was heading his way but stopped. The air suddenly felt thicker. The room appeared disjointed. For a split second, she thought she saw Leathan out of the corner of her eye. She spun to face him, but he wasn't there. The air became lighter and the disjointed visage vanished.

"What just happened?" Seth's keen gaze was locked on her.

A tingling sensation rippled through her body then vanished. "I don't know. It was weird."

"Tell me."

Starting to shiver, she said, "It felt like I was suddenly in two places at once. I'd swear Leathan was standing right beside me."

Seth's hand touched her shoulder. "Are you warmer now?"

The moment he touched her, the chill vanished. "Yes."

"I think they're trying to make contact with us...you."

"You mean...as a ghost?"

"That's exactly right," Calum declared as he strolled into the room. "In your own way, you two now haunt this house."

Seth's hand fell away. "I've already been dead once. Not in the mood to do it again. What do you mean we're ghosts?"

Nausea rolled through Alana and she sat.

"I don't think you've ever been technically dead, Seth," Calum replied. "And to your cousins in the future, you are but ghosts of the past now."

"So this is sort of like what Devin experienced in the Georgian? Then I should be able to make contact with my cousins telepathically."

Calum slowly paced the room. "This is nothing like the Georgian. That dealt with different dimensions. This house, the Revival, is by far my greatest creation. My greatest trap. This house is officially the most haunted house in New England."

Seth ran his hand over his face and shook his

head. "And how is that? I've been in the Victorian and Georgian. They were far more screwed up than this house."

"Are you so sure?" Calum asked casually. "After all, you first saw this house in spirit form."

Alana had never felt sicker in her life. "I barely know you Calum so I kinda apologize for being rude but get to the point. I want to go back to my time and so does Seth."

Calum grinned and said, "Of course, m'dear! But in all sense of the word, as far as everyone in the twenty-first century is concerned, you are very much dead."

"Oh God." She put her head in her hands.

"But you're not!" Calum declared.

Her stomach flipped and she eyed Calum warily. "You make less and less sense."

"He's always been good at that," Seth said caustically.

"Well, as far as any of them realize at this very moment, Seth is still dead and you are haunting this house. Everything that happened there in the future has been erased from their memories by my acquaintance, Adlin. As far as they know, Devin received that phone call from Alana and that was it. They're all there now searching for Seth."

Numb-like, Seth plunked down beside her. "They still think I'm dead?"

"Well of course they do, lad. Because you are. In a fashion."

Before Seth could speak, Calum shook his head and said, "Don't look so crestfallen. It was all very necessary you see. Adlin helped resurrect you and you, my dear boy, brought your cousins here. As it should be. The reaper would wipe you out too quickly if he had you all in one place."

"So all that for nothing... I'm still dead," Seth muttered.

"No. No. Not really. Not here anyways!" Calum said, a wide grin swallowing his face.

"And what exactly happened to me again?" Alana asked.

Calum removed his top hat and said, "Nobody really knows."

Seth frowned. "Nobody really knows?"

With a shrug, Calum offered a heavy sigh. "Indeed."

"What does that mean, exactly?" She asked.

"That's the thing," Calum said in an I'm-so-sorry fashion. "Nobody really does know."

"Oh, fun," she muttered under her breath and said sarcastically, "As long as nobody knows, all is well."

Seth appeared incredulous. Calum's face came alive and he smiled. "I knew you'd take this well! I told Grace, she'll take this well. Don't you worry!"

"Tell me, Calum," Seth growled. "What's next for us? What are we supposed to do now?"

"Absolutely nothing," Calum said. "Death, the reaper, still comes. But I've no idea when or how it will appear. All I know is that it can now be easily trapped... because you are here."

"That's reassuring," Seth muttered.

"Indeed!" Calum said.

"What about the stone that'll unlock the creature? The one connected to the warlock's magical aura?" Alana asked.

Culum shrugged. "It's yet to be found."

This statement brought a deep frown to Seth's face. "Yet to be found? You hid it. Where is it?"

With a shrug, Calum said, "I simply do not know, my lad."

"What do you mean you don't know?" Alana piped up. "How could you not know?"

"Well, I don't know everything," Calum said.

"Yes you do," Seth returned.

"You might think so, lad, but no. Surely you learned that at the Georgian."

"I learned you were more cunning than ever at the Georgian," Seth returned.

"Poff!" Calum waved away his negative words. "That house was confusing. As were its dynamics."

"And this house isn't?" Alana asked. "Are you out of your mind?"

"Not quite yet," Grace said from the door. "Calum, why don't you give them some time to acclimate. This is so very much to take on."

Alana frowned. Every time Grace was near she seemed to zap the life out of her. Or at least every other thought but the fact that her mom was nearby.

"Indeed, lass." Calum nodded at them. "We will talk again soon. For now, no harm can touch you. All is well."

Before Alana could say just how she felt about that statement, Seth's deep voice cut through her thoughts. "Would you like to know more about being a necromancer?"

CHAPTER SEVEN

No woman had ever offered him a heavier frown. A look of absolute defeat.

"Really, Seth?" Alana stood and walked to the window. "I don't have my iPhone, do you? There's no quick access for you to throw out a definition. I know you were as shocked as I was to learn that I was a necromancer. I know you were just as much in the dark as I was about what that meant."

Seth was tempted to lie back on the bed and be his usual casual self but the truth was... he didn't feel like his usual casual self. He felt edgy and eager. Never before in his life had he wanted to put someone's fears to rest, to make the pain go away... to somehow explain it all away.

"One thing I know without doubt, Alana. You are not evil."

All she offered was her profile as she studied the curtains. "I don't think you can be sure of that any more than I can be."

Before he could speak again, her sad gaze met his. "They left clothes on the bed for us. We're supposed to change."

For the first time in his life, someone had noticed something before him. He glanced at the bedside. "We don't have to do what we're supposed to do."

"No," she whispered. "That's half of what makes us who we are, eh?"

Seth worked at not frowning. Why should he when she wasn't? It seemed Alana wanted to make the best of this situation. That despite the news given, she was willing to… live here for now? He ground his teeth and considered. Really? Would they make it that easy on Calum and Grace?

"I think we'll be making it easier on ourselves," Alana said.

His eyes shot to hers. Had she heard his thoughts? Of course not. Impossible. "I'm not wearing those clothes."

Her eyes fell to the tub in the corner of the room. "You don't have to."

Seth watched as she unclothed. Holy heck. He'd remembered how she looked on the mountain. How incredibly beautiful. Now, as she took off everything nonchalantly, without a care in the world, he felt his cock harden. Even so, he knew trying to have sex with her again so soon would be a very bad idea. Alana's mind couldn't be further from intimacy.

And there was that whole "let's be friends" thing.

Seth's eyes were glued as her porcelain white form crossed to the tub. Damn, the woman was fine. She might not have the body of a Playboy bunny, but his eyes couldn't get enough of her tight, high ass and the little waist leading to perky breasts. In this light the areolas were more of a dark reddish brown, the nipples tight…and lonely. His eyes skimmed down her legs. Shapely, he'd imagine they'd look amazing in heels. How had this woman remained single for so long?

Alana cleared her throat and his eyes met hers. "You've "been there, done this," remember?" She sank down into the water. "We're just friends."

Seth shrugged and said, "I'm only human."

"Barely." Sinking down, she immersed herself in

the water.

"Ouch."

"Please." She rolled her eyes. "Are you really offended?"

"Not yet."

He watched her bathe for a moment. Lucky for him, whatever Adlin had done when reincarnating him had left him clean and refreshed. Good thing or he never would have kissed her. Though nobody had said a word, he'd come out of his coffin smelling like brand new, teeth miraculously brushed. That a condom had been in his jeans pocket had been a little too easy. But who was he to complain?

"Just get dressed. I'm not looking," Alana said.

Seth frowned. No lie. Her head was tipped back, the lines of her face at rest. She had no desire to look at him. Or so it seemed. Let's see. He stood and took off his clothes. He was sure to pull his shirt slowly over his head, then peek. Nope, her eyes were firmly shut. Let's see. Without seeming like a wuss, he shimmied off his pants and left on only his boxer briefs. No doubt about it, he looked damn fine in a set of briefs.

Still, her eyes remained closed.

"How do you suppose I wear this?" he asked.

The hint of a grin touched her lips but she didn't open her eyes. "I'd say, one leg in front of the other."

Oh, she was something. "I meant what they expect me to wear beneath."

"They expect you to wear what you're already wearing beneath, Seth." Her smile grew wider. "Just get dressed."

Grumbling, he turned away. Sure, whatever. He pulled on the stiff slacks and buttoned up the starchy white shirt. "I feel like I'm dressing for the prom."

Alana's voice sounded almost dreamy. "Funny, how well they dressed in this time period. Guess we sorta lost that in the twenty-first century, eh?"

"I don't care what we lost. This blows."

But even as he turned, Seth realized she wasn't affected in the least. Alana's eyes remained closed. Slow drips of water rolled down her smooth throat. Suddenly, he felt as though he were in spirit form peering at her from beyond. Always to admire, never to touch. "Alana."

Awe hell. He'd whispered! What was the matter with him? Warlocks didn't whisper.

But she heard him. Alana's eyes opened and slowly swung his way. "Well, look at you."

With a mad scowl, he brushed back his hair with his fingers. "Not my best look."

"Matter of opinion."

Before he could appreciate her for too long, she dunked under the water once more and rose. Hell, she was smokin' hot. He'd be damned if he let her see that he thought that. He turned and eyed the room. Water swooshed behind him. She stepped out of the tub and he heard the sound of a towel wiping over skin. Good. She needed to dry off. Seth kept busy studying absolutely nothing as she dressed. Finally, silence reigned.

"You ready to go?" he asked.

"I guess."

Seth didn't look back but opened the door. He studied the hallway beyond until he grew bored and looked at her. That took about one second.

"Well?" She stopped and waited, as though she knew damn well he'd look her way.

Holy hell. Alana looked amazing. She wore a pale green dress that dusted the floor and cinched in at the waist.

"My butt looks huge in this. Glad bustles went out of style," she remarked.

"Aren't you supposed to wear that too?"

Alana eyed the bed with disgust. "I'm so not wearing a corset."

"Don't blame you. Besides, you don't need one."

"Yeah, yeah." But she smiled a little at the compliment and slid on some old fashioned shoes.

"Well, if you're not wearing the corset, I'm not wearing the frock coat."

"You know fashion!" She replied.

He frowned. "Actually, I don't. Not sure where that came from."

Her brows drew together. "And I'm not sure how I managed to get myself tied into this dress so quickly. It was as if I'd been doing it for years."

Seth ignored the strange feeling of trepidation, but smiled and said, "Guess we really are ghosts!"

"Ha ha." Alana sauntered his way, hips swinging before she stopped short. "Did you see how I was just walking?"

"How could I miss it?"

"Strange," she murmured. "I don't...walk that way...but this dress. I don't know. Weird."

"Works." He grinned.

"See, this is good." Alana nodded. "We get along much better when we're friends. You're a pretty nice guy after all, Seth."

"Humph. If you say so." But the compliment met its mark and made him happy. As to the friend part, they'd see about that. For now, however, he'd go with it. Couldn't hurt.

"Let's go downstairs. We haven't had a chance to really look around down there yet," she said.

"Sure." Seth followed her down. Darkness had started to fall and with it, the interior now seemed to come alive. They'd done a heck of a job decorating it. Dimply lit wall sconces lined the hallway and a huge chandelier hung over the downstairs foyer. The numerous diamond leaded windows seemed to reflect the lights a thousand times over.

"All the same furniture," Alana commented.

"Yeah? I didn't get to see much of it in the future...the sheets and all."

"Right," Alana said.

That was it. Guess she wasn't ready to explain why the house had looked so unlived in. Eventually he'd get it out of her. After all, friends liked to talk.

"Some really expensive items here," he remarked.

"Money was something Grace always seemed to have enough of."

As they walked through the arched doorway to the dining room, Seth eyed the Oak court cupboard that was so ornately designed. How was it that he knew what it was called? Again, that uneasy feeling threatened to overwhelm him. It seemed every room had a chandelier, each grander than the last. And strangely enough, each room seemed to suit Alana. She looked as if she belonged in this era...in this house. He supposed she did. More than ever, he felt drawn to her as he followed her from room to room. He remained several feet behind her as her skirts dusted the floor and the lighting reflected off her hair.

Suddenly, she stopped. "Strange seeing it in one

piece again."

"What?"

"The mirror." Alana nodded at the tall, decorative mirror hanging in a short hallway. "That's the one that broke. The one that told me to read the journal."

"Ah." He put his hand on the small of her back and they continued walking. "You've got to love time travel."

"Matter of opinion."

"Right."

They entered the kitchen. A large paneled canopy with rope style molding was the main feature. A large vented hood made from hammered copper perched over the island cooking center.

"It hasn't changed much," she commented. "Just minus the modern day appliances I suppose."

"I think I'm going to miss your potato chips and granola bars."

Alana grinned. "No doubt about it!"

"Want to go outside again?" he asked.

"This is really hard for you, isn't it? Being inside."

"I'm working on it," he said. "Can you blame me?"

"No, I guess not."

They walked out the same backdoor she'd so recently stumbled out of when she called Devin. The air was cool and a three quarter full moon lit the yard.

"What did you mean when you asked Devin if he'd felt the same as you when he turned?"

Seth had hoped she hadn't caught that. "Long story. One better told by Devin."

"Why don't you tell me?"

"I don't know. I guess I feel wrong about it."

Surprisingly enough, she nodded and let the matter drop. Good thing. About the last thing he wanted to tell Alana was what happened to his cousin. Nope. He'd leave that alone.

Though she'd been beautiful by the home's lighting, she was stunning by moonlight. Her hair appeared much darker and her skin lighter. Combined with the long, flowing dress, she seemed almost ethereal. How ironic. Instead of heading for the rock, she veered into the gardens. They were amazing. Nothing like how they looked in the twenty-first century.

"How is this possible?"

"What?"

"The gardens. It's as if she planted everything years ago but that can't be. The house seems too new. It smells so new. And obviously, it is new."

"You've got to keep in mind that things aren't always going to make sense." He sighed. "Everything's likely to get more confusing before becoming clearer."

Alana fingered the stem of a vine running around a garden post. "I suppose."

"I'm sorry."

She glanced at him. "Why are you sorry? None of this is your fault."

Seth shrugged. "It's more my fault than yours. If you'd never met me, you wouldn't have gotten sucked into Calum's curse."

"That's one way of looking at it." Alana kept strolling. "If you'd never met me, you would've never ended up at Grace's Revival because without doubt, she's a part of this house."

"They both are," Seth agreed. "Seems they're pretty hot for each other too."

"Mmm." Her stroll became slower, as though she drifted. "Do you hear that?"

"Hear what?"

"I don't know. Some sort of music."

"No, I don't hear anything."

Suddenly she spun, her eyes nearly white. Seth stumbled back. When she spoke, her voice sounded melodious, foreign... a little creepy. The temperature plummeted. Her breath came out in foggy wisps. "Beware the black rose. It will rip from you your very center. It will take from you your heart."

Seth pushed fear aside. It had no place here. "Who are you?"

Alana, or whoever possessed her, slowly pointed in the direction of the mountain. "It will take from you your very heart."

What the hell was it talking about? "I don't understand. What black rose?"

The temperature rose and Alana's eyes cleared. "I'm sorry. What were we talking about?"

It took everything in him to hide his shock. She'd been through enough and he truly didn't want to freak her out further. "Eating. I said I was hungry."

"Really?" She frowned. "I could have sworn we were talking about roses."

Keep a level expression, Seth. He shook his head. "Nope. My stomach growled. I'm hungry."

The look of confusion vanished from her face. "Okay. What do you suppose we eat here? Not exactly the era of microwave ovens and munchies."

Chuckling, he said, "Too true. Let's see if we can find Calum. Maybe he can help us out."

Alana offered a delicate snort. "Couldn't hurt."

When they walked back in, conveniently enough, Grace was fluttering around the kitchen. Seth sensed Alana was as uncomfortable as he was as they watched her. Not discomforted by the fact she was cooking away but by the way Calum assisted. Their flirtatious banter wasn't meant to be viewed by others. When Calum leaned close and whispered in her ear, his hand slowly cupping her ass, Alana cleared her throat.

Calum didn't rush to remove his hand but turned a lazy, mischievous gaze their way. "So how was your stroll in the garden? Grace has done such a wonderful job with it."

Alana's eyes narrowed slightly. "Just how old is that garden exactly?"

Grace turned her head a fraction, offering them her profile. "Older than the house."

A strange shiver ran through his body and he knew Alana had experienced the same.

"The garden was planted before the house? I don't understand," Alana said.

Grace dried her hands and turned. "It's nothing to worry about dear. Why don't we sit down and eat. It will be a nice family reunion."

"Nothing to worry about?" Seth shook his head. "If it's nothing to worry about, why don't you just tell us what you mean."

"Now, now. No need to get everyone upset," Calum declared. "We'll eat and chat civilly over dinner about all of this."

Grace smiled warmly. "What a lovely idea."

Alana's mouth hung open by this point. His too probably. These two seemed like a couple out of a cheesy fifty's program. Play nice and pretend everything and everyone is shiny and happy. Damned odd. "Are you two serious?"

"Are you hungry?" Calum countered, a somewhat sly glint in his eyes.

Did he know what'd happened to Seth out in the garden? Good chance. But for now, he was cornered. "Yeah, I'm hungry."

"Good then!" Grace turned around and grabbed a bowl of what looked to be freshly baked bread. But when would she have had time to bake? They'd been in the garden no longer than fifteen minutes.

Alana and Seth followed Grace and Calum into the dining room.

"How the heck?" Alana asked.

Seth agreed. The dining room table was now set to the hilt with fine china and burning candles. A roast steamed invitingly from its platter. Whipped potatoes and bowls full of various vegetables lined the table. Everything smelled amazing. "I'm with Alana. None of this was here twenty minutes ago. I don't get it."

"My boy, it was well underway twenty minutes ago. Perhaps you were in the garden longer than you thought," Calum said.

"Unlikely," Seth said.

"I can assure you, we have been putting this together for you two for some time." Grace nodded at Calum when he pulled out her chair.

Seth didn't hesitate but pulled out Alana's chair. She gave a small nod of thanks and sat. Had he ever in his life pulled out a chair for a woman? Who the hell did that nowadays? Then again, it wasn't nowadays and the gesture had come so naturally to him. In fact, he couldn't help but wonder why the polite gesture had become all but extinct in present day. Seth shook his head. What was he thinking?

"You're overthinking all of this," Calum said.

Seth's attention snapped to his predecessor. Had he heard his thoughts?

Calum smiled and sat. "You both have traveled through time and now reside in a very haunted house. It's little surprise that you lost track of time."

"I must say, you cut a dashing figure in that outfit, Seth," Grace said. "You and Calum could be brothers!"

"They really could," Alana murmured.

Surprised by her input, Seth's attention turned her way. Every inch the nineteenth century female, she sat, back straight, with her hands folded in her lap. She appeared so pristine and beautiful. What had happened to his dare-devil Alana?

"It is a very haunted house," Calum said. "But one in which we can all enjoy a good meal."

Why did it seem Calum somehow answered his every thought? No doubt he did! Devious warlock. Yet, Seth couldn't help but settle into his surroundings. The ambiance was perfect and the food delicious. Why fight the feeling? Being polite was working for him. Who knew? All his concerns seemed to vanish for the moment and it felt pretty good.

"So, in celebration of your arrival, we have a gala planned for tomorrow. One hundred of our closest friends will be joining us. We thought to open the ballroom," Calum said.

"Ballroom?" Alana asked.

Exactly…what ballroom?

"Well, this one of course!" Grace said. "I know you've always seen it as a dining room, but it clears out rather well. Look at the size of it."

"Speaking of how I see things," Alana said. "Where am I? I mean, where is the younger version of me?"

"With a family member for a bit," Calum provided. "Until we get this all figured out of course."

"Of course," Alana said a little too quickly.

Seth was less concerned with the who's and why's by the minute. This food was delicious. He couldn't remember the last time he'd eaten a good, home-cooked meal.

"It will be divine. I already have an orchestra scheduled and a beautiful dress for you to wear," Grace gushed to Alana. "It's time you truly enjoy this home. Become the woman of this house."

Alana smiled softly and continued to eat.

Seth knew somewhere in the back of his mind that things were off. He knew he should be questioning all of this. But the food was too good and the company so… refined? Why rock the boat. This felt great, looked great and above all, tasted great!

Even odder, they all proceeded to chat idly for the rest of the meal. The weather was perfect. The house was the envy of Vermont. The project of building it had gone so smoothly. The couple who had built it had fallen in love and now lived here. It was all so grand.

Near the end of the meal, Calum said, "Seth, I thought perhaps on the morn I'd teach you more about being a warlock."

He'd said it as casually as he would, "Could you pass the tea?"

And in response, Seth nodded and replied just as casually, "I'd like that."

The women nodded. The men smiled. It was all quite cordial.

Until the next morning.

CHAPTER EIGHT

"What the hell happened to me!" Alana stared into the mirror, dumfounded.

Thump. Grunt. Within seconds, Seth appeared at her bedroom door, groggy and bleary eyed. "What's the matter?"

"Look at me!" She screeched.

His eyes rounded. She didn't blame him. Alana turned back to her reflection. While her face was the same, her hair was now long, silky and jet black. And her skin? No more freckles. It was smooth and perfect. Putting her hands over her mouth, she shook her head. This is impossible. I'm imagining this.

Seth ran his hand over his face and shook his head. "Wow!"

"Wow? Wow! Are you serious? What happened to my hair?"

Seth shrugged. "I don't know."

"Me either. This is crazy." Alana looked at the nightgown she was wearing. "And so is this for that matter."

A slow grin crept onto his sleepy face. "I don't know. You look sorta cute in it."

"Sorta cute? Pft!" She stomped across the room to the bed. A bed she had no recollection of sleeping in.

"What is happening?" Grace had arrived beside Seth and her eyes widened at the site of Alana. "Oh dear."

"Oh dear is right," Alana said. "Any clue why I'm looking more and more like Morticia Addams?"

Seth chuckled.

Grace waved a delicate hand in the air and shook her head as she entered the room. "I have no idea who you speak of but I think you look striking." Running her hand down Alana's hair she said in wonder, "It's so thick and shiny."

"Like yours," Alana muttered sarcastically.

Grace nodded, "Well, yes, but it's far more wavy and becoming on you."

"Whatever." Alana pulled away. "I liked my hair...and its length. Do you have any scissors?"

"No!"

Startled, she looked at Seth. The look in his eyes was so intense. "I'm sorry, Seth. I don't do long hair."

"But it does you," he said evenly. "You look... wonderful."

Alana narrowed his eyes. She looked like Grace! Damn men. "No, I don't."

"Why does she look like that?" He asked Grace.

Grace continued to shake her head, a warm smile curving her lips. "I have no idea."

"I dare say, what is all the commotion?"

Nobody paid much attention to Calum but continued to stare at her. This was unreal.

"Oh my!" Calum's eyes grew rounder and rounder as he headed her way. Stopping within a foot, he studied her carefully. "Well, this is unexpected."

Despite the fact she'd changed overnight, Alana couldn't help but notice the startling resemblance between Calum and Seth. They were damn near twins! How had she not seen that before? Sure, they'd looked alike. But now, in the early dawn light, their similarities were striking.

The back of Calum's finger shot up and lightly stroked her cheek. "My Lord, look at your skin. No more marks."

"They were freckles," Seth muttered, though he stared at her transfixed. "And I liked them."

"Yes, yes, of course." Calum strolled around Alana and eyed her as if she was an undiscovered life form. "The rest of you remained the same. How curious."

"Good thing for that," Seth added and winked when she looked at him.

Yet she saw the worry in his eyes. That meant more to her than anything. Because of that worry she said, "I just need time to get used to it. I'll be okay."

"But of course you will, dear." Grace stroked her hair. "I'm sure this is temporary."

Seth's gaze remained glued to hers, his steady confidence much needed. "You look amazing either way, Alana."

She welcomed the squeeze of his hand when it came, the brief nod of his head and steady lock of his eyes. I'm not alone. He's here with me. It's going to be okay. But it was hard to feel okay when your appearance literally changed overnight. It felt like part of who she was had been ripped away.

"You are every bit the woman you were yesterday," Calum said. "I'm sure the hair will not remain this way."

Alana narrowed her eyes. Had he read her mind? Anything was possible in this house.

"I do think the dress I have for you to wear will look just as lovely on you," Grace said.

"What dress?"

"The one for tonight's gala, my girl!" Calum said and grinned.

Huh? "I have no idea what you're talking about."

"Could you guys give us a few minutes alone?" Seth said.

"Of course," Grace said and ushered Calum from the room.

The minute they were gone Seth shut the door.

"What the hell are they talking about?" Alana shook her head. "I'm feeling super fuzzy. The last real thing I remember was walking in from the garden last night. I know that they cooked a meal for us in record time. After that, I only remember bits and pieces."

Seth leaned against the door and stared at her oddly. "It was all really strange. The dinner, the way you acted, everything."

"So you remember everything?"

"I do. But like I said, it was weird. I wasn't... myself."

Alana couldn't help herself. She strode to him and clasped his forearms. "I need you to be more specific, Seth. Please. I'm scared. More scared than I've been through all of this."

"I know you are," he whispered. She didn't fight him when he removed her hands and wrapped her up in a hug. No way around it, Seth was wonderful at hugging. For a good minute, she allowed him to comfort her until she pulled away.

"What happened last night? Tell me."

His eyes shadowed slightly. "Nothing overly terrible. We just weren't ourselves. You were so complacent and... well, not you. And I didn't care. It was all so cordial. Almost as if we'd sat at that table many times discussing the day."

Alana leaned back against the dresser and rubbed her arms. She recalled so little. Different impressions crossed her mind. How handsome Seth had looked... like the perfect nineteenth century gentleman. Shaking her head, she looked at him. Why would she have been attracted to a more subdued version of Seth? After all, despite his obvious issues, she'd always enjoyed the excitement he offered. Wasn't that the main attraction between them? That they like to live on the edge?

"Why are you looking at me like that?" he asked.

"Like what?"

"As if I'm a new species."

"I wasn't."

"You were."

She tried not to smile. "Sorry. I guess I was wondering about why I would find a calmer 'you' alluring."

"A calmer me?" He snorted. "No such thing."

"Hmmm."

Seth narrowed his eyes. "Don't get too comfortable with the idea."

Alana couldn't help but grin a little. "So what's this about a gala? And when exactly did I agree to go to it?"

Shaking his head, Seth said, "Just Calum and Grace doing what they want. A party for us. Or so they say. Something tells me all of this has more to do with them than you and me though. Could be wrong but I doubt it."

"Seriously, are they nuts? We've traveled back in time with a reaper coming to kill you and they want to party?"

With a shrug, he said, "They're odd as hell."

"You don't seem that freaked out about it."

"Why should I be?"

Alana rolled her eyes. "Um, death is after you. Time to party!"

Seth's expression clouded briefly but he soon grinned. "There are worse things to do. Besides, I'm kind of curious about this dress you're supposed to wear."

"Another dress," she muttered.

"You don't look too bad in a dress." He winked.

"It seems they're all I'll be wearing here." Walking to the bed, she picked up the simple tan colored dress.

"Mmm." Seth walked over. "Can't really climb mountains in that, eh?"

"If I ripped it to thigh level I could."

Chuckling, he said, "If you ripped this to thigh level and climbed a mountain, I'd be right behind you."

"Aren't you funny." Alana tossed the dress on the bed and nodded at the door. "Go get dressed. I need to get out of this room and I don't want to be alone when I wander this house again."

Seth edged a little closer, the look on his face uncharacteristic. For a split second, she wanted to mock him for looking so concerned about her but she paused. There was something to this. Something to him caring so much. But what? Her heartbeat crawled into her throat as she watched him. He wasn't looking directly in her eyes, but he was looking at her. An evasive Seth. Who knew?

"Go," she reminded, a bit too sharply.

Jerking his head in what seemed a remembered

nod, Seth met her eyes briefly and left the room. Alana stared at the doorway. Had she offended him somehow? Impossible. Seth didn't get offended. Did he? No way. Seth was Seth.

With a solid thump, she sat on the edge of the bed and pulled the dress onto her lap. Her body felt simultaneously charged and weakened. It wasn't the most pleasant feeling. If given a fight, she'd kick ass, but would she have the energy? Nothing was right. But somehow, nothing was wrong.

Ugh! She lay back on the bed and again stared at the ceiling. Seemed she did that a lot in this house. How was it she could remember so little from last night? Worse than that, if this house was so haunted it turned her hair black and made her freckles vanish, why wasn't she inherently more petrified? Truth told, though it'd freaked her out at first, she wasn't all that bothered by it now. It was as if the feeling had been a minor tooth ache numbed by the Novocain of complete nonsense. Growling, she sat up. No need to lay here and overthink things.

With a quick tug and pull her nightgown was removed. The fact she was without bra and panties right now was irrelevant. Alana crawled into the simple dress and buttoned it up. There was nothing to brush her new hair with so she ran her fingers through it. There was no way she wasn't pulling it back from her face. Ripping the sash off a tieback for a curtain panel, she wrapped it into her hair and tugged. Low ponytail intact, she left the room.

Seth met her in the hallway and they headed downstairs. About halfway down, the air seemed to thicken. Suddenly weak, she stopped and leaned against the wall.

Seth stopped beside her and held her arm. "You okay?"

"I don't know." Nausea rolled through her and she sat on the stair. Seth sat beside her. "Everything looks fragmented."

Alana blinked and narrowed her eyes. "Oh wow."

"What?"

"It's Devin." Leaning forward, she watched him trudging up the stairs. His form was transparent as if he was a ghost.

Seth frowned. "What are you talking about?"

She nodded. "There. He's walking up the stairs toward us but he's not really looking at us.

"I see nothing." Seth squinted as if that'd help him see better. "Wish I had some equipment with me."

"Devin's holding something. I think it's what you called an EMP (Electro Magnetic Phenomena) detector."

"No shit."

"He's getting closer, about three stairs down." She leaned back instinctually as he approached. "Holy," She whispered, "He's walking right through us!"

The air chilled dramatically as he did. Seth must've felt it to because his body shivered slightly. Alana turned to watch Devin continue only to discover he'd stopped and spun. The EMF detector had started whizzing and all five lights on it were now lit.

"He stopped," she reported. "The EMP detector is going nuts when he...well...moved it through us somehow."

"Damn!" Seth stood and turned. Now the men were facing each other, separated by a few steps. "Devin, can you hear me? I'm right here? C'mon man!"

"He's not responding to you but he's taken out a digital recorder."

"I can't believe I'm in this position again," Seth growled.

"He just asked who's here," She said.

"It's me, Seth! I hope that thing works. We're still here in the house but we've traveled back in time about 140 years."

"The EMP detector is still going nuts. Devin's asking if you're Seth," she said.

"Of course I'm Seth!" Seth stepped up a stair. Startled, Devin did too.

She'd never seen anything stranger.

"Devin backed up a step. I think he senses you," She said.

"Really?" Seth took another step up. Devin did the same. "Did he do it again?"

Nodding, she said, "Yep, keep doing it."

Sure as heck, every step he did it, Devin did the same. All the while Devin asked questions. Ones that Seth, of course, didn't respond to. The moment they both reached the top step, the EMP detector stopped whining and all five lights turned off.

"What's he doing now?" Seth asked.

"The EMP detector stopped so he's heading back down the stairs. It looks like he's trying to pick up a reading again."

As he walked past her Alana yelled, "Devin, stop! We're here. Seth and I are here!"

But he didn't respond and continued down the

stairs.

"Did he hear you? What's going on now?" Seth asked.

"No, doesn't seem like he did. In fact, he just faded at the bottom of the stairs." With him vanishing so too did her dizziness and nausea. Wiping sweaty palms on her dress, she took a deep breath.

"What a mess." Seth sat next to her again. "You doing better? You look better."

Nodding, she said, "Yeah, I'm alright." She shook her head. "It's strange that I see them and you don't. They're your family."

"It must be because you're a necromancer," Seth responded.

Uneasy, she said, "Not sure I like it."

"Don't think you have much of a choice."

"What was it like for you when you learned you were a…warlock."

"I thought it was great." Seth nodded down the stairs to where she said Devin had vanished. "But Devin hated it. Took him a long time to accept the gift. He looked at it as evil. Something that had changed him against his will."

"I get that," she said. "Not so sure I'm too happy about my new gift either. In fact, I'd be fine with losing it."

Seth nodded. "I know you would. But maybe after Calum tells you more about what you're capable of you won't feel that way. After all, you like things that get your blood pumping. Guarantee that this'll do it."

Alana eyed him. "But you forget one thing. You loved the paranormal long before you became a warlock. I didn't even believe in it. Now that I do, can't say I'm crazy about it."

"Just give it time. You'd be amazed how intense it can get."

She shook her head and stood. "Safe to say I know how intense it can get. Main reason I don't think I like it much."

Seth continued down the stairs with her. "We'll see."

"No choice," she muttered.

"Ah, there you are," Calum said from the dining room. "Come. Sit. Eat."

Alana stared at the elegant table. Breakfast had been served.

Seth muttered under his breath, "Here we go again."

"This is nothing new, eh?" she asked, proud of herself for remaining so calm.

"Nope. We ate here last night." He nodded at the table. "Same sort of spread."

"Really?" She shrugged and sat down. "I don't feel like I've eaten in centuries."

Seth sat across from her and glanced around before saying to Calum, "I thought you were having the party in this room."

"Oh, we are," Calum said. "The room transforms quickly. Just a matter of moving around some furniture."

"Moving around some furniture?" Alana said incredulously. "I've never seen a dining room with so much stuff in it."

"You sound as if you think the room cluttered," Grace said, her tone almost injured.

"No. No," Calum said. "Impossible to clutter a room this large."

"Matter of opinion," Seth said around a bite of egg.

Grace eyed the room as if trying to see what they saw. "I do like odds and ends."

Alana tried not to chuckle despite herself. The room was overdone.

"It's half your charm," Calum assured, his gaze lingering on Grace's face.

It was so odd seeing her mother young and flustered by the appraisal of a man. She again struggled to remember Calum. Granted it was over a hundred years ago but wouldn't she remember him somehow? Was magic that powerful?

Time to stop asking herself that when the answer was clearly 'yes'. With a heavy sigh, she pushed the food around on her plate.

"You should eat, girl. Your strength is so very important," Calum said.

"Oh yes, very important," Grace seconded.

Seth nodded as he chomped down another mouthful.

"How can you possibly be hungry after what just happened on the stairs?" she asked.

Grimacing, he swallowed. Before he could say a word Calum said, "What happened on the stairs?"

Seth shook his head and kept his eyes on her. "Meant to tell you to keep that between us."

Why? "Seems to me we should keep the guy who built this house in the loop."

"I couldn't agree more." Calum narrowed his eyes at Seth. "Care to share, lad?"

Seth grumbled to himself then said, "We saw Devin on the stairs. I mean Alana saw him as a ghost. He sensed we were there. Just like Leathan had upstairs yesterday. This was far more intense though and lasted longer."

"He had ghost hunting equipment," Alana added. "It responded to our presence."

"See!" Calum grinned. "Just as I said, you two are ghosts to them." His gaze once more fell on Grace. "Amazing, isn't it, love?"

She smiled softly, her eyes alight. "Positively. It is just as you said it would be."

"Said it would be?" Seth frowned.

"Of course, yesterday," Calum said a little too hastily. "This is by far the most haunted house in Vermont and you two are part of it!"

"I'd rather enjoy it from the twenty-first century," Seth said sharply before commencing to another big mouthful of food.

"Eventually," Calum said dismissively and turned his attention to Alana. "I promised to tell you more about your new gift."

"Not now," Grace said. "We're eating, darling." A small pout curved her full lips. "Makes for poor dinner conversation."

Alana wondered if Grace realized she hadn't touched her food. It seemed her mother preferred to pretend everything was perfectly normal. Setting aside her food, she sat back and nodded at Calum. "Now's as good as any time for me."

"Very well then!" Calum smiled wide.

Seth frowned but said nothing. How could he between bites? Seemed the freaky situation they were in didn't bother his stomach at all. Then again, he was probably used to eating during offbeat situations. He must've had to eat during the hauntings at the Victorian and Georgian. How, she couldn't imagine.

"The gift is hereditary," Calum announced.

Everyone's eyes swung Grace's way. "Yes, yes. I possess the gift. But not nearly as strong as Alana."

Calum continued. "As you know, Necromancy is the ability to communicate and oftentimes raise the dead."

"Which is why I was so easily able to communicate with Seth," Alana said, her mind spinning. "But why was he the first? Despite the hundred or so years I can't recall, why didn't I communicate with... the dead, in the years I do remember?"

"As to the years you do remember, are you absolutely sure you haven't?" Calum said.

"Pretty darn sure," Alana responded.

"He makes a good point," Seth said. "Didn't you think I was just a voice in your head?"

"Well yes but I knew you, had watched you die, or so I thought. Pretty traumatic stuff." She absently swirled egg yolk on her plate. "Seems to reason you'd be my own inner voice going a little loco."

"I understand your reasoning and surely you understand now how easily you may have misinterpreted other spirits over the years when they tried to communicate. In Seth's case he was persistent and quite obviously part of your journey here," Calum said.

Alana's fingers felt a bit numb so she set down the fork. "You mean to say that dead people have been talking to me my whole life? That when I thought I was thinking for myself it was really others talking to me?"

Calum nodded once. "That is indeed what I'm saying. Interesting, isn't it?"

Nausea rolled through her and she pushed away the plate. "Not really. Kinda makes a girl feel insane."

"Yet you're not insane, sweetheart," Grace said softly. "In fact, you've handled everything far better than I ever did."

Alana didn't know what to say to that. She wanted to shout and scream, rant and rave. But more than anything, she wanted to get the hell out of here. Again. But this time she stopped herself. It was time to stop running from every difficult situation. Besides, in this reality, where the hell would she go?

"Tell me more about being a necromancer," she said to Calum. "I need to know I'm not evil."

"What's with you and Devin about that?" Seth shook his head.

She rolled her eyes. "I'd think that'd be obvious."

Calum's eyebrows lifted and he said, "Evil, as I've said before, is much like beauty, it's all in the eye of the beholder. Everyone's take on it is different."

Incredulous, she looked from Calum to Seth and back again. "You two aren't right. Hope you know that. In no reality is evil misunderstood. Evil is evil and it's bad. Seriously bad."

Before Seth could speak, Calum waved away his potential rebuttal and said, "Never mind all that. The more important thing is that you are now aware of your abilities and can learn to control them."

Alana took a deep gulp from the water perched lazily by her clenched fist on the table. "Any chance I can skip it altogether? I'd really prefer not to."

"You can't avoid what's part of you," Calum responded sharply.

When her eyes shot to his, Alana was surprised to see that his serene expression had vanished. In its place, a face made of harsh planes and too-intense eyes.

"What he means to say," Grace said, expression the grimmest it'd been since their arrival. "Is that some things are unavoidable."

Blood started to thump faster through her veins. How dare they look at her the way they were. As if she'd had this 'gift' all along and taken the easy road by ignoring it. With an angry shove, she leaned forward and rested her elbows on the table.

Glaring at Calum and Grace she said through clenched teeth, "Everything that's happened to me and to Seth for that matter, in this house, is unavoidable because of you two. I know it's Calum's curse but it's becoming very obvious that it's Grace's curse too. And because of that, it's my curse! So don't you two sit there with those superior, I-know-it-all expressions on your face because I don't deserve it."

"What do you deserve?" Calum replied evenly.

Alana tried to get her anger under control. "To not be here. This isn't my time. This is all a lie."

"This is your time," Grace said, her motherly sweet persona all but vanished. "And you are here. It's time you accept that."

"It's time?" she sputtered, enraged. "Time?"

Before she could blow, Seth smoothly intercepted. "I think we need to keep things low key. Too much overflow heading Alana's way. One way or another, we all need to get along through this."

Believe it or not, Seth's statement made the heavy thud of her heart slow some. Who knew Seth could be a peace keeper? She sure as heck didn't. He was right though. They needed to get along. She didn't have to like it. Sitting back, Alana nodded. "Seth's right." With a deep breath, she looked at Calum. "Tell me more about my ability."

"Quite right." Calum nodded, obviously pleased with both her attitude and curiosity. "It is not your gift to communicate with the dead that is so spectacular, my girl, but your power of divination through that whom you have summoned."

Seth's mouth dropped open the minute hers did. What?

"That is right," Grace said. "Through that divination you can see the future or any hidden knowledge. You can obtain so very much."

Another sip of water was needed. She downed the glass in one large swallow. When she lowered the glass it was to find everyone staring at her. Of course it was her turn to respond. What fun. Twirling the glass slowly with one hand she silently cracked one finger knuckle after the other on her lap before saying, "I can see the future? How's that work when I'm in my past?"

Grace smiled and said, "You'd be amazed, my dear. The past and present are easily intertwined. A wise necromancer knows that the past is but a reflection of the future. It's all repetitive."

"So we never really learn from ourselves," Alana muttered.

"We do," Calum said, "but not in the obvious sense. As humans we're more content to keep the drama flowing so we do mess up time and time again. If not, we get bored. Just our species."

Was that true? She'd never been much of a deep

thinker. In her world, she did everything she could to find the next thrill. She did everything she could to not overthink things. For the first time, sitting at that table over a prim and proper breakfast, Alana knew it was time not to run but to think very clearly. To not be afraid and run but be confrontational. Funny, in that singular moment she realized for all she'd always thought she'd dived into danger head first, she'd been nothing but a coward. Running into danger had kept her from dealing with what was right in front of her.

"If... and I mean if, the dead have spoken to me over the years, how do I learn to separate them in my mind. How do I learn to tell the difference?" she asked.

Seth looked at her with a careful mix of respect and interest. He understood that she was at the precipice of understanding something far beyond what she'd ever been capable.

"It is a matter of truly understanding who you are," Calum said. "Once you do, the voices that do not belong in your mind will become much clearer."

"I thought I already had a pretty good idea about who I am," she replied.

"I think you're getting a better and better idea very quickly," Calum said. "Am I wrong?"

It took everything she had not to appear startled. Calum definitely had a way of understanding someone. Then again, he was a warlock. She offered a haphazard shrug.

"Well, my guess is that you seeing or sensing Leathan and Devin is just the beginning. It's your gift beginning to become more apparent."

"Super," she said dryly. "I guess I hope that they continue to show themselves instead of simply being voices in my head. The whole voice in my head thing is creepy."

"Time will tell how your gift manifests," Grace said.

Obviously. "How did it happen for you? When did you first realize you were…this?" she asked Grace.

"When I became pregnant with you."

A strange sensation rolled through her. "Really?"

Grace nodded. "Pregnancy can sometimes make a woman more intuitive. In this case, it ignited a dormant gift within me."

"That's intense." Seth scooped the last bit of food into his mouth.

Alana frowned. "That must've been pretty scary. What did my father think?"

She'd purposefully not brought up her father. A man who she knew nothing about.

Grace's brows rose slightly. "I'm afraid that he was not around long enough to know of it."

Ah, so Dad had bailed. Honestly, she had little desire to learn much more about him. She was frustrated enough with her mother right now.

"You going to eat any of that?" Seth asked, nodding at her plate.

"No, it's all yours."

Seth didn't hesitate but slid the plate his way.

Grace frowned a little. "You really should try to eat something, Alana."

"Not hungry. Sorry," she said listlessly and looked at Calum. "Is there anything else I should know about my new gift?"

"Not at the moment," Calum said. "The more you get used to it, the more you will understand."

"I have just one more question for now," Alana said. She really didn't want to ask this but had to.

"Yes?" Calum said.

Ignoring the severe apprehension building quickly she asked, "If I can communicate with the dead does that mean that I can communicate with death. Will the reaper try to talk to me?"

Calum didn't hesitate for even a fraction of a second. "I'm counting on it."

CHAPTER NINE

Seth had to admit he was pretty proud of Alana.

Instead of taking off like she usually did, she sat calmly after Calum said what he said. Incredulous and more than pissed off, Seth said, "You counted on it?"

"Well, of course," Calum responded evenly.

"So she's bait. Just like the other women were," he ground out.

"I'd think by now you would have realized that the women are part of the reason the curse is unraveling. It would only make sense that they possess a lure... a way to draw out the monster"

"You ass. So you're using Alana to draw death? I would think me being here would be draw enough," Seth retaliated.

"Regrettably, no. Any more than it did in the other two houses," Calum said.

Seth scowled and eyed Alana. Though she'd gone paler she seemed pretty composed considering. It was odd seeing her with dark hair and no freckles but it didn't bother him. In fact, he was seriously drawn to it... which was odd. It didn't escape his notice that she strongly resembled Grace now. No lie though, Grace was hot. Though he hadn't said a word, he'd seen the very slight changes in his own appearance as well. He was looking more and more like Calum. Somehow, this was a bad thing. But why? How? Outside of the obvious.

"What about the stone?" He asked. "That still

hasn't been found. Or has it? What'd you do with it, Calum?"

"Now that I can't say," Calum said. "Especially with Alana sitting here."

Seth started to respond but Alana shook her head. "He's right. If he says where it's hidden, the reaper will discover the truth through me."

Calum and Grace looked at her with approval. Seth sat back and crossed his arms over his chest. "You seem uncharacteristically okay with all of this, Alana."

"No choice." Though she sighed, he noticed that some color was returning to her face. "What Calum says makes sense."

Seth hated to admit she was right. For that matter, he hated to admit that Calum was right. She might be getting good at not fleeing but he figured she could use a little escape right now. "Want to go for a walk, Alana?"

As he suspected, relief flooded her face and she nodded. "Yeah."

Before he realized what he was doing, Seth stood and pulled her chair out. There was that whole gentleman thing again. Though Alana seemed a little thrown off she thanked him. Naturally, she headed for her dependable rock.

"No," he took her hand. "Let's walk through the woods. Put some space between us and this house."

"Alright," she said. "Not really dressed for it though."

"Who cares?" He pulled her along, more than aware of the feel of her hand in his. It was weird. Usually he didn't notice something like that.

Though color dusted the tops of her cheekbones,

the unmistakable vibrant life that usually entered her eyes when outside wasn't there. He didn't like that. What to do? Hmm. Strangely enough, the answer to his question materialized.

Seth pulled off his shirt.

"What are you doing?" She murmured, eyes scanning his chest. He didn't miss the admiration.

"Going for a swim."

"What? It's got to be all of sixty degrees out here!"

"So?" He pulled down his pants and grinned.

Her eyes rounded slightly and she blushed. Totally unlike Alana. But he wouldn't be swayed. "Come on."

"No. I don't think so."

"Look at this." He grabbed her hand and pulled her to the edge of a cliff. Though it wasn't anything a dare-devil would be interested in seeing that it only hosted a mere thirty foot drop into the water, it was better than nothing. She seriously needed some life pumped into her.

Seth inclined his head toward the water. "Jump."

Alana shook her head. "Naw."

"Fine. Let it all get to you. Stay as safe as you can." He didn't wait for her answer but dove off the cliff.

As expected the water cut like a frigid knife. Mountain water at this time of year might as well be iced. He loved it. After he surfaced, he floated on his back. Alana stood at the edge of the cliff high above. Her long black hair blew in the wind, its silky length shiny beneath the glowing sun. He already knew what she'd do but enjoyed watching her from this angle.

A brief look of frustration passed over her face

before Alana quickly shed her dress and dove. She hadn't given him much time to enjoy, but Seth watched her perfect naked form from the moment it left the rock all the way down until it vanished beneath the water. Even then, he watched her swim beneath the water, her body a slender, graceful piece of perfection. When she surfaced, the pinched look had vanished from her face. In its place, his Alana...the live-on-the-edge girl he'd jumped with.

"This is perfect," she exclaimed.

"My thoughts exactly," he murmured and grinned.

Not bothering to cover her breasts, she shook her head. "One track mind."

"Least it's on track. How about yours?"

"What do you mean?"

"You seem off. Or hadn't you noticed?"

"How would I notice if I'm off?"

Seth swam closer. "Didn't it occur to you that you normally would've beaten me off that cliff? That you wouldn't have hesitated for even a second?"

"Yeah, so. Guess I'm getting smarter. The water's freezing."

"You don't seem bothered by it now. You seem pretty happy to me."

"Gotta admit," she smiled. "I feel pretty good. Thanks for this."

Hovering within a few feet of her Seth grinned. "Anytime."

Despite the fact they were both naked, he clearly saw that she intended to keep their 'just friends' status intact.

Alana sunk beneath the water for several moments before she resurfaced. Though it seemed like she wanted to say something she didn't. Instead, her gaze skimmed the water toward the mountain. He didn't miss the brief flash of concern that lit her golden eyes then vanished.

"What is it?" he asked.

"What is what?"

"Whatever I just saw in your eyes. Let me in, Alana. You've learned a lot of crap in a very short time. I want to know that you're okay."

She seemed a little taken back by his comment. "I'm fine."

"Why do you seem almost offended that I asked?"

Alana shook her head. "I don't know... it's not like you to...care."

Now he was offended. "Huh? How could you say that?"

She shrugged, her slender shoulders popping up from the water. "See, you're losing track of who you really are as much as me."

"Damn." He leaned back in the water. "I see you're back to your normal self. Not sure I like it."

"Don't really care if you do." Swimming to the water's edge, she perched against a rock, tilted her face to the sun and closed her eyes.

Well, if she thought they were back to normal, fine. He swam over, stood and braced his hands on the rock on either side of her shoulders. Very slowly, her eyes opened. Oh yeah, his Alana was back full throttle. She didn't look shocked nor did she bat a lash.

"You're standing a little too close."

He leaned his face closer. "So?"

"Friends," she said carefully.

But he didn't miss the catch in her voice. Or the way the gold of her iris's flared to life. "Right."

Slowly, inch by inch, he let his eyes wander down her body and licked his lips.

"Stop," she whispered.

His eyes shot to hers. "Stop what?"

"You know what."

"Did you hate what we did on the rock face yesterday?"

"You know I didn't. But we talked about this. It's just not a good idea for us to be more than friends."

Seth ran the back of one of his fingers down her arm. "I wouldn't mind being both."

"Never works out well," she said softly.

He enjoyed the way her chest heaved as he continued the lazy stroll with his finger. "Maybe not with other men."

Despite the freezing water his cock was working with him. It wasn't his style to sit back and not take what he wanted but for some reason, he needed her to come to him this time. He wanted her to want it as much as him. Though only a foot or so remained between them, she did nothing to close the distance. He'd almost bet she would back up if she could.

"And don't forget," she reminded. "You don't have a miraculous condom on you this time."

He shrugged and leaned in a little bit closer, eyes on her lips. "I don't need a condom to kiss you."

Alana's eyes widened then flickered to his lips. "With you it doesn't stop at a kiss." She shook her head. "Besides, it's not a good idea for friends to kiss. Sort of defeats the whole purpose."

"Matter of opinion." But he wasn't going to push it. Instead he moved away, walked onto the shore and said over his shoulder, "I know damn well you're checking out my ass."

"Arrogant bastard," she muttered.

Seth grinned and looked up at the cliff, then looked her way, allowing himself a healthy eyeful of her nude form getting out of the water. No way around it. She was far hotter than Grace. The way she moved. Not languid and sexy, but with an enticing straightforward stride that made her honed fitness obvious how active she really was. But he knew she had sexy in her. He'd seen it when her body had writhed beneath his on that rock yesterday.

"Not going to be fun trekking through the woods in our bare feet," she commented.

"This would be one of the many benefits of being what I am," he responded. Within moments their clothes were in a pile at their feet. He grinned at the startled look on her face. "You'd be amazed at what else I can do."

Stepping into her dress, she said, "I'm sure."

Seth climbed into his clothes and walked over to her with a quick stride. Before she realized his intentions, he wrapped one arm around her back and cupped the back of her head with his free hand. Tilting her head, he kissed her soundly. Though she was stiff for a second, she soon softened. Relishing her sweet taste, he wrapped his tongue around hers, deepening the exchange. All the 'let's-just-be-friends' drained right out of her and she melted against him. The minute she did he pulled away and said, "Told you you'd be amazed."

Though Alana's eyes narrowed, the corner of her lip quirked. "At least you're consistent."

He gave her space. "Can't help it." Seth nodded northward. "Let's keep walking. Kill some time."

With a good twist, she rang out her hair and followed. Though their shoes weren't the best for trekking through the forest they were both adept at moving in this environment so it didn't slow them down much. It felt good to be out here with her. Without arguing that is. But before he'd died they'd never really argued. No. They'd always had a great time together. Seth stopped short at how much it really bothered him that they might not get to spend more time together after this... even if they were just friends.

Alana stopped beside him. "What's the matter?"

"Nothing." As if he'd tell her what he was thinking. Doubtful she'd take him seriously anyways. "Just debating which direction to head."

"I have an idea. Follow me. This should be right up your alley."

They veered right and tromped through the leaves and roots, angling sideways until she paused and planted her hands on her hips. "Pretty sure I'm in the right area. It looks a little different around here. Guess over a hundred years will do that."

Seth went down a little further and looked around. All he saw far and wide was tilted forest and tons of trees. Then he spied something apparently at the same time as her because she came down from the other side.

"There it is."

All he saw was the side of a rock exposed to the elements. Due to rain water run off, a deep pathway had been carved into the ground beside it. They rounded the corner and soon enough he spied what she'd been looking for, a crude cemetery.

"Old family plot," she murmured. "Missing a stone or two obviously."

"Doesn't look that old." Seth had always loved cemeteries. The older the better. He crouched in front of one of the gravestones and dusted off the surface. It read, "Sadie. 1805-1825."

Alana seemed almost aimless. "Well, I suppose it wouldn't be that old in this time, eh? Weird."

"I'll bet." He peered at the other stones. "Doesn't look like many lived past fifty."

"Didn't have the same medical care," she commented.

"Why are they buried up here. So far from most of the surrounding houses?" he asked.

"Never really knew." She knelt in front of headstone and shook her head. "This stone doesn't have an inscription on it. Just a..." Leaning forward, Alana squinted. "It looks like a flower."

Seth joined her and felt a thrill of interest run through him. "It's a rose. A black rose."

"Yeah, so." Alana shook her head. "I don't recall this being here in the future. How could that be?"

Good question. Seth ran his fingers over the rose. The fact that Alana had mentioned a black rose in the Tudor's garden and now this gravestone was here with a rose on it meant something. He knew he should probably share with her but he still got the feeling that it was just another thing that'd freak her out. The black rose was a mystery he'd figure out on his own. At least he'd try.

"It's strange not seeing Grace's stone here." Alana stood and leaned against the rock face.

Naturally, her mom would be buried here. It was

hard to imagine. Seth looked up at her. "You okay?"

"Sure."

Somehow he doubted that. Leaning against the rock beside her, he eyed the ten or so stones. "I suppose in its own unique way this is kind of a cool place to be buried. On the side of a mountain."

Alana nodded but said nothing.

"You seemed interested in bringing me here earlier. Now, not so much. What's going on, Alana?"

She shrugged. "Not sure. Something about seeing all these stones so much newer. And, believe it or not, Grace not being here, seems really wrong." Alana nodded to where her plot should be. "It sort of seems desecrated even though I know damn well why she's not here. Make sense?"

Seth squeezed her hand. "Sure."

Normally, he would have mocked. But he saw the seriousness in her eyes. The odd sadness. It made him uncomfortable and... concerned? Awe hell, he really was cracking up. Besides his cousins, he didn't get concerned about others. Pulling away his hand, he cleared his throat and said, "So you want to head up or down?"

"Is back to the future an option?"

He grinned. "Eventually."

"My thought? The quickest way is straight back down to the house."

"I suppose."

"What time do you think this gala's at?"

Seth felt an odd jar in his bones and was surprised to see that the sun was sinking. How could that be? "Is it me or did the day fly by way too fast?"

Alana frowned at the horizon and rubbed her arms as if she shivered. "We haven't been gone that long have we? Why does it look like it's late afternoon?"

"Don't know. Let's get back though."

They didn't bother with small talk as they walked. Seth guessed that her mind was reeling like his. It was one thing to be thrown back in time, another to have time pass like a too-fast-draining-hourglass once here.

When they walked into the house all was calm. The setting sun cast long spikes of orange down the hallway. The scent of lemon-oil filled the air. They stopped short at the dining room entrance. It had been transformed from grandeur with too much furniture to downright majestic with a select few pieces.

"Wow," Alana whispered. "It looks like a ballroom!"

Seth grinned. "Damn. Who knew?"

"I told you as much," Calum declared from the far doorway.

"Yep, but we didn't believe you," Seth said and walked into the room. It was decked out. Not in the way he'd expect but softer. There were sprigs here and there. Even bowls full of berries. It was elegant but earthy. Both he and Alana should have thought it totally bizarre but they didn't. Somehow it worked.

"Now that's always been your problem," Calum admonished.

"It looks incredible," Alana said.

Calum bowed slightly and nodded. "Much thanks my dear."

"So what's up with us losing time?"

Alana didn't seem overly surprised by Seth's question. Calum on the other hand looked almost... affronted? And conveniently enough, didn't answer his question.

"What time is the party supposed to start?" Alana asked.

"Soon," Grace said.

Seth glanced behind him and hoped Alana didn't catch the look of admiration that had to be on his face. Grace looked amazing. Already dressed for the gala, she wore a long dark chocolate colored dress that hugged her figure and made her skin glow.

"I need to get dressed."

Seth was surprised by the low octave of Alana's voice. When he looked her way he was more surprised to see that she gazed up the stairs, as if she was eager to go up them, to get dressed in an outfit that wouldn't suit her at all.

"Come then!" Grace declared and swooped Alana up the stairs before Seth could comment on how oddly smooth it was all going.

"Do not look so baffled," Calum commented.

"It's just shocking, that's all."

"What's that?"

"Are you serious? You don't see what's shocking about this?"

"I haven't a clue what you are talking about." Calum waved away Seth's next words and nodded outside. "The odd passing of time probably has to do with the haunting."

"That's your answer for everything," Seth said.

Calum shrugged. "I would think by now that you would be used to this sort of thing, lad. Nothing is bound to make sense within the curse."

"See, that's the thing." Seth glared. "It'd all make a lot more sense if you weren't so continually evasive."

"I tell you what you need to know." Calum admired himself in a mirror. "I created this curse and it's important that I remain in control."

"Yeah, yeah, I get it. We're all pegs in your game. But I can't help wonder how much control you really have. Seriously, why not just destroy the creature when it comes rather than trap it?"

Calum arched a brow at Seth in the mirror. "I would have thought you figured that out by now."

Seth rolled his eyes. "Right. It takes a combined effort to destroy it even though you're far more powerful than all of us put together."

"You've got to remember that they're after my descendants, not me. A more apt payment in their eyes. It's all become such a complex web now. One I must finish."

Though he'd always been the cousin who most enjoyed becoming a warlock and wrangling through this curse, Seth finally understood why Devin and Seth had gotten so aggravated. It involved a woman they cared about. And despite what he told himself, he knew his feelings for Alana were growing. Had been growing for some time.

"How will you know when the reaper is close? How do you intend to trap it?" Seth asked.

"With the stone of course," Calum reminded. "And as I've said before, the reaper is by far the most powerful and stealthiest. My methods of trapping it are quite risky."

"Great." Seth paced like a caged animal. Energy built in him like a volcano getting ready to blow. He needed action. This waiting around shit wasn't for him.

"Regrettably I cannot seek it out nor can you, lad.

Death always finds the person, never the other way around."

Seth nearly growled. "How the hell do I fight death? I mean a vampire and werewolf are visible albeit nasty creatures but a reaper? Seems impossible. How do you kill something that's already... dead?"

"A vampire is dead. You all fought that. Them I should say," Calum said. "And you beat them. You did not even know they existed and still you beat them. My hope is that the same rules apply with a reaper."

"But I need my cousins to succeed and they haven't technically been born yet," Seth said.

"You have a necromancer at your disposal. I'm quite sure she'll tie all of this together for you," Calum assured.

"Another pawn in your game. How convenient."

"She is here for you, because of you," Calum replied. "I did not figure Alana into my equation." He frowned and looked out the window. "Or her mother for that matter."

"Speaking of. What about Anna? I thought you were in love with her. She was irreplaceable," Seth commented. "She's all you talked about in the Victorian and Georgian. Hell, she came to you as a ghost in the Georgian! Wasn't she the love of your life?"

Calum went perfectly still, his body language suddenly pulled tight like a bow. "My feelings are none of your concern."

"You made them part of all of our concerns when you wrote about it in your journal," Seth reminded.

"It was the only way to get you to travel back," Calum said through clenched teeth.

Interesting. It was hard to rile up Calum. This topic apparently did.

"Listen, I don't judge you for loving another woman. You're human after all. Kinda. And Grace is pretty damn hot. But what about Anna? How can you so easily—"

"No." Calum's posture grew tighter. "This subject is best left alone."

"Is it really? This is your love Anna we're talking about."

Seth grinned at the mirror Calum had just been looking in. "Adlin! About time you made another appearance."

The Scottish wizard grinned. "It's an odd haunting this one. Harder to get in and out, but worth a shot when Calum gets talking about romance, aye laddie?"

Calum spun on his heel and nodded his head in wry acknowledgment. "Seems an avid interest of yours, old man."

Adlin grinned, his reflection clearer than it'd been in the future. "I prefer consistency."

Eyes narrowed, Calum said, "Of course you do."

"Interesting, this romance between you and Grace," Adlin commented.

"Quite unexpected," Calum said.

"Aye. I can't help but find it curious."

If possible, Calum's eyes narrowed even further. "You speak as though you know something I do not."

"I always know something that you do not," Adlin assured with a wink. "Because, might I remind you, I have been around far longer than you."

"So being dead is considered 'being around' these days, is it?" Calum asked.

"Hmph. You should talk. You're not precisely alive yourself, now are you?"

"More so than you, I'm sure," Calum said.

"Enough," Seth said. These two wouldn't shut up if you let them. "Adlin, have you communicated with Devin and Leathan? Do they know where I am?"

"Nay, sorry lad. If you think it's tricky here you should try being there. The house is classically haunted and busy. I am fairly certain however, that they know you're here. Seems they've made some contact with Alana?"

"Yes. Exactly!" Calum declared.

"Exactly what?" Adlin asked.

"She's a necromancer."

"Is she really?"

"Indeed!"

"How wonderful!"

"Okay, enough you two!" Seth shook his head. "Try to stay focused, eh?"

"We are focused," Adlin replied defensively.

"Naturally," Calum said, equally wounded.

"At least in your own little world," Seth muttered.

"Well, I'll say," Calum said.

"When did he get so moody? Wasn't he the fun one?" Adlin asked.

Calum shook his head and looked helplessly at Seth. "At one point."

Now Seth was talking through clenched teeth. "Guess it happened when I thought I was dead, being without a body and all."

"Oh, there was that," Adlin allowed.

"I'd nearly forgotten," Calum agreed.

"How exactly was it that you knew?" Seth asked and then reconsidered. "Nevermind. After all, you're in control. You know everything."

Again Calum ignored him and asked Adlin, "Will you be attending the gala?"

"I'll certainly try." Adlin was about to say more but his image faded.

"Oh bugger." Calum shook his head. "Hauntings. They're so inconsistent."

Seth watched Calum putter around the room and couldn't help but think back to the haunting at the Victorian and how far they'd all come. Back then Calum and Adlin were arch enemies, Adlin's disgust for Calum's turn to dark magic a palpable thing. But somehow through the hauntings they'd formed a lukewarm friendship. Good chance they didn't even know it. As far as Seth could tell, where Calum was determined to see him and his cousins through this nightmare, Adlin was doing the same for Calum. And Adlin had a motive. Damned if Seth knew what it was. Maybe something to do with Calum's love, Anna? So this infatuation Calum had with Grace had to be stumping Adlin. Sure as heck was stumping him!

Though Calum had essentially done all of this to protect his descendants, it was primarily because those descendants came from Anna. He'd loved her so deeply. So why was he so easily swayed by Grace?

Calum headed for the door. "The gala will start soon. I've left a change of clothes in your room."

Seth frowned. For all they'd talked he hadn't got a single straight answer. Had he really expected to? Before Calum could make his escape, Seth asked something he really needed answered. "Tell me one thing, what is the black rose all about?"

Calum slowed at the door but didn't look back. "You'll know very soon. And when you do, your life won't be worth living."

CHAPTER TEN

"It's beautiful. But it won't work with my coloring," Alana said dubiously as she stared at the dress in Grace's arms.

"Perhaps not your original coloring, dear," Grace said, her tone tentative and gentle.

"Oh, right." Alana rubbed her lips together. "I forgot."

"Come, let's get you into this."

Alana didn't think twice about changing in front of Grace. After all, she'd been her only family member. The fact that she was her mom and not her grandmom would still take some getting used to. As she slipped the silky cranberry fabric over her body, she knew this dress would be amazing on her. Grace did up the little buttons on the back then turned her toward the full length mirror. Amazing was an understatement. Both the color and fit were made for her. At least this version of her.

"You look so lovely," Grace murmured and made small adjustments. "Would you allow me to do your hair?"

Alana nodded. One part of her still wanted to tell Grace off but another knew that that'd be silly. For whatever reason, she'd been given a chance to see another side of her grandmother/mother. To travel back in time and get to know her on an entirely different level. And, no matter how strange, Grace had been nothing but kind to her. This woman, her mom, cared. Or at least she had.

Within minutes Grace had piled her hair on top of her head, allowing only a few wisps to escape. As Alana watched the hairstyle unfold in the mirror, she had to admit it was flattering. It had enough elegance to get by but spoke more of whimsy and romance with a sharp edge of sexy. The next thing she knew, Grace was patting her face with various things. Makeup she supposed. But this stuff was no modern day Cover Girl. The compacts were tiny and decorated. Something you'd find in your great-grandmother's drawers. Maybe.

Alana sort of felt outside herself as Grace continued. She watched her mother's elegant hands flitter around and smelled the sweet perfume she wore. The same she'd always worn.

Grace turned her back toward the mirror. "Now look at you. Perfect. Beyond lovely."

Is that me? Alana stared at herself in the mirror, completely stunned. Yeah, she wasn't herself but this... this transformation was incredible. The cranberry made her skin shimmer and her eyes shine. The subtle way Grace had applied the makeup made her eyes look larger and more mysterious, her lips fuller and inviting. And her cleavage... was that really her cleavage? Yep. That was one thing she could call her own. In fact, her body shape hadn't changed and this dressed loved it.

She meant to say thank you but instead said, "What did I do with my life in over a hundred years? Where did that little girl go?"

Grace's eyes moistened and she whispered, "I wish I knew."

Alana shook her head and turned to face her mother. "How do you not know? You created this.

You raised me as your granddaughter. Please, I need to know the truth. I feel like part of me is missing."

Shaky, Grace slowly sat on the edge of the bed. "Part of you and me... is missing." With a deep breath she continued, "We lost time. That's all I know. We lost time."

Alana wanted to shake her silly but decided that being gentle was a better angle to take so she sat next to her. "When? How?"

"Calum," Grace whispered. "He somehow made it all happen... my grief is terrible. Somehow I take you with me and we're there... in the future and I'm older. You no longer remember me as your mother." Her teary gaze turned Alana's way. "It was strange and sad on so many levels."

Alana frowned. "But didn't I as a little girl wonder where my mom had gone or why you were older? It makes no sense."

"You didn't seem phased in the least," Grace said softly, her expression distant. "In fact I remember waking up that morning. You crawled into bed with me as you did every morning and I cuddled you close. As I stroked your hair I remember the shock I felt as my older hand ran down your hair. I felt such panic but didn't want to scare you so I sent you downstairs to start the water boiling for tea."

It had happened that fast? Impossible. Shaking her head, Alana asked, "You mean you grew old overnight?"

"Yes," Grace whispered. "Overnight."

"That's hard to imagine."

"More so than you think." Grace's eyes flitted to hers. "Do you know the feeling you had this morning when you looked in the mirror?"

Alana nodded.

"It was just like that. But instead of a different hair color and skin I was… aged. My youth had been stolen from me." Grace wiped away a tear and offered a wobbly smile. "But you had not."

It was hard to imagine what that must've felt like. "Well, how does Calum die? What's going to happen? You know so much."

"That's the thing." Grace shook her head. "I really don't."

"What do you mean you really don't?"

Grace rubbed her lips together as Alana so often did. "It is only my gift as a necromancer that I know he dies. And it is my gift that allowed me to continue on. You see this man Adlin helped…"

"Ah, Adlin. I've met him."

"Have you?" Grace asked, surprised.

"Briefly."

"Ornery old fellow."

Alana chuckled. "Yeah."

"I wish I could tell you more."

"Me too."

Grace took her hand. "I do think that this will all end well."

Though she wanted to pull away her hand she didn't. "I hope you're right. Right now it seems unlikely. I have another question."

Grace nodded.

"How did you know I'd be coming? I mean me as an adult."

"Calum told me. It was as simple as that."

Alana shook her head. "I don't think anything is as simple as that."

If she saw an odd flicker of wisdom spark in

Grace's eyes it vanished as soon as it appeared. "I can only tell you what I know, dear."

There was more to this. Alana knew it. But as each moment passed she felt less interested in searching it out... at least for now. Maybe later. The sensation should have alarmed her but it didn't.

"Ah, do you hear that?" Grace asked.

"Hear what?"

"The band has started and so has the gala."

"Band?" Wow, they went all out.

"Come, let's get jewelry on you then off we go," Grace said.

Alana nodded and let her mom wrap her wrist in a gorgeous diamond bracelet, then a necklace. It took a minute or two before Grace pulled away. Gazing in the mirror, she was shocked by the simplistic beauty of the piece. Edging closer to the mirror she realized that it was a rose. Finely threaded in silver or platinum, its leaves stemmed out across her skin. The rose was in full bloom, the petals a timid but stunning fan against the alcove where her collarbone met. From point to point the piece wasn't much larger than her thumbnail.

"It becomes you," Grace murmured.

Alana stared at the rose. It did somehow work for her. It was so beautiful though. It'd work on anyone! "Why did you really throw this gala tonight?"

Grace didn't miss a beat. "Because it seemed a good way to lighten the mood."

Alana bit her cheek. Lighten the mood? Okay. Whatever. Seemed Calum and Grace remained in their own little world because for her and Seth the only thing that'd lighten the mood would be returning to their own time.

The music was very radio-station-gets-stuck-on-classical as they walked downstairs. But the sound was smoother and echoed through the house as if the walls emitted the very sound. As if the house itself played the music. Alana didn't do enchanted fairy tales but this moment, walking down the stairs, into a room full of gawking admirers sort of felt that way. As if she'd been designed for their eyes only. But her eyes were looking for one person.

Regrettably, he was nowhere to be found.

Typical.

"Hey."

On the bottom stair she turned and looked up. Why should she own the Cinderella moment when Seth was hot enough to steal the moment with his super sexy self. Damn. He looked so fine. Dressed head to toe in a black suit and tie done nineteenth century style, his black hair was sleeked back and his blue eyes piercing in an all-too-naughty way. He had the sort of looks that made women freeze frame then tumbled into his bed.

Seth was all steaming hot sex appeal with a mad dash of elegance. And... her eyes drifted lower.

"Alana?"

Blinking, she turned a drifty gaze Grace's way. "Yes?"

"This way, love."

Instead of taking Seth's hand when he walked down the stairs, as seemed not only proper but essential to her femininity, Alana absently followed Grace through the crowd of foreign faces. When she tried to turn back, Grace took her hand and pulled her further, deeper.

Away from him.

The room seemed to explode with light and life. But wasn't that always the way? People laughed and smiled and danced. It all felt so normal and natural. It felt as if she belonged here. Candles burned everywhere, even in the chandeliers overhead. Wax dripped here and there. A small drop hit her forearm which only led to the pure excitement that was building inside her.

Alana said what came to mind. "It seems like I'm late to the party. People have been here for hours, haven't they?"

Grace turned and looked directly into her eyes. "It does not matter. What matters is that you enjoy yourself."

Oh, she did. As though walking on air, Alana floated through the crowd. They all seemed to split before her in awe. The women looked away. The men didn't. This was, in its own way, exhilarating. Refreshing. She'd spent her whole life wrapped up in avoiding people and indulging in extreme sports. Now it felt like she was releasing a deep breath of air that she'd been holding for far too long. Look at me. Admire me. Adore this. I am beautiful and not running. In fact, I'm walking right for you.

"May I?"

Without hesitation, she took Calum's arm and allowed him to lead her onto the dance floor. For the first time in her life she didn't want to run in the opposite direction. No, she wanted everyone to watch. See her. After all, she was worth seeing.

"You look lovely," Calum said and spun her onto the floor.

"Do I?" She flirted. It came so naturally.

"You know you do, love."

Spinning in Calum's arms was an easy thing. He could have been Seth they were so similar.

"But I'm not him," he murmured close to her ear.

"Hmm?" She said startled. But she kept dancing. She kept spinning.

"Here then," Calum said at some point.

Then she was dancing with Seth.

No words were said. In fact, they didn't even look at each other. They just moved and spun and danced. Though their bodies didn't touch, she felt his heat, his incredible strength. Then, after what felt like only a few seconds passed, the music ended.

But he didn't let go.

"It's not all that bad," he said so softly she barely heard him. Seth quiet? That made her eyes rise to his. Their beautiful blue depths hit her first. She could swim in them forever. That endless blue.

"Alana, are you okay?"

Though his lips moved his words seemed a million miles away. With a heavy swallow she tore her gaze from his, only to have it fall to his lips then down his neck.

"Alana?"

The throaty way he said her name instantly locked her eyes with his again. "Yes," she whispered.

His arms tightened and pulled her closer. The heat from his body intensified. His tongue, brief and flickering, wet his lips. Those perfect, well-formed lips made to kiss a... Alana squeezed shut her eyes. Her body was on fire. The burn between her thighs so intense she was surprised her body once more swayed alongside his. It should be limp and twitching on the floor!

"Alana?"

"I'm fine," she croaked. Time to be strong. Time to rise up.

"Alana?"

Nope. Screw strong. She wanted to have sex right here, right now! With him. All he needed to do was whip her out of this room into a little alcove. That was all it would take.

As if he heard her, Seth's free hand cupped her head and pulled it against his chest. The next thing she knew they were in the room adjacent, his body nearly pressing hers against the wall. While she figured for sure he'd take much needed advantage, he didn't. Instead, Seth cupped her face. Though his voice remained husky, she detected the concern.

"Snap out of it. Be here. Now. With me."

Alana closed her eyes, aware only of the length of his body, the pure closeness. "I know it's you."

"I'm not so sure."

"I just told you."

"What I wanted to hear."

She rested her hands on his chest and stared at his strong neck. "No, what I wanted to hear."

His finger found her chin and tilted her mouth toward his. Instead of kissing her he hovered and whispered, "I did it wrong the first time. I'm so sorry."

Her heart skidded to a halt. What was he talking about?

"You know what I'm talking about."

Alana swallowed. Right, he was a warlock. She squeezed her eyes shut then slowly opened them. "How did we get here? Did you just use magic in front of everyone?"

Seth shook his head. "No. I walked you right out

of there. You don't remember, do you?"

"No." Alana shivered. "One second we were dancing, the next we were here. I actually walked out of the room with you?"

"Yep." Tilting his forehead against hers he said, "You seemed out of it…drifty. Sort of like you were under a spell."

"I think I must've been," she murmured and shook her head. Totally crazy… all of this.

"How do you feel now?"

"Okay I guess."

"You sure?"

Alana nodded slowly, touched by the concern in his eyes. This place really was transforming Seth. Not that he was a complete jerk before but he definitely wasn't this compassionate.

"We should go back," she said softly.

"I'm concerned about how this place is affecting you," he said.

"There's not much we can do about it."

"But to be under a spell like you just were is something I can't control or protect you from, Alana."

She sighed. "I didn't seem in danger. If anything, I was…" Her blush deepened. "Pretty aroused."

"Aroused?" Seth's lip curled up slightly. "So you're being haunted into wanting me. Can't complain. Maybe I do like this house after all."

Eyes narrowed slightly she said. "Even I know I shouldn't be hiding in a corner with you. Let's return."

Seth watched her closely for several more moments before he nodded, took her hand and led her back into the crowd. The candlelight suddenly seemed extra bright, the crowd not nearly as appealing as it'd been.

"There you are," Grace said warmly, her hands together as though she'd been praying.

"There they are," Calum agreed. "Our guests of honor."

Seth fell away. The feeling of him leaving her side felt like the stilts had been removed from her non-existent legs.

"I wondered where you went," Grace declared.

As if her brief exchange with Seth had never happened, Alana's legs gained feeling and strength ran through her body. "Just needed a break I guess."

Seth seemed to fade away into the crowd with Calum. Grace nodded at the dance floor. "You looked lovely out there."

"Thanks. I guess."

"How did you feel?"

Amazing. Beautiful. In love. What? Alana backed up a step and shook her head. What was she thinking?

"Alana, are you well, dear?" Grace said, concerned.

Though she shook her head no, Alana whispered yes. Was she seriously falling for Seth that hard? There was no way. Was there? No way. It had to be the haunting.

"He's very handsome," Grace said.

Alana blinked absently at her. Handsome? Sure, that was a given. But why would Grace say that right now?

"Would you like to dance, miss?"

It took Alana a moment to realize a man had approached unseen. Blond and lanky tall, his eyes twinkled as he held out a hand.

"Go on, then." Grace nodded at the man. "Jackson is quite the dancer."

Without giving it too much more thought, Alana took his hand and allowed him to lead her onto the dance floor. From there it became a steady stream of men. She wasn't sure where one ended and the next began. On occasion, she'd see Seth dancing with one woman or another. How could she have fallen for him? Because the more she danced the more she knew she'd done just that. Every guy felt wrong. Every guy should have been Seth. Ugh! She'd lost it… again.

About five songs later and five perfectly decent guys, she was ready to take a break. With what she hoped was a warm smile at the current man, she said, "I'm going to sit the next one out if you don't mind."

A perfect gentleman, he nodded and stepped away. Turning, Alana found herself right back in Seth's arms.

"You've been busy," he commented.

He smelled citrusy and sporty and fresh. "You too."

"I had to play nice."

"Right."

"You jealous?"

Alana rolled her eyes and grinned, but said, "You want me to be?"

Ugh! Why the hell had she said that. Way to go, girl. This whole 'friends' thing just wasn't sticking.

"Maybe. It depends if you were hauntingly aroused with them as well."

As if he'd declared love, her face burned. Would her blush show true like it had when she was a redhead? Hopefully not. "Well, I'm not."

"Good."

Too much, too fast.

"Listen." Alana swallowed. "We're just caught together in extreme circumstances. Naturally, I'm drawn to you more than usual."

Seth chuckled. "Sure, Alana. Whatever you say."

"Really," she assured. "You're all I have of the twenty-first century."

"Well then, admire away in a purely platonic fashion." He grinned and winked. "I like watching your face turn red."

She bit her lower lip to squelch a grin. Guess he had her pegged... at least a little bit.

"We dance well together," he commented.

They did, better than she would have thought. "Question for you."

"Yeah?"

"How do we know how to dance to this music?"

"I've been wondering that myself." Seth looked at the dancers around them before his serious gaze settled on her. "Want to know what I think?"

"Wouldn't have asked otherwise."

"It's part of the haunting. Like Calum said, we're part of the haunting."

"I don't understand."

"Well." Seth frowned and shrugged. "We're ghosts right? Wouldn't it make sense that we're part of this era now and that we'd inherently know how to dance like people in this time."

The last thing she wanted to truly consider was that she was a ghost. But when she looked at the serious expression on Seth's face she realized she had no choice. It was either accept or go insane. What fun. "You truly think we're ghosts?"

"What choice do I have?"

Seth had barely finished his statement when Alana caught something over his right shoulder. Some sort of form... transparent form.

"What?" Seth's body slowed, his eyes alert. "What is it, Alana?"

"I think I just saw Leathan," she whispered. "He was right behind you."

Seth turned but she grabbed his arm. "You know you won't see him. Come." She grabbed his hand and they walked off the dance floor.

"Can you still see him?" Seth asked.

"Yep." Alana nodded at the center of the dance floor. "He's walking through the dancers, doesn't even see them. "There's an EMF detector on the floor. It's going nuts. He's talking into the recorder. Asking it questions."

"Can you hear what he's asking?"

She shook her head. "No."

"He's trying to make contact. You need to get back out there and respond!" Seth pulled her back onto the dance floor. "Come on."

It'd be about the oddest damn thing she did in her life but she swung into Seth's arms right where Leathan was standing and started to dance. As though she was talking to Seth she said, "Leathan, Seth and I are here. Can you hear me? It's Alana."

Seth slowed their dance. "What's he doing? Is he responding?"

"Shssss." Alana watched as Leathan spun slowly next to them. He knew they were there. She knew he could feel it. "We're still right here. Take your time, Leathan."

Leathan stopped moving and clicked off the

recorder. With a quick rewind he replayed, his eyes growing rounder and rounder before he yelled, "I've got them guys! Get in here!"

She clenched Seth's arms. "They know we're here."

"Tell them we're okay."

Alana tried to keep her eyes from moistening. It was intense knowing that Seth's family was so close and he couldn't talk to them. It was disturbing to see how emotional he could really get. "I can't right now, he's playing back the digital recording."

"And?"

"My voice is playing back," she whispered. "But it's a little garbled."

"Seriously?"

Alana nodded but put a finger to her lips. A minute or so passed before she said, "I'm still here, Leathan. We're at a party. We're okay."

Seth spun her slowly, waiting and whispered, "Should I talk?"

"No," she whispered.

She could tell by the eager shift of his eyes that this was killing him.

"It's a dance," she replied to Leathan's question. "Seth and I are dancing."

"What's happening now?" Seth asked.

"They're all here. Leathan, Devin, Isabel, Andrea and Dakota. They're setting up a ton of equipment. They're continuing to talk to us, one at a time. They seem excited."

"No doubt." Seth slowly spun her again and pulled her closer. "Keep talking to them."

"There are at least a hundred people in this room with us. Are you sensing them?" She asked thin air but made sure it looked like she was talking to Seth.

Meanwhile, Leathan's ethereal form appeared, then vanished, then reappeared.

"Can you hear me?" She repeated.

Leathan did another replay, clicked the machine off and said, "Yes! Yes, I can hear you, Alana."

Alana grasped Seth's arms even though they continued to dance and said, "Do you know that Seth and I are here? Please don't leave. We're right here….right here by you."

Devin nodded. "We know, lassie. We're glad you're together. Doubly glad we made contact."

"Yeah, we're glad we're together too. Couldn't imagine being here without Seth."

Isabel seemed to clear her throat before saying, "Have you seen the reaper there?"

Alana shook her head. "No. Just Calum and Grace. Have you seen it in your time?"

Leathan's face turned grim. "A few times now. But it's different than the other creatures we fought."

Seth's brows lowered in question and Alana mouthed silently, "I'll fill you in later." Then she spoke to Leathan. "How so?"

"It doesn't seem to exhibit the same blatant anger. We're assuming that's because Seth isn't here." He paused a moment. "Or it knows where Seth is and it's just taking its time. Enjoying the build-up. Have you found the stone yet? We've looked everywhere but have had no luck. Didn't really think we would."

The last part of his statement sounded far away. All five started to fade. Alana said, "You're vanishing. Can you hear me?"

But she knew he hadn't because the last thing she

saw was them scrambling to adjust the equipment, all five talking at once.

Then they were gone.

"Damn," she whispered.

"They're gone, eh?" Seth sighed. "Well, at least you can make contact with them here and there. So what's up? What did Leathan say?"

"Pretty much that the reaper isn't as nasty as the other creatures you faced. It seems to be toying with them... I think. He didn't get a chance to talk much about their encounters with it."

"Well, at least it's not doing what it was doing when I was still there. Not sure my cousins could fight it without the three of us being together."

Alana nodded. "Which leads me to believe that it's not particularly concerned with them..."

Seth frowned. "Which most likely means that me, Devin and Leathan with our combined strength would be unable to defeat it."

"Exactly," she said. "Because if you could it'd only make sense that the reaper would finish them off now to avoid a formidable threat in the future."

"Not very comforting," Seth said.

The song came to an end and they took advantage of the break to leave the dance floor. Seth got them each a cup of some sort of punch that obviously contained alcohol. Alana took a small sip and watched Calum and Grace dance. They were absolutely stunning together. No doubt she and Seth had looked pretty damn good out there too. After all, they looked more and more like the other two by the hour. Or at least it seemed to her tired mind.

In fact, as she watched the couple spin, Alana would swear she saw them flicker. After rubbing her eyes, she looked again. Of course they were still there, spinning and laughing and gazing at one another in complete adoration.

"I could use some fresh air. How about you?"

Fresh air sounded perfect. Alana nodded and followed Seth outside. The air was unusually muggy and while the moon was nowhere to be found the numerous candles from inside lit the garden with soft splashes of warm, secretive light. The flowers flipped in a light wind. Life shifted and swayed with abundance, as if this particular garden preferred the discreetness of dark to the vibrant glow of daylight.

Seth took her hand and they walked down the garden path. "It's sort of strange how calm I feel right now. As if I'm not quite myself and don't really care."

"I understand," she murmured. And she really did. As the breeze caressed her hair, its delicate fingers twisted the dress around her body. Night was tempting here…erotic somehow.

"You feel it too," he said.

"What?"

"How arousing this place is."

There was that word again... arousing. She drifted behind him, hypnotized almost. "Mmm hmm."

"I don't remember that being here." Seth nodded at a veranda.

Neither did she but Alana thought it complimented the garden perfectly. Not overly large, the wooden structure nestled in a corner with luscious vines growing all over it. The sweet smell of rose and honeysuckle grew stronger as they climbed the stairs and entered. Plush cushioned seats lined either side. How enchanting. As Seth pulled her into his arms rain began to fall.

"I did it wrong the first time," he whispered, repeating what he'd said indoors.

She knew what he was talking about and shook her head. "We both did. We were venting."

"Doesn't make what I did any better. You should have been someplace like this the first time we were together, not on a mountain face... not like that."

"We were letting off steam."

"Maybe you were but I'd be lying if I said I was." His thumbs caressed her cheeks. "I just wanted you right then and there and I always take what I want, typically without worrying about the repercussions."

A sharp ripple of awareness shot through her body. "You took what I wanted you to take. I could have said no and if I did you would've listened."

Despite himself, a confident smirk appeared. "You really don't know me that well yet, do you?"

Alana couldn't help but grin. "I know you well enough."

Seth pulled her to one of the benches. "Come, sit."

Without hesitation, Alana sank down next to him. The rain and wind increased but barely touched them in their little alcove. "This place is amazing."

Seth nodded but his eyes remained glued to her face. "You sitting there with the rain misting behind you seems so familiar. Like extreme Déjà vu."

"I know. Same here," she said. "Strange. I don't remember this veranda ever being here but it all seems so normal. It must have been here when I was a child and that's why."

"Makes sense."

There was more to say. None of this was quite right. But none of this was quite wrong either. When Seth leaned over and kissed her, none of it really mattered. The world could fade away for all she cared.

And it pretty much did.

Which made them completely blind to the fact that death circled their private alcove waiting…watching…smiling.

CHAPTER ELEVEN

Seth pulled Alana's small body up against him. For the first time in his life he was truly aware of a woman. He buried his face in her hair and inhaled the sweet smell. He ran his hand down her slender arm and marveled at the baby soft texture. In some small way, it felt like he was making love for the first time. In fact, it didn't even occur to him that he hadn't thought of it as sex.

The rain fell heavier, its mist blowing in on the warm wind and mixing with the slight friction between their bodies. Though the darkness seemed to increase outside, a fire felt as though it brightened in their fraction of reality.

Alana ran her fingers through his hair; her gentle lips parting as his tongue very lightly skimmed her neck then her ample cleavage. He flicked his tongue into the deep alcove between her scrumptious breasts and braced his hands on her slim hips when she arched, lightly but firmly pinning her in position.

His erection throbbed eagerly, ready to be free from the uncomfortable confines of his pants. But it wasn't time. Not yet. Running a sure hand up her leg and thigh, Seth flicked his tongue up her neck feather-light before hovering over her lips. Eyes closed, her chest rose and fell quickly as if she enjoyed his lips so close but not touching. As if she enjoyed the sweet promise of what was to come. As if she enjoyed the taste of his breath in her mouth.

Slowly, carefully, he ran his hand up over her

clothed thigh, belly, and then gently cupped her breast. Again, he marveled at how perfectly it fit in the palm of his hand, how amazingly round and firm it was. Ever so slightly, he rubbed the pad of his thumb over the protruding nub of her nipple beneath the fabric of her dress. Her eyelashes fluttered when he flicked his nail over it. But she wasn't looking... just breathing him in.

It was incredibly provocative.

Fanning his hand over her chest, Seth felt the heavy thud of her heart beneath his palm and closed his eyes. When he did, the delicate silk of her lips touched his, so feather soft it felt like a flower petal brushing his lips. For the first time ever, his lips tingled, came alive... throbbed.

Alana's hand covered his and her tongue entered his mouth. Slow, curious, she traced the outline of his tongue before she flattened and slowly wound around once. Remaining still, he relished the pure sensation of feeling her lips trembling against his. Bit by cherished bit, he ever so slowly joined his lips to hers because he had no choice. She tasted amazing. A swirl here, a twirl there, his tongue sucked her in and his lips fused to hers.

A low throaty moan rumbled from within her chest and vibrated beneath his palm. Clenching his hand over her chest, Seth suddenly wanted to hold onto this moment forever, hold onto her forever.

Nodding as if she'd heard his thoughts, Alana stood and swung her leg over his hips. Seth helped her pull up the dress so she could comfortably straddle him. Instead of giving him back her scrumptious lips, Alana stared intently. Her hair was damp, some tendrils clinging to her neck and face.

Her eyes were large and dark in her pale face.

Neither talked.

Words didn't belong here tonight.

Still her chest heaved as though she'd sprinted a mile, the delicate material straining against the ample mounds of her cleavage. Seth reached up and ran his finger across the small pearls of moisture on her skin then slowly licked it from his finger. All the while, her shadowed eyes watched his movement. Sexy, like a stormy siren, she reached beneath her skirts and touched herself. His mouth dropped open. As if she had all the time in the world and she ruled this moment, she continued to touch herself, her head dropping back in pleasure. Full lips parted, eyes closed, the sheer plane of her neck glistening with dew.

Never, ever, in all his time on Earth and with all the many women he'd been with had Seth seen something so incredibly alluring. He grasped her hips and involuntarily thrust against the warmth between her thighs. There stood a damned good chance he was going to pre-ejaculate in his pants.

She knew. A small smile formed on her lips and Alana pulled free her hand. So slowly he thought he was going to die with want, she brought her fingers to his lips. With near greed, he pulled her digits into his mouth and closed his eyes again. Sugary sweet, she tasted like perfection. Eventually, she pulled free her fingers and traced one gracefully around the outer edge of his lips. Then, one button at a time, she undid the front of his shirt as he reached around and nimbly undid her buttons.

All the while, he thrust up against her core, immensely pleased by the way she bit her lower lip.

She was as eager as he. And he was almost certain she didn't have on any sort of panties. As if to confirm his suspicion, she moaned and curled her fingers into the dark dusting of hair on his chest when he thrust a bit harder.

The next throaty hum from her throat snapped the last of his restraint. With nimble fingers, he unbuttoned his pants and allowed his cock much needed freedom. Alana breathed heavily and leaned forward, giving him the perfect opportunity to guide her where he needed her. Burying her face in his neck, she slowly sank. His cock twitched and he dug his nails into his thighs instead of slamming her into position.

A small whimper of pleasure erupted as she forced herself down further and further until…

"Holy hell!" He cried and grabbed her hips. The pleasure was so intense he nearly got off right there and then. Seth had never felt this before. His cock throbbed inside her as if he'd already let go. His whole body shook as he held her in position. If she moved even a smidge right now, he knew he'd blow. Head falling back against the cushion, he breathed deeply and tried to focus on the heavy rain, the steady mist blowing across his cheeks.

Carefully, as though she understood, Alana leaned forward and cupped his cheeks. Inch by inch, she angled his head until her lips met his… and kissed him for the first time. Or at least it felt that way. Almost in a chaste way, she kissed him. Angling, light, she kissed him. Her smooth lips pretended they were that of a virgin. Seth cupped her head and took the gentle offering. He took the reprieve she'd given him. Through the heavy blood rushing through his head he could hear the suckle of her kiss, the swoosh of her dress in the wind.

And it was only when she'd convinced him that her sweet kiss was enough that her hips moved.

Seth nearly gasped into her mouth.

Holding back was no longer an option.

Reaching under her skirts he grabbed her backside and thrust up harshly. Alana squeaked but didn't shy away. Her hips twirled and she thrust back. Hands holding onto his shoulders, she began to ride. Seth ground his teeth and met her thrust for thrust. Her hair fell free and fanned around them. When her tongue snaked out and licked her lips Seth nearly howled.

But not yet.

Abruptly, he stood and spun, then kneeled. This position pinned her back against the corner railing of the veranda, but still cushioned by the seat. Unable to grasp him anymore, she grasped the post above and behind her. With a sharp tug, he had the front of her dress down. While her breasts spilled free, he thrust again. And again. She cried out. He cried out. Somehow they slid down until he knelt on the floor and she sat on the cushion.

But even that wasn't nearly close enough.

When she fell back on the seat he came over her. Rain and sweat steamed off of their skin. Her legs wrapped around him and he buried deeper, more evenly. The thrusts, the passion, all became more intense. Seth felt the soft plushness of her breasts press against his bare chest. He heard the increasing whimpers erupt from deep inside her. He felt the clenching tightness of her core around his overly sensitive cock. And when he thrust that final time and his body locked up in unbelievable pleasure, he heard the loud keen of her release. Even then he couldn't push far enough into her. He couldn't get enough of her grasping pleasure. The overly intense feeling of their hearts slamming against each other.

Seth wasn't going anywhere but inside of her.

That was the last thought he had as the rain lulled him to sleep.

When he awoke, it might have been minutes later but he suspected it was several hours based on the lightened sky. But the light was very dim and rain still fell. Alana was curled up beside him, still dressed from the waist down. Damned if he wasn't ready to have her again. Gently, so as to not wake her up, he pulled free the dress and admired the smooth planes of her body in the predawn light.

Beautiful.

Shedding the last of his clothing, he once more lay beside her on the bench, his front to her back. Seth inhaled the scent of her skin as he ran his hand up her thigh, then over her hip. He liked the way her hip bone joined with the lean muscles of the side of her stomach. He liked the firm definition of her arms formed from mountain climbing and extreme activity. Dusting the back of his knuckles beneath her breasts he was again surprised by their size. An A or B cup would better suit her athletic body. Not that he was complaining. The C cup was fine. He peppered kisses over her shoulder and found his way to the delicate lobe of her ear where he gently nibbled.

Alana responded by pushing her ass back against his groin. Whether asleep or not, her body knew that there was an aroused male nearby. Moving back just a scant few inches, he let his knuckles walk slowly down the steps of her spine, as though every stair was treasured, new to the touch. As he knew she would, Alana arched, pushing her firm ass tighter against him.

"Seth," she whispered.

A small knowing grin on his face, he cupped one cheek in his hand and squeezed. When her leg lifted in invitation, Seth turned her onto her belly and crawled over her. Before she could comprehend his intentions, he lifted her hips slightly and slid in from behind.

This time she didn't play coy or take it slow. This time she cried out and pushed back in 'take-me-now' welcome. The fact that she so adamantly wanted him back inside of her aroused him even further. Frenzied, he braced on his hands and thrust almost violently. Needy couldn't begin to describe how he felt.

When Alana came within seconds, her cry muffled in the cushion, his cry wasn't far behind. Seth came so hard he crushed her and couldn't help it. His body was useless. But she'd come hard too based on the heavy clenching of her body. Exhausted, content, he fell beside her and pulled Alana's sweat soaked body flush against his. Kissing the side of her neck, he closed his eyes.

"Seth," Alana whispered. "Seth, are you awake?"

Heavy lidded, he pried his eyes open to daylight. Alana's golden eyes looked back. At some point they'd faced each other and... cuddled? Seth blinked and found he didn't really want to move. He kind of liked it here.

"I don't cuddle," he said softly. Now why had he said that?

A small smile started to blossom on her face

before her eyes widened and she sat up. "Oh heck! We're naked in my mother's garden!"

Not nearly as concerned, he grinned and sat up too. "Oh no. Not that."

Alana's eyes widened further and she shook her head. "This can't be good."

"You're an adult. One stuck in another time no less. Wouldn't worry."

"That's not what I'm talking about."

Seth looked in the same direction as Alana and froze. What the fuck?! He jumped up, pulled on his pants and stumbled out of the veranda. He couldn't be seeing straight, could he?

Alana pulled on her dress and stumbled down beside him, her voice weak when she said, "Tell me we're having the same nightmare. Please, tell me."

The Tudor house was downright decrepit. For that matter, so was the garden and all the trees. He spun and looked at the forest. It was…dead? Not in a New England winter sort of way but in a horror movie on crack sort of way.

He closed his eyes then reopened them. Everything was the same.

Dead.

"Seth, I'm scared."

Bile rose up but he swallowed it. Alana didn't need to see him afraid. He was the ghost hunter and warlock. This was his thing. Facing death was his thing. Straightening his shoulders, he turned her way and froze once more, his eyes widening.

"What is it?" Alana stepped back a fraction. "You look like you're staring into the pits of hell, Seth. What is it?"

"Your necklace," he murmured.

Alana's hand came to her necklace and she frowned. "What about it?"

"Black rose," he said. "It's a black rose."

Fingering the pendant, her frown deepened. "It wasn't black last night. Why is it now?" She bit the wobble of her lip. "And why does this shock you?"

"I'm sorry. I should have told you. I just had no idea." Seth made himself touch the pennant.

"What the hell are you talking about?" She tried to rip off the necklace. It wasn't budging.

Seth stopped her and loosely gripped the rose in his hand. The night in the garden came back to him. When she had in another state and voice said, "Beware the black rose. It will rip from you your very center. It will take from you your heart." When he'd asked Calum so recently what the black rose meant and he'd responded, "You'll know very soon. And when you do, your life won't be worth living."

Staring at the rose centered pennant that had changed colors overnight he said calmly, "This has to do with why we're here."

She pulled away and paced a few steps, fear in her eyes. "What do you mean?"

Wiping a hand over his face, Seth shook his head. "I don't know."

Alana stood before him in an instance, her eyes fiery bright. "You have to know. You're the warlock!"

With an even look, he continued to shake his head. "But I don't. Sorry. I should have told you sooner about this. I didn't want to frighten you more."

Hair frazzled, dress falling off her shoulders, Alana placed her hands on her hips. "Too late for that. Tell me what you know."

All of the romanticism of last night had vanished, as though it'd never existed. Then again, how the hell could he even for a second worry about that when the shit they'd been thrust into made it irrelevant. So he told her what she'd said in the garden and what Calum said not that long after.

Alana's hands slid down her hips as though the resolve to keep them in place had vanished. He didn't blame her. Heavy news. Because he wanted the defeated look off her face, Seth said, "It's all part of the curse. We're in this together and we'll figure it out. You're not alone." And for good measure. "And I've got more power than most men."

Tears clouded her eyes briefly before she blinked them away, looked at the sky then nodded once. With a tug at the sleeve that'd slipped over her shoulder, Alana turned her attention to the house and said, "It looks terrible. Everything does. We need to find Calum and… Grace."

Seth already knew Calum wasn't here. He could feel it deep down inside. That wasn't a good thing. Had they somehow traveled in time again? If so, where'd they go? Death itself?

"Almost."

"What'd you say?" he asked Alana.

"Almost." She knelt and fingered a dead flower. "It almost had life and color in it. I could've sworn."

"I see nothing but black," he responded.

"Nevermind." Alana stood and started to walk toward the back door.

"I didn't mean to-"

"It's okay," she said over her shoulder. "Let's go see."

But he knew that they weren't going to find

anything. As they walked into the house it only got worse. It looked as though someone had spread several centuries' worth of dust over everything. Strangely enough, it was even sadder than how it'd looked when he first saw it. Sheets covering years of neglect would've been preferable to this.

This was just… death at its best. As though sadness had swooped through and devoured everything. The gloom felt intense, like a heavy cloak that settled over his shoulders when he entered. A tear slipped free from his eye. Damn! Wiping it away he almost growled. Being depressed was about the furthest thing from his nature. This was the reaper at work.

"Grace! Calum!" Alana yelled as she went through the rooms. Again she yelled, "Calum? Grace?" and took the stairs two at a time.

Seth knew she'd find nothing. It was all gone…life, light, everything.

Eventually, Alana trod down the stairs, her skin even paler than normal. Sitting down beside him on the bottom stair she looked aimlessly around the vast foyer. Several minutes passed before she said, "What do we do now?"

He took her hand and squeezed. "I don't know. I'm sorry."

"Have you sensed the reaper? Is it here?"

"No. But then again, not really sure what I'm supposed to sense. Nothing's jumping out." Seth sighed. "All seems pretty…"

"Dead," she whispered.

"Sad," he said.

"Really sad," she agreed. "Like I just want to cry and cry, then give up."

"Same here."

They sat that way for a long time, depressed before Alana finally said, "I know this seems... I mean I know I always run... but can we leave, run, get out of here?"

Seth felt so listless that he really didn't care. "Naw, why bother?"

"I just need to." But even as she took a few steps, Alana slumped to the floor and stared aimlessly at the door.

While he knew that wasn't like her he got it. Leaving his current position seemed a total waste of time. So he continued to sit and stare at the door like her.

Day turned into night. Night turned into day.

Eventually, Alana lay down and rolled a few times, putting herself closer to the door. "It just seems like... I dunno."

Seth had long ago propped himself against the wall. He'd long ago ignored the rumble of his hungry stomach. "Huh?"

Laying on her back, knees bent, Alana stared at the ceiling high above. "Maybe it'd be better to look at the sky."

With a wide yawn, Seth shook his head. "This works fine for me. I'm comfortable."

"See." She continued to gaze at the ceiling. "Me too. But why?"

"Why what?" he asked lazily.

Alana's head lolled to the side and she narrowed her eyes. "Why are we so comfy? Seriously."

"Um, isn't comfy good?"

"Is it?" Her gaze returned to the ceiling. "Maybe you're right."

"Am I?" Seth wasn't so sure but he was too damned relaxed to care.

Alana stretched and rolled a few more times toward the door.

"What's with you all over the floor?" He asked, smiling. "Why not stand?"

Even as he said it he wondered. But as he wondered the curiosity faded. And faded. Until he really didn't care.

Another day passed. Another night.

The next time he woke, Seth was surprised to find himself lying on the floor next to Alana, much closer to the door. He rolled over and cuddled up next to her. Alana shielded her eyes with one arm and pushed him away with the other. "No. No. No."

Flopping uselessly aside, he shrugged. "Whatever."

With arms flailed she grabbed the door jam and tugged herself over the eve. Seth watched her nonchalantly. As if she was a fish gasping for water, Alana started to buck and pulled herself further.

"No. No. No," she blustered over and over again.

Heck, she's wound up. About to roll over and nap, her voice grew louder, "No, Seth, no! Wake the hell up!"

Shit. He was about to cover his ears to her screeching when something hard hit the side of his head. Ouch! It barely occurred to him to lift his hand to his head.

"Seth, wake up! This house is screwed. Please wake up!"

House. Right. Screwed? Naw. Why would it be? It was her house.

"The reaper, Seth. It's got you. You've got to

fight now. Right now."

Oddly enough, the strange octave got through to him better than the yelling. The reaper? Got to him? But how?

"You're lying on the foyer floor, Seth. You have been for a day. You would've been on the stairs all this time had I not dragged you."

Tilting his head toward the door, Seth was momentarily blinded by daylight. Somehow, Alana was outside now, her tired body crumpled against the door, a hand held out beckoning. "Please, come to me. You have to. I can't come get you. It's too strong."

What was she talking about? Seth yawned again. Maybe if he slept a bit he'd understand.

"If you go back to sleep I might never get you. Wake up! Get out now, Seth. For me, Leathan and Devin, for your family."

Her? His family? Oh, they could wait. Seth was about to roll over when he swore he heard Adlin of all people say, "Listen to her, laddie. Hear me now. You'll die if you don't leave."

Seth nearly rolled his eyes when he heard Alana's low whimper. Blinking, he weakly shaded his eyes and looked back at the door. Was she crying? Why would she cry? Alana didn't cry. Went against her tough ass exterior... didn't it?

"Seth! Get the fuck out now!" She screamed.

Like a fire had been lit under him he instinctively started to roll toward the door. A loud screech started to fill the house, as if it came from the very walls, the very floor. Seth bit his lip until it bled and willed his limbs to pull him closer to her. Within feet of her the ground started to vibrate then shake and shimmied him backwards.

"Not. Yet. Bastard."

Adlin's voice almost hurt his ears it was so loud. As if a wave came from behind, the floor buckled and undulated and he was pushed right to Alana. She grabbed his arms and pulled him, her legs moving so fast that before he knew it she caught his chin on her kneecap seconds before his face landed in her lap.

Seth instantly wrapped his arm around her waist and muttered, "Grace, you saved me. You saved me."

Alana cradled and rocked him in hers arms, tears running down her face. "Of course I did, Calum. Of course I did."

***

If a complete mess had ever been made it was happening now.

Adlin, wizard, ghost and former chieftain of the MacLomain Clan, stood over the two at his feet and shook his head, his gaze flickering from the front door of the Revival to the couple on the ground.

Without a flicker of a doubt, he'd thought he'd seen just about everything but apparently not. Calum, meddlesome warlock that he was, had gone and created himself something that even he himself couldn't control. Had he expected that Adlin could?

Hands on hips and white robes billowing in a phantom wind, Adlin stared up at the dead house. Aye, indeed it was dead. As was everything around it. But not everything beyond that. Life still flourished, things still moved and breathed in this world he'd left behind.

He'd watched over Calum these last several years. Aye, he'd even helped him despite how opposed. But now? What to do. How to help? Calum had created a puzzle that had somehow involved his heart.

Adlin sighed. Calum was not totally at fault.

"Well then, what will you do now?"

With a small smile, he turned to his beloved, Mildred. She'd been a welcome part of his life with the MacLomains even though she was originally from the twenty-first century. "Now what are you doing here?"

Her shifting ghostly form shrugged. "Where else would I be when you are playing with matters of the heart?"

They shifted closer together and he said, "Perhaps I've gone a bit too far this time."

Mildred gave a warm smile. "I doubt it."

"Well, lassie, it's a wee bit o' a mess."

"Is it now?" She glanced down at the couple sleeping on the ground. "Perhaps if you told them the truth, it wouldn't be such a mess."

"Ah, the truth." Adlin sighed away his next words.

"Yes, Adlin, the truth. Because I don't think Calum or Seth knows it, never mind everyone else."

Adlin arched a brow at her. "You know you're not supposed to be in this story, right?"

A twinkle lit her otherworldly eyes. "Oh, I know. I couldn't help myself. Besides, a woman's voice in your ear never hurt anything, now did it?"

His heart skipped a beat and he winked. "I suppose not."

She patted his hand and continued to the eye the couple. "You suppose right."

Before he could once more tell Mildred how much he loved and adored her she nodded at the couple and vanished. He would see her again. After all, every MacLomain tale somehow belonged to her.

Adlin sat on a nearby rock, again so thankful for the life and afterlife that God and the Fates had given him. Soon it would be time to share something devastating... with his friend.

CHAPTER TWELVE

The birds chirped first.

Then the wind blew across her face.

"Alana...Grace." He nudged her. "Alana, wake up."

Her eyes opened slowly and she smiled, "Calum?"

"No, it's me, Seth...I think."

A small knowing smile caressed her cheeks. "Of course you are."

He covered her hand with his. "Why are we out here? What happened last night? Last thing I really remember is the veranda then crashing in..." His eyes fell to the house. His words died.

Alana sat up. "Well, I guess we are right back where we started then."

"I'd say." He jumped to his feet and held down a hand. She accepted and he pulled her up.

"We're going to need to fix it you know."

Seth snorted. "Um, yeah, ya think?" Laughing, he lifted and spun her. Alana laughed and pleaded that he put her down. Oddly enough, she felt refreshed. In fact, she felt amazing.

"Let's do what we do best first though," he said.

"That is?" She grinned, her smile wide, eyes full of life.

"Come." Before she could respond, Seth grabbed Alana's hand and started to pull her toward the rock before a throat cleared and they froze.

"Before you kids run off aren't you the least bit

curious why you look nothing like yourselves now? Or do you find you look exactly the way you should?"

They turned to find Adlin with his arms crossed over his chest, shaking his head.

Alana looked at Seth, then Adlin. "He looks great to me."

"Who exactly does he look like though?" Adlin asked.

She laughed. "Uh...Seth."

"Ah, so for the moment, you're Alana. Why do you suppose you called him Calum when you awoke?"

"Slip of the tongue I guess." Alana shook her head. "What are you getting at?"

Adlin looked at Seth. "And you called her both Alana and Grace. Find that curious? She sure didn't at the time."

Seth shrugged. "We'd been looking for them. Their names were on our minds."

"More so than you'd ever imagine," Adlin agreed.

"What do you mean?" Alana asked.

"I mean-" Adlin seemed to pause for effect before looking at her. "That you are possessed by Grace." Then he looked Seth's way. "And you by Calum."

Alana couldn't help but chuckle and glanced at Seth, then Adlin. "You're kidding, right?"

"You clearly have not looked like yourself for several days, Alana. Does this information overly surprise you?"

It felt like a lump was stuck in her throat and she whispered, "I thought it was just part of the haunting."

"Well, it is dear child," Adlin said. "In some part."

"In some part?" Seth asked. "Explain."

"Well, I'm quite sure that Calum intended to possess you, Seth." Adlin began to pace. "But what he didn't expect was Grace possessing Alana as well."

Seth scowled. "You mean to tell me that Calum is... in me?"

"He has been all along, laddie." Adlin rolled his eyes. "You don't exactly look like yourself anymore either. And your personality, the ability to dance... well haven't you noticed the changes?"

"Yeah, I suppose. Guess I figured it was the house doing it. Or the reaper somehow." Seth's eyes narrowed. "How the hell did he possess me when he was literally right there?"

Adlin looked skyward in exasperation. "Are you really all that curious after everything else you've seen him do through these hauntings? Calum is powerful... and clever." Adlin sighed. "A little too clever this time," he muttered as an afterthought.

Alana felt nauseous. "So you mean to tell me that I'm possessed by my own mother?"

Seth flinched. Adlin shook his head. "No, actually, you're not."

"What?" Seth and Alana said at the same time.

Adlin was about to speak when Seth strode forward until nose to nose with the wizard. "What exactly do you mean old man?"

"Ah." Adlin rocked back on his heels. "My old friend, Calum. Glad to see you can emerge at will."

"What I can and cannot do is none of your

concern."

Adlin's brows lowered slightly. "Everything you do is of my concern. I have decided I like you despite your constant ability to meddle."

"Well, I'll say. You should talk!" Seth barked. Or was it Calum?

Despite her near panicked state, Alana felt a sharp edge of exasperation. "Clearly, Seth isn't himself... maybe even Calum, which by the way is crazy. No matter, I need you both to focus. What do you mean my mother isn't possessing me after you already told me that Grace is possessing me!"

Seth nodded sharply. "Out with it, old man."

"Why do you think you so instantly fell in love with Grace?" Adlin asked 'Calum.'

"Have you looked at her? She's stunning. Absolutely beautiful," Seth responded.

"You are one of the most powerful men I've ever met," Adlin said. "And still you did not see what stood before you... or should I say who."

Seth frowned. "Grace stood before me."

"A lass materializes on your worksite one day and because of her beauty and leadership alone, you instantly adore her. Really think about that, lad. Isabel was as stunning as Grace with all the same qualities. Why not her? Or the dozens of others you've come across in your travels?"

Seth pinched the bridge of his nose. "Love happens. You never know when or where it just does. Even a supernatural creature like me can fall victim."

"Can you then? Just like that? Look at Grace, Calum. Really look at her."

Alana felt like a deer caught in headlights when 'Calum's' sharp eyes turned her way.

"Who is she?" Adlin asked. "It's imperative to all of this that you see who she really is."

By instinct, Alana took a step back as 'Calum' took a step forward. All that could be heard was the rustling of dead leaves overhead. Suddenly, the pupil's in 'Calum's' eyes flared and anguish crossed his face. "No...it can't be."

"Who?" Alana whispered.

But even as she asked, Adlin vanished and 'Calum' staggered then fell to his knees. What the heck? Because she so clearly saw Seth, she rushed over. "Are you okay? Seth... Calum? Whoever you are?"

Seth brushed her away, shook his head and croaked, "I'm fine. Just feel really confused."

Alana crouched in front of him. "Calum?"

"No, I'm Seth. But I think I was Calum. It was strange."

She touched his cheek. "I'll bet."

Seth paused another moment before he nodded his head as though he'd come to some sort of internal conclusion. "I'm not sure what we're supposed to do next but going back into that house isn't an option. By the way, thanks for saving me."

"I had little to do with it. More Adlin." But she smiled anyways.

"Oh no, it was definitely you." He stood and she followed. "I don't know how you did it but you managed to get out of there. Sheer will and a good mind I'd say. Because I would've stayed there doing nothing until I died."

"Trust me, I felt the same way. But something kept nagging me that it just didn't feel right. Must've been Adlin."

"I don't know. You're more powerful than you think," Seth said. "Death is sort of your thing. Makes sense you might be able to think more clearly than most when in its presence."

"Not the best of compliments but thanks I suppose."

Seth took her hand. "Come on. Let's try to get out of here. I have a feeling we'll only be able to make it so far but let's go as far as we can. This house is officially too creepy for me."

Alana released a deep breath. She couldn't agree more. On both counts. Though opposed to it she knew they needed to talk about what they'd learned from Adlin. Or at the very least, what he'd learned. "So who exactly is Grace?"

"I'm not sure." Seth squeezed her hand. "But she's definitely not your mom, Alana."

"How can you know that for sure?"

"Because Calum does now," he said softly.

Though the day was warm and humid, she shivered. The idea that they were possessed was unbelievable. "I don't feel any different. Shouldn't I feel different if I'm possessed?"

"I guess not. Seems we switch when we switch. Pretty painless." Seth pulled her further into the forest. "But I've gotta say, the whole topic is something I'm trying not to overthink right now."

"Agreed." Yet the thought was terrible. Seriously. At any given moment another woman could overtake her? And influence Seth? *I mean really. How could she be so sure Grace was with Seth or Calum at any given time? Yep, Seth was right, best to not overthink it.*

"It's not really dusk, eh?" Seth said absently as

hey trudged deeper into the forest.

Alana looked up through the tree cover. "No, not really. More of a brooding storm."

"Exactly."

"We'll need to find shelter… and food." Surprisingly enough, she wasn't all that hungry. Instead she felt incredibly energized. "How long do you suppose we were in the house?"

"I've been trying to figure that out," Seth said. "Based on my lack of hunger I'd say a few hours but I know it had to be days. I remember it getting light then dark over and over."

Nodding, she replied, "Me too."

"We've been able to walk further than I thought it'd let us," Seth mentioned.

She could tell he was a million miles away and making small talk for her benefit. It had to be hard to possess magic and have nothing to use it against… to be so aimless.

"Seth."

He glanced her way. "Yeah?"

"It'll be okay. We'll figure this out."

A brow arched and the corner of his lip inched up. "So you're as worried about me as I am you then?"

Of course! How would he really know that though? "Yep. You're my partner in crime… or at least…this."

Seth squeezed her hand in reassurance. "I'm good. You're good. We'll get through this."

Amazing thought to think it'd all started out so simply as a jump off a cliff. The search for a quick rush had turned out to be the beginning of the longest, most petrifying rush they'd experience. Now they were beginning to climb the mountain again. The house, or should she say, the reaper, had let them come further than she would've thought.

"Everything's still dead," Seth commented.

"It's depressing." Alana sighed but kept her chin up.

"Well, black is my favorite color so it's not so bad that everything's dark."

Biting back a grin, she said, "What about all the gray that's with it?"

"That I could do without."

He stopped short and looked down. They had arrived at the cliff they'd jumped off of yesterday.

"It's dry," she whispered.

"Yep." With a firm expression, Seth nodded once and pulled her after him.

Like him she didn't glance back. Why bother? Death had swept away everything and left in its wake a dismal lack of color. Neither said a word as they climbed. After what seemed like hours of endless movement, Seth stopped and shook his head. "This is it."

"This is what?"

"The spot we climbed to after we had sex for the first time. We've walked past it several times but it keeps reappearing. I think it's the border of our unseen prison."

Alana blinked. How had she missed walking by the same place over and over again? She knew why. Her mind was all wrapped up in their situation, the fact that they probably wouldn't survive this. Not particularly interested in whining about their circumstances she slid down against a rock face and propped up her knees. Seth however seemed restless and roamed the area.

A low rumble of thunder bubbled and burped across the sky. The horizon lit up with a long streak of deep reddish-white heat lightening. The black bellied clouds seemed to roil and thrust within the light, casting shadows across the bleak gray lands below. Seth stood—his silhouette tall and strong—against the writhing backdrop. It almost seemed for a second that he could reach up and swipe his muscled arms across the sky and remove the blackness. Was there blue sky behind all that? A shining sun? Seth had always seemed the dark, intense type. The thought of him bringing out the sun seemed more than far-fetched.

Eventually, he turned and came to sit next to her. After a few minutes of comfortable silence he said, "I wish I had the power to make the sun come out for you."

It had to be the most romantic thing a man had ever said to her even if he'd meant it in a purely literal fashion. So she said what seemed appropriate. "I wish we weren't in a position that you felt the need to say that." Alana cringed. For all she'd thought she was saying something romantic in return it'd sounded blah. Really blah for that matter. "What I meant to say is that if I had to be in such a crappy place, it's good to be here with you."

Seth laughed. Not a chuckle or snort or some semblance but a full out laugh which made her smile. "Thanks, Alana."

A little help from Grace wouldn't hurt, all that old fashioned romance. The minute she thought it, she brushed it aside. She didn't need someone in her head to help her with a man.

"It's hard to guess when night might be here but we need to find more shelter than this," Seth said.

Alana watched his handsome profile as he gazed out at the horizon. She couldn't help but wonder if this contemplative man beside her was all Seth or a little bit of Calum too. As if he heard her thoughts, Seth's eyes swung her way, intense and searing. In that one blazing moment she knew he was all Seth and felt almost guilty for thinking otherwise.

"Do you see Calum when you look at me?" he asked.

"Are you reading my mind?"

"No, just your eyes."

She bit her lower lip then said, "I'd be lying if I said I didn't look for him in you now."

"But do I look that much like him?"

"Honestly? Yeah. But you're not quite a match. You have a restless energy he doesn't have."

"Is that a good thing?"

"For me, yes." Alana looked at the clouds again. "I think in the long haul Calum would bore me."

"He has restless energy too. You need to really know him. From what my cousins say we're the most alike."

"Are you really?" A cloud slipped beneath another streak of lightening. "I haven't seen that."

"Maybe you're afraid to see it."

"I'm not afraid of you, Seth."

"But maybe I'm afraid of me."

Alana looked at him but he only stared at the sky. What an odd thing to say. "Why would you be afraid of you?"

Seth blinked and shook his head. As if he hadn't said it he jumped to his feet and held down his hand,

"We've got to find shelter."

Just like that he'd shut her out. The interesting thing? She'd never realized that Seth hid something until now. Fear. Of himself? Or of something he'd done? Alana had no clue but intended to find out.

Alana stood and looked around. "Any idea where?"

Seth nodded. "Follow me, but first." He knelt and grabbed a sharp rock. With a quick jab, he punched a hole in her dress just below her ass and then ripped the fabric all the way around. No joke, she found the assertiveness a turn-on and his actions a potentially wild move for things to come.

"Surprised you didn't use magic to accomplish this."

A wicked grin erupted. "Now what fun would that be? C'mon, let's go. Lose the shoes."

Not only did she do that but she tied the remainder of her dress between her legs, creating shorts. Her outfit was far from perfect for nature but the fabric did have a good amount of stretch to it. And thank any god listening, she had on panties!

This time he didn't take her hand but sidled along a path that edged the cliff. Most would have freaked out. This particular path was all of six inches wide with nothing but a wall of rock on one side and a sheer drop that fell hundreds of feet on the other. However, Seth and Alana moved along it without a care. Even with death all around them, it still didn't scare them.

When the path grew even narrower, they still sidled along. Thump. Thump. Her heart started to pound louder and louder. Now this was risk. This made sense. Enough with all the paranormal activity.

Give her mountain sport any day of the week. Eventually, Seth sat and she followed. They lifted with their hands and dragged their butts along the craggy surface.

Suddenly, Seth stopped, leaned his head back against the rock and smiled wide.

She couldn't help but smile too. "Why are you so happy?"

Slowly, he tilted his head forward and looked at her while he swooped his arm in a gesture that engulfed the land below. "This. You. Love it."

Before she could respond he fell sideways, angled his body slightly and grabbed the top of a man-sized hole carved into the side of the mountain face. This movement made half his body swing over the thousand-foot drop before he shimmied his way backward, inch by inch disappearing into the hole.

It was the only way to get into the man sized hole he'd found.

As he vanished the rain began to fall. Heavy, swollen drops slapped her skin and face. Alana nodded, up for the challenge. Any good climber knew things were about to get a whole lot trickier when one added in the element of moisture. And any good climber knew that they should be able to depend on themselves. Actually, they should embrace it. That was half the thrill and honor of being up so high above the world.

Reaching inside her top, she dried her hands and without hesitation, leaned sideways and grabbed the top of the hole as Seth had, digging her nails into the rocky surface. The rush began. Pure exhilaration filled her and she swung her body out.

But she'd misjudged her momentum.

Her body kept swinging on the wet surface and her nails scraped… and scraped. With a determined growl, Alana froze. Seth wasn't here. This was her moment. Inhaling deeply through her nostrils, she carefully walked her pointing finger as far as it could reach. Nothing. So she tried her pinky finger. There was a small indent, so she anchored it, bending her finger into a hard ninety degree angle. But a pinky finger couldn't save a life. Centimeter by centimeter, she searched with her thumb.

And found a slight notch.

That's all she needed.

Two fingers locked in as securely as possible—despite the searing pain—she ever-so-gently shifted her core. Now wasn't for the thrill of the ride but for pure survival which in its own way made the soul sore. Rain began to pound harder, making vision nearly impossible. All she had was the feel of the rock around her. The pure natural essence of it… the do-or-die attitude found at this altitude.

Alana had found her own little Heaven in the midst of hell.

Her body slipped a little. She found purchase. Once she did, that was it. By shimming her body in combination with finding enough finger holes, Alana was able to first pull her face out of the driving rain, and then her body into what felt like a decline into pitch blackness.

Perhaps she hadn't escaped hell after all.

By instinct, Alana welcomed the blackness much as she had when the rain blinded her and braced her arms and legs on either side of the slim downward tunnel. Seth didn't yell up. She hadn't expected him to.

This was what they did.

Or at least what they had done before he died.

Wiggle by wiggle, implementing every muscle in her body, Alana made her way down with nothing but the thought of, "I can't go back the way I came," motivating her.

It was, by far, a dare-devils best case scenario.

About ten minutes later she started to hear the roar of water. No way! Excited but too smart to rush, she continued on until she reached the light at the end of the tunnel, which as far as she could tell, was lit by a very dim source. Carefully, because she now somewhat understood the dimensions, she turned herself over by finding niches and moving a slow inch at a time. When she finally got to where she could see ahead of her, there was about a foot left to go. Almost drooling with anticipation, she sidled forward until she could see.

Pure beauty.

How could this exist? Why ask that. She knew damned well that the Earth was full of secrets, most especially mountains, even the less grandeur ones. But this mountain had a beautiful belly with a wealth of perfection well hidden.

Alana perched at the hole of an inner cliff that fell hundreds of feet into what she estimated to be a fairly deep body of water. Waterfalls fell randomly. Some poured as if the mountain was determined to keep itself clean inside out, and some trickled gently as if wanting to keep the peace within the great beast.

What really amazed her was how well it was lit. She'd like to say it was brightened by black but that would be impossible. The best way to describe it was neon. Black owned everything but the water and the rocks. They were nearly white. A soft white much like the glow of a twenty watt bulb… but everywhere and definitely bright enough to compliment the black.

"Well… aren't you going to drop?"

Seth had spoken softly from somewhere but she heard him clearly.

"It's almost too pretty from this angle," she replied with a sure grin.

"I think I'd really like to see you drop." Now his tone was all seduction. "I think you'd like it too."

Oh, this man did know how to turn her on. With a wide smile she took in one last eyeful then pushed herself out of the hole to her waist. There was no way to run and leap. It would be straight free-falling. Luckily, the hole jutted out like a misshaped nose. It was all air between her and the water. Now or never! With a shove that she knew would scrape her legs, Alana pushed herself over the edge.

Falling. Falling. Falling.

Alana straightened her body into the perfect dive and relished the roar of the cave and wind passing her face, the pure freedom of knowing that she was diving into water she'd never touched. The exhilarating feeling of knowing she might not survive the dive it was so high up. But she would survive. Because she knew what she was doing, Alana went into 'selective attention' mode. It was all about visualizing how she'd land at this point.

She straightened her arms then swung them to generate power, then once more rigidly pointed her hands and feet. The speed she hit the water would be extreme but she knew it was deep enough by the way the light lit the water. If a random rock broke the light further down she'd never know. At this speed it'd be too late.

Alana would be dead.

Grinning, she raced down, incredibly alive in the pure feeling. In what seemed a split second, she sliced through the surface of the water and spiraled downward in a woosh of underwater weight and bliss. Her body slowed and the weight of the water started to flow around her body easing the propulsion. The water was just deep enough that she came to a stop within inches of the bottom.

Laughing inside, she spun and let her back thump softly to the bottom. It was nearly as dark down here as it'd been in the tunnel. Releasing a few bubbles through her mouth she slowly rolled forward and pushed off the bottom with her feet then casually made her way to the surface. When she broke the surface, Alana continued to laugh, the joyous sound echoing far and wide.

"I really do love you."

Alana spun to see Seth crouching on the rock shore, smiling.

"What?"

He shook his head. "What, what?"

Swimming toward him she asked, "What did you say?"

"Nothing." Seth reached out his hand and helped her out. "I didn't want to ruin your moment."

"I could have sworn," she started but stopped. He really had said nothing. She could see it plainly on his face. No worries. That was okay. Alana nodded and started to wring out her hair. "That was amazing! Why didn't you tell me?"

Seth grinned. "I didn't want to ruin it for you."

Alana smiled and laughed. She couldn't help it.

"You were right. The thrill of doing and seeing it all on my own was the key."

"Right." He laughed.

"Hell yeah!" She untied and twisted the water from her torn skirt. "How did you find this place? Wait, nevermind."

Seth winked. "Every once in a while the warlock is coming in handy here. I knew about it before everything died here. The truth is, my magic wasn't working out there but now it works in here."

"Good thing." Alana ignored what that might mean for them and turned to look back at what she'd seen from so high above. It was almost as stunning from below. Water crashed more angrily from this angle and where it wasn't crashing it was glistening and trickling in a slow steady stream, following the varying paths it had made in the rock face over millions of years. It was no less than absolutely breathtaking.

"This lighting isn't natural," she whispered.

"No," Seth said in her ear. "That is mine. My magic is black and somehow when it meets deep earth, its reflection is white."

Leaning back, she welcomed the feeling of his strong body behind hers. "Although you don't think you have much power... you do."

"I'm flattered."

"Well deserved flattery." She turned in his arms and looked up. "Thank you."

Wet, his hair remained plastered to his head, making his eyes seem somehow more intense than usual. "For what?"

"For being you." Her gaze fell to his lips. "And for all of this. For allowing me some freedom from all the fear."

His long black lashes nearly shadowed the deep blue his eyes had turned while they studied hers. "You nearly fell off a cliff, sidled down a tight, black sixty-eight degree angled tunnel then plummeted hundreds and hundreds of feet into icy cold water and you're thanking me for freeing you from the fear." With a solid grasp his large hand cupped the back of her head, rested it against his chest and he whispered, "Anytime sweetheart. Anytime."

Alana didn't mean to but she wrapped her arms around his wet waist. The muscles in his back clenched beneath her fingertips. The warmth of his body flooded hers. Seth suddenly seemed more amazing than ever. He was her perfect fit. She hugged him even closer not because she wanted to but because she had to. Did he even know how great he'd become?

His chin rested gently on her head, a strange sort of comfort...a loving sort of comfort. They stood that way for what seemed a blissfully long time. So long in fact, she'd swear the moisture between them had evaporated by the pure body heat.

About to pull away, she stopped. "Do you smell that?"

"Smell what?"

"Like a flower." She melted against him. "Heather."

"I didn't think you'd taken the time to smell it. You were so angry that day, Grace."

Alana blinked but even as she did she fell away somehow. "Why do you call me, Grace?"

Seth... Calum inhaled deeply then exhaled. "I'm sorry, Anna. It's in my nature to test."

"Even me?"

"Even you."

No. No. No. Alana pushed away and stumbled back, shaking her head wildly. "Anna," she shouted. "I know that name."

Before she understood what was happening, Seth had her wrapped in his arms again. "You are not Grace, you are Anna."

Blinking rapidly, she breathed in the scent of his skin. So familiar, so much a part of her life... her love. "I dinnae ken," she murmured.

"Nay," Seth said. "It's Calum. I'm here. You are Anna. You are my wife. You always were. Please try to remember. Please don't be confused."

As if she'd been stabbed with a knife, Alana pushed away and stumbled back, turned her head and held her rolling stomach. Her body felt foreign and sick and so very, very sad. "Nay. Nay. Nay." She whispered the words over and over again.

"Aye." Seth... or Calum came and scooped her up so fast the world spun. "You found me again, Anna. In another life, in another body. I'm so sorry."

Alana clutched her arms around his neck. The world spun so rapidly her body hurt. "No. You died. Left. Gone. Impossible."

Then darkness fell sharp, cool with relief. It was as though she'd just slipped into a dream when Alana jerked awake. She was cuddled in Seth's arms. He sat back against a rock, his blue eyes black and distant.

Not Seth at all.

"Calum?"

Seth's eyes turned her way, so sad it hurt to look at them. He nodded.

Alana wanted to scream and shout. Make all of

this go away. She wanted Calum back in his cocky and overly arrogant body and Seth… just back. Just him again.

"You…her," he whispered. "I thought she was gone."

Clueless, Alana nodded and responded softly, "Of course you did."

"I'm still not sure how this happened. Did you die?"

Alana stared back at his sorrowful eyes completely unsure how to answer. "I don't know."

"You must have. That's the only way any of this would make sense. You took her body."

This bothered her. She was deceiving. "I am Alana, Calum. I'm not Anna or Grace or whoever you think I am."

As if the Devil had snapped a finger, Calum's eyes shot to hers. "You are only one of two people now, Alana or Anna. Grace never was… for me."

"I don't understand." She shook her head even as he pulled her closer.

Calum's eyes went from sad to serious in an instant. He held up his wrist and closed his eyes. Alana watched in amazement as a stick crawled up his arm and closed into what looked like a leather band. His eyes popped open. "This arm band will only turn black when Seth wears it. White when I do."

Alana looked from the white bracelet to Calum's face and nodded slowly. "Okay."

"Go to him," Calum said.

As she watched in amazement, he slumped back against the rock. Alana bit her lip and willed away the tears. What was this? Heartache from every angle obviously.

"No," Calum grunted. His eyes shot open and looked at her. "No."

"I'm sorry?" She asked, still not entirely sure who she talked with even thought the wrist band was black.

"It's me, Alana," Seth replied. "What happened?"

She shook her head, "I honestly don't know."

Seth studied her face. "I lost time. We were just standing and hugging. Was it Calum?"

Nodding slowly, she said, "Think so."

"Fuck," he muttered, set her aside and stood. He pulled at the wrist band. "What the hell is this?"

Hopping to her feet, Alana said, "Calum put it there so I'd know if it was you or him. It's okay, Seth, he didn't hurt me. I wasn't injured."

"Not the point." Seth grumbled and walked to the water's edge. "These moments down here are for you, from me, and that bastard is stealing them."

What? Wow. Really? "Seriously, Seth? Are you that oblivious?"

When he turned and looked at her, Alana's legs buckled and she fell flat to the cave floor. Seth's eyes were completely jet black, his voice deep, husky and foreign when he roared, "Get back to the house!"

But the words weren't meant for Seth's body and shot out of his mouth like an oily whip. She watched as the black, inky sliver whipped across the room and vanished into the hole that she'd so gleefully jumped from earlier. Alana gasped for breath as she stared at the ceiling.

This was pure horror.
This was the reaper.

She watched and watched, completely dumbfounded. It was as if she was on the cliff all over again but this time she was afraid of heights. This time she couldn't move she was so paralyzed with fear. Not a toe or a finger budged an inch.

This was absolute terror.

"Alana, Alana! Can you hear me?" She felt her body being shaken but tearing her eyes away from that hole in the corner was nearly impossible. "Alana, please, it's me, Seth."

It took everything she had but Alana pulled her gaze free. When her eyes met Seth's she released his name on a deep sigh. "Seth. No house."

Seth yanked her up against his body and though he whispered she swore he yelled, "No house. No Calum. No Grace. Just you and me, Alana, that's it!"

"It was here... the reaper. In you somehow."

"I'm sorry," Seth said angrily.

"Why? It's not your fault."

"It's as if I can't control what or who's entering my body or when. I hate this feeling. I can't protect you." He stroked her hair and said, "That's why I'm sorry."

"Well, stop it." Alana wiped away a frustrated tear. "I get that you're angry. I am too. But there's nothing we can do about any of this."

Seth grunted in frustration. "There better be something. I don't want this to be all that's left when I just found you."

Alana trembled and because she couldn't see the wrist band from this angle she mumbled against Seth's chest. "Calum?"

"No," Seth said softly.

Alana pulled back slightly and looked up, not

entirely sure how to respond. But when she looked into his eyes she knew. "We'll make it through this. There are too many extreme sports left we've got to try together."

It almost looked like he would grin but he didn't. "And much more than that."

CHAPTER THIRTEEN

Several hours later, Alana sat on a rock ledge and watched Seth forage for food. The chances of him finding anything down here were slim to none. But she wasn't hungry anyway. Maybe being in such a dead place and technically being considered ghosts meant that they didn't need basic nourishment. Or maybe it had something to do with the fact that they were possessed.

They hadn't said much after he'd made the comment about just finding her. The truth of the matter was him saying that scared her almost as much as the predicament they were in. Seth had almost sounded like he wanted a relationship with her and the Seth she knew was incapable of commitment, never mind love. Wasn't he?

His current feelings had to have something to do with this place. They'd been through hell together. That could do funny things to people. Make them feel things they didn't really feel. She'd heard that when people hooked up under extreme circumstances it never worked out. Then again, his cousins had met Isabel and Dakota under nasty conditions and they all seemed happy.

But Seth? Really? She'd be damned if she'd even get her hopes up. Alana pulled up her legs and rested her chin on her knees. Now there was the real problem. A nugget of hope… that hope even existed. Her feelings for Seth had always been strong. From the moment she'd met him skiing early last winter.

She'd never forget the way he'd looked when he'd sauntered up to her group at the top of mount Killington. There were far more extreme spots but he'd ended up there in his black ski suit which made him look like a dark God against the blinding white snow. Her pulse had skittered through her veins at the sight of him.

His eyes were bright blue as they skimmed her small group and landed on her. Then he'd spoken, his deep voice a sexy vibration that rumbled right through her. She'd almost got off on the sound alone. "Which one of you wants to race... backwards?"

But he hadn't been looking at anyone but her when he'd asked. Later she'd learn that her friends had felt the strong urge to back away, almost as if compelled by the pure directness of his possessive gaze. Naturally, his challenge met its mark. Though the slope wasn't the toughest, Alana still knew it was a bad damned idea to go down it backwards, especially if unfamiliar with the terrain. So naturally she replied, "You're on!"

That nutty race down the hill, which he'd won, marked the beginning of several such encounters they'd have in various sport challenges around New England. Seth had quickly become her best friend. Who knew if he felt the same but they had a blast together. Sure he'd hit on her a few times but that was Seth. Flirting was a staple part of his personality. And women never minded. If Seth was nearby and interested, they'd be his in less than five minutes. She however, continued to shoot him down. It was that same old story, why ruin the friendship for a quick fling?

With a heavy sigh, Alana reflected on how far

away those simple—although she thought them complicated at the time—emotions were. She'd do anything to be back there, suffering from the endless fantasies of a man emotionally unavailable. This new Seth, the guy who thought he wanted her, would vanish if they made it through this alive. She didn't doubt it for a second.

"No plant life. Nothing. Wish I could summon food but that's always been Devin's trick."

Alana jumped. Somehow Seth had ended up leaning back against the rock beside her, arms crossed over his chest. She'd been so deep in thought she hadn't heard him approach.

He looked up. "I startle you?"

"Yeah."

"Must've been deep in thought."

"Yep." *You have no idea.*

His gaze returned to the water. "Pretty sure we should be starved right now," he remarked.

Was it her imagination or was there an uncomfortable tension between them? Oh no. She closed her eyes and shook her head, then looked at Seth. "Were you listening to my thoughts all this time?"

"Yep."

He'd answered so casually she almost didn't believe him. Regardless, her face burned with embarrassment. "That's an invasion of privacy you know."

"Sorry. It just sort of happens sometimes."

"I doubt that."

He released a long breath, pushed away from the rock and stood in front of her, bracing his hands on either side. "You evaded my earlier statement."

Alana focused on breathing. Leave it to Seth to face this head on. She'd rather go forage for food. So she moved forward making it clear she wanted to get down.

Shaking his head, Seth said, "Nope. You're staying right here and talking to me."

She glanced at the wrist band. He was definitely Seth right now. But she knew that. "Fine," she muttered and pushed back until the back of her kneecaps hit the rock.

"Not for a second have I forgotten the way you looked that day on Mt. Killington," he said.

Alana's heart stopped beating. While she wanted to look anywhere but at him she didn't. His gaze was so intense her world seemed to freeze altogether.

"That blazing red hair of yours, those golden eyes, how could I have looked at anyone else?" Then that direct gaze seemed to be looking into the past. "That white ski suit, those curves. You were a beacon on the slope. The closer I got to your group the more excited I became. I'd never felt anything like it."

Alana swallowed, unsure how to respond. But he continued.

"I didn't doubt for a second that you'd take my challenge. I'd been watching you on the slopes that day. A natural. Almost bored with the simplicity of it though." He shook his head and smiled. "You were my perfect match."

How had she never known this? They'd talked plenty... as friends. Perhaps that was it.

"I was bored," she said.

"How could you not be?" He rolled his eyes. "It wasn't exactly live-on-the-edge material there."

"A little ice would have been nice," she

conceded.

"A few more jumps."

"At least a few severe wind sheers."

"But we found our fun," he said.

"Wearing the wrong skis was the key. Made it really treacherous." She grinned.

"Oh, and here I thought it was the path with too many trees."

Alana laughed a little.

"That," he said and nodded at her.

"What?"

"The laughter. We've always had that. Remember when we reached the bottom, how hard we laughed?"

"That was mostly you," she reminded. "Because not only had you kicked my ass but I'd taken a few good rolls at the end."

Seth grinned wide. "Heck yeah. You thought you were all that. In the end you were just a petite crazy redhead with her skis up in the air."

Sitting up straighter, she narrowed her eyes. "I'd never been so irritated in my life."

"Which is why you immediately re-challenged me."

"It turned out to be a pretty long day, eh?"

He shrugged. "I don't know. Seemed like it flew by to me."

"Naturally, you won the next few times down until I finally beat you."

"And we were politely asked to leave the slope."

"I'm still surprised we managed to get in three more runs."

They'd immediately left for another slope and skied until the next place closed. It was probably the best day of her life.

"Since that day," Seth continued. "You've always been on my mind. You're my best friend too, Alana," he said softly.

"I never knew," she said just as softly.

"Now you do. No more evading my earlier statement. I want to know what you were thinking when I told you I'd just found you, that I wanted more."

Her poor heart had just seemed to resume beating when he asked. But she knew how to handle Seth. "You listened to my thoughts. I'd think the answer is pretty obvious."

"So you think I'd let extreme circumstances dictate how I feel about you?"

"Listen." She tried again to get down but he wasn't having it. Now she was getting aggravated. "You and I both know you, Seth. You're acting crazed right now."

He pushed forward between her thighs, efficiently locking her in place. "Fuck the cliché. People really do change."

"Okay, then tell me this, how many women have you slept with since we met?"

"None."

"You're lying."

"I don't lie."

"You do now."

"It's always a challenge with you, Alana. Every single time. Then when you're done challenging you run."

"Go to hell."

"I'm in hell. With you. We're in hell. And you can't run anymore."

"Neither can you." Alana glared at him. "Because believe it or not, that's what you do too. Jumping off anything you can find, putting yourself in danger constantly with stupid stunts. And you don't stick with one woman because you're afraid of something."

"What do you think I'm afraid of?"

"You tell me."

This time she didn't have to try to push him away, he turned and strode to the water, where he stopped, back turned to her.

She jumped down. "Point proven."

"You didn't prove a damn thing."

"Sure I did. You run too. You can't commit." Alana didn't walk to him but stayed where she was. They'd never been so honest with each other and distance felt safe.

Seth crouched and ran his hand through the water. "Since the day I met you I haven't slept with another woman. Believe me, I've tried. But you're always there. At night when she's in my arms it's never her but you. Again and again." He shook his head and released a small wry laugh. "And when a man's with the wrong woman his body knows it... regrettably."

He was in front of her so fast she barely saw it. "And I mean regrettably. It blows wanting a woman who's full of nothing but fear. You're untouchable, Alana. So the only thing you ever saw in me was that I'd never be able to commit to you."

She crossed her arms over her chest and ground her teeth. "A better approach would've been to avoid other women."

"Please. Really? Why? There was no hope with

you."

About to storm off, Alana stopped. No more running. "So for all that you live on the edge you're nothing but a coward." She was about to say that he never even tried but he had, several times.

The anger softened on Seth's face. "You never took me seriously. Maybe I deserved that."

"You definitely deserved it."

"Do I now?"

She shook her head and leaned back against the rock. "I'm sorry. I don't know. I just don't know."

"Yes you do." Seth turned and pulled off his shirt. All that perfect male flesh unraveling before her made her totally lose track of the witty rebuttal that'd been forthcoming. Her toes curled when he pulled off his pants. Wow. His backside was so perfect. Nothing but pure muscle from head to toe. His body was one hundred percent athletic perfection.

"Come join me," he said over his shoulder.

No. Heck no.

Yeah right. Who was she kidding? Alana undressed while walking and licked her lips every step of the way. Seth disappeared under the water. This water should be freezing. It was before. Why was it warm now? Almost like bath water.

"Because I made it that way."

Alana turned to find Seth directly behind her.

"Not real good for my dick otherwise."

Her eyes rounded not only at his statement but by his obvious erection.

"You bounce right back, don't you." But she wasn't backing up.

Seth held up two fingers. "Two things you should know. Things I should have already told you. The first, I can control whether or not you become pregnant, at least when I can use magic. Second, I've been tested for all STD's."

How romantic. She rolled her eyes but couldn't stop a grin. Up front, say-it-like-it-is Seth. "You're rather presumptuous. How could you even think I'd want to sleep with you after what we just talked about. "

Now he grinned. That perfect, sexy, arrogant grin. "Don't kid yourself. You want it even more now."

Damn, he knew her too well. "Sex friends. Fantastic."

"Oh no." He reached out and cupped her cheek. "No more friends."

"Mm hmm." Alana didn't believe him for a second. Still. He was beyond gorgeous and she'd already slept with him twice. What harm could one more time do? "Swim first."

Cupping her other cheek he leaned down and brushed his lips lightly over hers. "Sure."

Alana pushed back into the water and realized for a fraction of a moment that her legs wouldn't work. Ugh, she was weak in the knees! Darn man. Sinking beneath the water she turned and pushed forward. The water felt amazing. Opening her eyes under water, she marveled at how everything looked. Shimmering and white with black crystals further down. If this was magic, it worked for her. Seth appeared beside her, all long and male and beautiful. It took everything she had not to propel herself harder through the water, not to race him to some unknown destination.

He wiggled a come hither finger and moved

closer. Before she could move away he pulled her mouth to his and kissed her. No easy task kissing someone under water but somehow it felt like he was breathing more air into her. Then he pulled away and gestured for her to follow him. Revitalized and in no need of air, she followed. They went deeper and deeper but it remained light enough to see. The swimming became turbulent as they pushed past the outer currents of one of the waterfalls. Eventually they reached a man sized hole and she followed him through.

When she finally breeched the surface she gulped a deep breath of air. Seth let out a whoop and laughed. "You weren't out of breath. I gave you plenty."

Grabbing the edge, she wiped the water out of her eyes. He was right. "Guess it seemed like I should!"

"Some definite perks to being a warlock." He winked and pulled himself onto a ledge. "Nothing quite like sharing air with you."

She grinned and braced her arms on the rock beside him which put her blissfully near the area of him she couldn't take her eyes off of. "Consider yourself privileged."

Seth leaned back, giving her a better view. "You know I do."

Alana licked her lips, her body shivering with awareness.

"Not that I want you to look away from what you're looking at but check out where we are."

Her cheeks burned only a little and she dragged her eyes away. Oh wow! How had she missed this? The small antechamber was cozy, intimate and amazing. They were on the backside of a raging white neon waterfall. Had it not been for the mere two feet of rock between them and the water they'd probably be swept over. On the other side was a shelf that was approximately the size of a queen sized bed. Behind that water streamed down the rock face, creating a constant flowing shimmer of water over the rock 'bed.'

Alana smiled. "This is something else."

"Even has a natural Jacuzzi," Seth mentioned with a wicked gleam in his eye.

Yes it did. The water around her bubbled, the current active enough from the raging waterfall to turn the small pool into a natural cauldron of stimulating… motion.

"How is it that you found any of this?"

Seth's face grew perfectly innocent. "I am a warlock."

"A possessed warlock at that." She nodded at their surroundings. "Did Calum have something to do with this?"

"Doubt it."

"Hmm."

"If he did I know nothing of it." Seth slid back into the water and came around her, an arm braced on either side, his erection tucked against her backside. His lips fell next to her ear, warm breath fanning her tender lobe. "Still focused on that 'friends' thing?"

Alana breathed sharply through her nostrils and said, "What do you think?"

He pulled his arms closer and brought his cheek next to hers. "I think you don't believe my sincerity."

Turning her head, her lips fell next to his. "You're right."

"You will eventually." He kissed the corner of her mouth.

Her muscles rippled when he pushed tighter against her and he feathered kisses along her jaw. Her body swelled with what felt dangerously like joy. Alana closed her eyes and tried to harden her emotions. But even as she did she turned and put her arms around him. Their lips met frantically and all other thoughts fled. None even mattered. As she kissed him, her best friend, she didn't care about anything but him. She wrapped her legs around his waist and let her hands slide over his broad shoulders.

Seth's hands lightly squeezed her butt cheeks then rode up her thighs. The water churned around them. His cock throbbed against her belly. When he nipped her lower lip she groaned and pressed tighter against his hard body.

"Water sex," he nearly panted. "Never good."

Alana squealed when he quickly spun her, put one hand under her ass and pushed her up onto the ledge. It didn't even occur to her to be embarrassed that her backside was in his face. Pulling herself up, she crawled onto the rock bed, thrilled by the water running beneath her.

"So damned sexy."

Alana looked over her shoulder to find Seth propped on the ledge watching her. Sitting, she crossed her legs in front of her and stared right back. He said nothing. She said nothing. They just sort of eyed one another. It wasn't a matter that the passion had gone away. No. It still existed. Stronger almost when they weren't touching each other.

"Back at ya," she said.

Whether or not he could hear her over the roar of

the waterfall didn't really matter. The lazy way his eyes traveled over her body was answer enough. Alana swore she felt his touch everywhere his eyes traveled, dark and erotic, languorous and slow, paying attention to every little detail. Though she was tempted to cover up she didn't. Instead, she shifted onto her side, allowing the water to slice down the curve of her breasts and lap at her stomach then gush over her hips to stream down her legs.

She'd never felt more sensual in her life.

"Come," she mouthed.

Seth didn't move, simply watched her as intensely as she watched him. It was a moment between friends, a moment between lovers. It was both comfortable and extremely exciting. Putting her legs in the right position to entice him didn't even occur to her. Curving her hip to appeal didn't occur either. It just sort of happened. Bracing herself, looking at him, that's all there was. It was simple. There were no insecurities. Sucking in her stomach didn't even occur to her. Why would it? This was Seth. He'd seen everything.

Eventually, he pulled himself out of the water and came over. His erect penis should have made her shy... something. But it didn't. He didn't. When he knelt and came over her, Alana fell back, the water sluicing past her shoulders.

His lips were within inches of hers when he said, "You had on pink panties."

Alana smiled. "I didn't mean to."

"But you did. Pale pink. Almost blended in," he whispered. "But I saw."

Spreading her legs, she whispered back, "You're right. They almost did."

When his lips closed on hers this time she was remembering the same moment as him. When she'd skied down the mountain alongside him, wiped out, and her snow pants had pulled down. The top of her panties had been visible, barely. Everything had been covered in snow. Of course Seth had seen, had been watching.

He shook his head. "You are." He stopped and kissed her, long and hard, their tongues twirling. When he pulled away, his blue eyes met hers. "More to me."

The feel of him over her, between her, his hot body touching hers, made it hard to speak but she did, had to. "No."

"Yes." Seth's lips touched hers briefly and his body fell solid over hers. "Yes you are."

She shook her head, ignoring the feel of his heavy, hot member against her opening. "No, I'm not. I'm just another."

Not what she meant to say. That sounded almost desperate. As if Seth sensed her confusion, he lifted slightly and said, "You've never been just another. And I'm not to you. Be honest with yourself, Alana."

Biting her lip she shook her head even as her legs rode his thighs. "Tell me you don't want more with me. Tell me I'm just another. I swear it's easier that way."

His brows lowered briefly but his eyes remained locked on hers. "Is that really what you want to hear?"

No. Yes. "It's something. Give it to me," she whispered.

His eyes abandoned hers and drifted down her neck, her breasts, before they harshly went back to hers. "No. Sorry. Not gonna happen."

Before she could fight him, he pushed forward. Alana groaned and shook her head but her groan turned into a moan too fast. Leaning down, her legs pinned on either side of him and his cock stretching her tight he said, "I want more from you. You're not just another."

Alana dug her nails into his shoulders when he pushed forward. Head thrust back, she bit her lip so hard it bled. She dragged her heels over the rough pumice of the stone before she lifted her legs.

"More. Please more," she whispered into his ear when he pushed a little further.

"Me. All of me. For you." Seth pushed so hard he filled her.

Alana dug her nails into his hair and groaned. Yet she still needed to know she was just another. She knew it was insane. Or not. She didn't want to get hurt. But even closed, her eyes rolled back into her head. She couldn't fight perfection. With a sharp exhale, she wrapped her legs around his waist.

When he started to move she first flattened her palms against his shoulders then slowly curled her fingers. She had no choice. Touching the top of her mouth with her tongue, Alana tried to fight the…oooooh. Clenching down on her lip hard with her front teeth, she whimpered.

Seth stopped and his hand traveled up her ribcage, his fingertips dusting the underside of her breast while his lips skimmed the top of her collarbone then somehow whipped down to the too sensitive tip of her breast.

Alana bucked wildly.

Seth groaned and swiftly swooped down to grab

her nipple with his teeth. She stilled as though caught in the jaws of a lion, he pulled back and thrust again. Whining, keening, she shook her head. Wrong. Wrong. This had to be wrong.

Then he stopped, leaving her throbbing and wanting. Alana turned her head to his, her cheek to his. "What, what?" she asked almost desperately.

"How do you feel, Alana?"

Paused, his cock buried deep inside her, every feminine part of her wanting him to keep moving so she said eagerly, "You. I want you."

Seth pulled back slightly, his eyes meeting hers. "Really?"

She had to be drooling. "Yeah."

"Fine." He leaned back slightly and her arms whipped over her head, tied by some unseen force. The water gushed harder. His eyes grew more intense. The air grew colder. Suddenly she felt the icy stone beneath her body, the glimmer of terror that flickered in his eyes, then the cold hard black. His eyes turned her way, his voice deadpan, lacking compassion. Fear started to fill her. Not arousal or lust but cold, hard fear. A distance she'd never felt before. Seth's eyes locked on hers as if he was a thousand miles away. "You still want this."

Mouth open, Alana almost shook her head no. It would only make sense. He petrified her right now. Taking a deep breath she tried to think, to focus. This was Seth. Seth. And he was angry all of a sudden. But why?

"Do you?" he asked again, his body immobile over hers.

Alana pulled her hands free from whatever unseen force had held them and swallowed. She'd been ripped from oblivion, perfection, by her friend. One who was inside her in more ways than one. Gentle, she cupped his head. He was both mad and afraid. And she was confused.

Seth was afraid.

Not of her. Never of her.

One second he was trying to convince her now he seemed to be pushing her away. Closing her eyes, she breathed deeply. Seth was afraid. Not only that, he was petrified. Alana kept her eyes closed but clenched his hair tighter with pure revelation. Biting her lip, she turned her head to hide the tear that slipped free. He didn't need to see that.

After all, she'd truly figured out what Seth was the most afraid of.

Before he could say another word, she locked eyes with him and made a motion with her head. "Just kiss me then."

She'd never know if he'd read her mind. It didn't really matter. Seth leaned down slowly and kissed her, his tongue sliding slowly yet desperately into her mouth.

And she kissed back just as desperately.

The eager thrust of his body in hers soon made the world spin away. They rolled until she was on top, moving and wild. Then he was on top. Panting. Intense. Sweat broke out on her body even as water rushed around her.

Alana couldn't help it, she grabbed his neck and pulled him close. "Too much. Don't want to get hurt."

Had she really just said that? They'd broken through an obstacle and she'd thrown up a wall almost immediately.

"Exactly," Seth said and stopped.

Just like that.

Alana tried not to cry out when he pulled away.

"It's too much," he said softly, his arms thrust over his head when he lay next to her.

No. Of course it's not too much! You should know that! Her eyes skirted to the wrist band, not white, but still black. "Are you serious, Seth?"

With a loose well-muscled shrug he looked at her and said, "This isn't for you. You deserve better."

"I deserve better?" Alana frowned and tried to ignore the heavy lump that formed in her throat. "So you're playing that card, eh?"

Seth's eyes went deadpan and he sat up. "Believe it or not, I am."

Alana sat up next to him in what had to be the best sex location ever. Her body had gone numb. He was completely serious. But what to say? I knew better. I should've listened to my instincts. She tried to swallow but couldn't. "Fine," she squeaked.

"Fine," he muttered.

Alana watched him slide down then disappear into the water with one obscene thought in mind. The warlock had shunned the necromancer. Truth was, the super-hot guy had shunned the freckled-faced redhead. Alana nodded to no one and stared at the waterfall blankly. Am I dreaming?

But she knew she wasn't.

And she knew why.

Still, it didn't make the fact that he'd pussy'd out like he had any easier. Alana seethed through her nostrils and shook out her hair. 'Is what it is' she said to herself. For all Seth thought he confronted shit, he really didn't. Damned men. She fell back slowly and let the water sluice around her.

Moments before he'd been here now he wasn't.

"C'mon, Alana. I can't keep it warm here," Seth said.

Alana sat up and glared at where he'd disappeared beneath the water. What a jerk. But even as she sidled down, she could admit that she'd been a little harsh. But weren't best friends supposed to be able to take that? Grinding her teeth, she shook her head. She was right. He was wrong. Sliding into the water Alana sighed. Seth had meant every word he said and she'd screwed it up.

In the water, Alana stopped. Confused... and angry. When had she become so insecure? Confidence had always been her thing. But Seth made her feel vulnerable and apparently doubt herself. Anger continued to flare. She looked around at the perfect cave alcove, one he no doubt made possible and shook her head. This... Seth... was all a bunch of bullshit. It'd all been part of this stupid curse. Never them. Two idiots who'd met on a mountain who liked to ski. Nope. Just a curse. A means to an end.

Clenching her fists, she growled and dove.

The harsh waterfall current pushed and pulled. Alana struggled against it until she found the right flow that'd work her to the top. She saw the surface. It glowed white. Nearly out of breath she pushed toward it. As she did, someone suddenly pulled her up and pushed her back. When they surfaced, Seth shook his head. Alana's back hit the rock surface within feet of the raging waterfall's outermost spray and she frowned.

Seth came close. His eyes narrowed to mere slits. "You know now," he said. "You know what I most fear."

She heard him over the waterfall. After several moments she nodded. For all she thought he made her vulnerable, it occurred to Alana just how vulnerable she'd made him. Seth was supposed to be the daredevil, afraid of nothing. But he was afraid of his own power. Better yet, what she'd think of its dark presence. But that wasn't all he feared.

"Good," he said.

Alana tried to brace herself but it was too late. Somehow he'd ripped into her. With a heavy groan she closed her eyes. Seth's voice, his heart, came close. "Lend me some escape."

"I don't want to be your escape," she whispered.

Too late though. He owned her. No escape. Alana wailed as he slammed her back against the rock wall. He'd found a foot hold and now he had her. In. Out. Fast. Slow. She couldn't keep up. Holding onto his wet skin wasn't an option…. Digging in with her nails was.

"Alana," he panted, aroused by her intensity.

"So much anger… at me," she breathed as he rode her up the slick wall. Forget how angry she'd been at him moments before. "You should stop this. It's for all the wrong reasons."

Dear God. Let this last forever. The feeling. Him. This. Forever. Energy and sizzling hot lightening shot through her body. Still, she shook her head. "No."

His warm mouth clamped over her mouth, his free finger tickled her clitoris. "No. Are you sure?"

Damn it. She wormed away from his finger, tried to push away from him. "Friends don't do this, Seth."

Grabbing her wrists he shook his head, the expression on his face serious. "You're right, they don't."

Alana couldn't close her eyes when he pushed her back against the rock, when their hands clenched together, immobile. She couldn't remove herself when he started to move again. Easy and careful at first, then a bit faster. She couldn't remove herself from the feeling that began to build deep inside. Eye to eye, he was unavoidable. Alana shook her head and said what should have stopped him. "You don't think you're strong enough to save me."

A strange gleam lit Seth's eyes, his muscled arms pulled her close and he drove into her. Alana yelled out and wrapped her legs around him. His mouth close to her ear he said, "I'm always strong enough."

Sharp pleasure ripped through her body and electrical currents shot up and down her limbs. She'd never felt anything like it. Seth braced himself and moved. Because she wanted, needed more, Alana climbed up him. With a sharp shake of his head, Seth held her in place and thrust up one last time.

Unable to hold on anymore, Alana screamed with release. So powerful was her orgasm that she didn't realize that Seth had yelled just as loud and was barely able to hold onto her. Apparently magic only came in so handy when dealing with jaw dropping sex.

There was no way to know how much time passed while he held her that way... the two of them draped against the rock wall being sprayed by the waterfall. It'd all fallen away. The anger, insecurity, everything... they'd been completely raw with each other both emotionally and physically. Resting her cheek on his shoulder, Alana kept her eyes closed long after the orgasmic burst of stars faded. It seemed even through the water and mist; she could smell his

unique scent... musky and masculine and all Seth.
She'd smelled it before when she'd worn his sweatshirt when they'd camped overnight after hiking.

Seth's breathing had slowed and his heartbeat had returned to normal. Still, he held her. Even as the water grew colder and colder, neither moved. His arm eventually slid up and wrapped around her waist, pulling her closer. A simple gesture, Alana relished the long hug he gave her.

Eventually, he pulled back. "Too cold now." A small grin erupted. "Guess keeping it warm this time got too hard. You zapped out my magic with something else."

Though she could barely hear him she got the gist and grinned as well.

"Let's get out of here."

Alana swam after him and was surprised to see him stumble when they got to shore.

She touched his arm. "You okay?"

"Yep." He yawned. "Used a lot of magic. Makes me tired." With a quick shake of his head, he said, "Don't worry. I won't sleep."

"Sure you will. But get those clothes on first."

As they dressed she watched his eyes sliding shut. It was hard to imagine how much 'magic' it took to turn all this water warm, never mind the light. Even as she watched him with concern, the massive cave grew dimmer.

"Damn," he muttered.

"Don't worry about it. We'll be fine." Alana gazed around until she found a spot that looked the most protected. Wedged between two rocks, they'd at least be sheltered on two sides.

"Gonna get dark." Seth slid down the rock and she joined him.

"I'm not afraid of the dark," she assured.

"Sure you're not." Neither talked about what was in the dark that was really so petrifying. She leaned her head on his shoulder and they held hands as the cave grew dimmer and dimmer.

"Sorry about all that," Seth said softly. "And sorry about my fear."

Alana repositioned their hands so that their fingers interlocked. "Believe it or not, your fear made me less afraid... of what we might have together. And as to you being afraid of not being able to protect me, even your family; you should worry at least a little bit. The fear will help motivate you."

Closing her eyes, Alana wanted to share, tell him something he didn't know. She wanted to include him in that small part of her that she didn't show the world. "I missed my grandmom when she died. Grace will always be that to me. She was so good to me." She opened her eyes. "It hurts... seeing her now hurts."

Seth squeezed her hand. "I know."

Alana stared at their interlocked hands and murmured, "It's the worst part of this haunting."

"Don't let it be," he said gently. "Look at it as some extra time." He squeezed her hand tighter. "I know that sounds weak but it's something, eh?"

"I suppose." She sighed. "It is something."

"Of course it is."

"I held the cross over my chest every night hoping she'd contact me."

Silence reigned until Seth finally said, "You thought the cross would help with that?"

She nodded. "She used to tell me stories about how the dead and living could communicate but that it was okay because God was there with them. I thought maybe…"

Seth leaned his head against hers. "Your bedtime stories were different, huh?"

Alana nodded.

"Now it's all making sense."

She nodded again.

"Good," he whispered. "And I like that you held the cross. It's good that you respected something."

"Someone," she murmured.

"Someone," he repeated then fell silent.

Darkness had all but fallen. Several minutes passed. She thought he was asleep when he mumbled. "Don't tell my cousins about my fear. I'll never hear the end of it."

With a small chuckle, Alana squeezed his hand.

Shortly thereafter, the cave went black and Seth's breathing slowed to a deep slumber.

Chapter Fourteen

One second she was in his arms… the next she was sinking down, down until she vanished beneath the dark water. He tried to illuminate everything but his gift wasn't working. Panicked, he dove after her. Screaming over and over again within his mind, "Anna! Anna! Come back! Don't leave me!"

Even as he struggled through the water toward her, someone else was pulling him back.

"Seth, wake up, it's me," she said urgently.

How was Anna talking to him even as she drowned? Torn, he looked down as he grabbed onto the very solid arms wrapped around him.

"Please, Seth, wake up."

It took several seconds for the stark terror to flee and black reality to drizzle in around him. Implementing his magic, the dim cave slowly resurfaced and Alana held him tight. He glanced at his wrist to see the band go from white to gray to black.

He put his hand on the back of her head. "I'm okay. It was Calum dreaming or… something."

Alana pulled back and looked into his eyes. "You were freaking out, flailing in your sleep. You sure you're alright?"

Seth nodded, readjusted to his surroundings and rubbed his eyes. "Hell, I fell asleep."

"I think I did too." Alana frowned. "I was in the water. It was daytime. Then I was sinking… drowning. You were there… I think."

"Calum and Anna," Seth said. "That was strange. It was as if she drowned. I…he… felt so much pain. I kept thinking it was you but knew somehow that it wasn't."

As the nightmare slowly faded, the memory of their time together before quickly resurfaced. It seemed Alana's mind had gone there too because their gazes locked. He'd come clean with her. Let her see the truth. All of it. But did she really understand how deeply his feelings ran? Words weren't his thing and he knew he hadn't conveyed the intensity of his feelings as powerfully as he'd felt them.

Seth had been shocked as hell that first day on the mountain. He'd thought for sure that they'd ski down the slope and she'd be out of his system. After all, she wasn't the first woman he'd thrill-seeked with. But she was the only one he'd ever wanted to continue finding 'the rush' with. Every rush possible. Alana had been the holy grail of women. Had he really known how much she'd impact his life, he would've probably skied in the opposite direction that day.

Figure the odds.

Alana had been a magnet since that sacred second he spotted her. For the first time in his life, though he knew he could impress any woman, he had to impress this woman. Heck if he didn't fight the feeling every step of the way though. While he hit on her because it was in his DNA, Seth hoped she'd reject him. Because he knew deep down inside that if she let him in, his world would change. Freedom and thrill-seeking and basically being the kick-ass guy that he was belonged to him. Girls could sample from the awesomeness of 'Seth' but that was it!

Alana had somehow, while rejecting him, become one of the few people he wanted to spend time with, all the time for that matter. Like a re-born moron, he'd finally understood why Leathan was willing to stay in a time-warping house with Dakota and Devin preferred the eighteenth century to the twenty-first as long as he was with Isabel.

Now it was too late.

The idea of another woman having a piece of him seemed repulsive. Alana consumed his thoughts. He figured that's the real reason why he haunted her when he supposedly died. Not because she'd been there when he hit rock bottom or the fact she'd been a necromancer, but because she'd been there all along, firmly entrenched in his mind.

Where else would he go when dead but to her?

"What next? How do we get out of this?" Alana asked.

We don't. I don't want us to either. But that's not what she was talking about. He arched a brow and grinned. "You really want to know?"

Alana's eyes rounded a little and he saw the fear in her eyes when she looked at the hole high in the ceiling. He couldn't imagine what she'd felt when she saw the reaper leave his body and vanish through it earlier. Had she not seen it, Seth knew she'd be thrilled. Instead of letting what the reaper did to her bother him, because it sure as hell did, he shook his head and nodded at the water.

"We go out a different way. Even more fun."

Relief softened her eyes. "Really glad to hear it."

Seth meant to stand. He meant to leave the moment behind but he couldn't. Leaning over, he brushed his lips over hers. Alana stilled when his hand came to her cheek. Slanting his mouth over hers he deepened the kiss then pulled away. Her lips were full and moist, ripe for more. He stared, transfixed, but didn't continue. Sometimes moments like this were as good. Just looking at her... wanting her. Had she really heard him when she first jumped into this cave? Those rare words he'd voiced?

Alana's eyes fell away as though she'd heard his thoughts. As though she'd hoped he'd say those words again. "We have to go face the house," she whispered.

Seth truly hated Calum's curse now. It wasn't fun anymore. How the heck did he ever think it was? *I need to complete this thing and free us all. There isn't room for fear. There isn't room for romance.* Nodding, he stood with her. No matter what came out of all of this, he would die to ensure she lived. And that his cousins, Andrea, Dakota and Isabel lived.

His was the last fight.

He intended to kick ass.

"Hope you don't mind getting wet again," he said.

"Sort of figured that'd be what you'd say," she responded with a smile.

There was his girl. Despite her fear of the reaper he saw the thrill of a new adventure lightening her eyes. "This one's tougher than the way in."

"Oh, you're telling me about it this time?" Alana put her hands on her hips and shook her head. "Now what fun is there in that?"

Seth eyed her up and down. "Because I'd hate to see you iced after all we've been through. I'll give you a hint. Keep yourself moving as slowly as possible this time. You're gonna run out of water before you run out of air." His gaze lingered on her legs. "And I'd hate to see you scratch up all that beauty even more than you already have."

Alana nodded and tied her dress again. "Got it. Lead the way."

For the all the emotional baggage they'd thrown at each other earlier, Alana bounced right back. And he loved it. This girl didn't deal in wimping out and overly-sappy moments. Unless prompted of course.

Seth dove into the water. He'd almost hesitated, sat her down and mapped out the route ahead so that she'd be less likely to get hurt. But she would've been insulted. No doubt about it. Alana might've opened up some about her feelings toward him but she, like he, would run in the opposite direction if he changed who he was… and she was.

This time she wouldn't need extra air. Swimming directly downward, he kicked until he found an opening about three feet wide where he turned his body and went through it feet first. This is where it got tricky. The rushing water popped him forward. Keeping his head angled up, he pointed his toes and kept his arms crossed over his chest. He knew that she'd instinctively do the same.

The tunnel narrowed and decreased its angle slightly. He'd estimate it to be about seventy-five degrees now which was still pretty dangerous when going down a natural rock waterslide.

Though it was a good thing that the stream became less powerful it was hazardous when it became shallower. The decline became less though, so by the time the water was almost non-existent, he'd slowed to a near stop. It carried him a few more feet before it went bone dry. Not surprising in the least. Everything outside of this cave was dry and dead. Water, no matter its proper function in nature, would not exist beyond.

Turning on his stomach, Seth slowly sidled backwards then stopped and waited. Within a few minutes, he saw her feet... turned down. Good girl. Though strange, the roar of the water was a dim echo here, like the sound of a seashell if you held it up to your ear.

Alana said, "I thought you said this would be fun. Why are you waiting for me?"

Seth thought about it for a second and told the truth, "Because I have more to say before you possibly die at the end of the tunnel."

Alana laughed. "And what would that be?"

"Don't die."

Then he kept on moving. While he might not be ready to say the words he meant he wanted the opportunity to. When his feet reached fresh air, he dug his nails into the rock on either side and carefully shimmied his belly until his hips were over the edge. Alana had stopped several feet ahead of him. Both knew if she lost her grip, which was a minimal risk on what was now was an eighty-five degree angle; they'd both plummet to their deaths.

Finding the ledge below with his feet, Seth carefully, one slow inch at a time pulled himself free. This maneuver had everything to do with correct angling, use of body weight, balancing and patience. This was a stunt that the bravest and most experienced would respect. If they didn't, all would be lost. The wind shear was slight which made the jaunt only slightly less death-defying.

Despite the urge to pull up and grab hold of the rock ledge, Seth took his time to balance on and feel out the rock face. Once he was sure he'd mapped it out properly, he stood erect and moved along the ledge, freeing the opening.

Within a minute, Alana's leg's appeared beside his face and like he had, she bent at the waist. Her height and weight were different so she had to move even more carefully so that her feet would have to drop several inches to the ledge, all while balancing as he had. Seth watched every move she made, ignoring the way the dress turned shorts struggled to ride up over her ass. This wasn't about sex or attraction. This was about survival of the fittest.

The muscles in her arms and neck strained. Every little sinew in her legs stretched and fluctuated as she found her balance. He watched with appreciation at the determination on her face. Seth saw not the black hair and smooth skin but the red hair and the pronounced freckles that appeared when she strained to achieve her goals.

Though it took her slightly longer, Alana eventually stood beside him. Her eyes were as bright as the sun, her smile wild and radiant. When she looked down, then at him, a chuckle bubbled in her chest. "You weren't kidding. This is more fun."

If he could've had sex with her at that moment, he would've. She was perfect. But he wanted a chance at the reaper and giving it all up now would give death an easy fight. Seth couldn't help but wonder why the monster didn't just take them. A good gust of wind would do it.

"You know why," Calum said from somewhere deep inside his mind.

Seth leaned his cheek against the cold rock. He did know why. The reaper wanted a fight. It wanted all of them. But more than that, it enjoyed the game. The human, albeit warlock, ability to want to fight intrigued death.

Turning his head, Seth began to make his way along the rock ledge. No need to tell Alana what to do. She knew. It was precarious and about as live-on-the-edge a stunt as they'd ever done. Why? Because they weren't tied off, without safety equipment and very soon there would be no ledge. Worse, they were completely unfamiliar with the mountain. Seth didn't bother adding the three thousand foot drop into his equation. A drop over thirty feet could kill the average person.

Could he manifest rope, safety equipment? Apparently not. He'd tried before they even hit the cave. Dead was dead in this land. That he could do anything in the cave was a miracle. If he could've fought the reaper from that cave he would've. But death wasn't ignorant.

They would fight at the Revival.

The sound of nail scrapping rock rang out and he froze. The blood in his veins turned to ice. His heart thudded heavily in his throat. Carefully, he turned his head.

A few bits of dirt fell down the cliff beneath Alana but she was secure enough. She winked. "Sorry."

Seth frowned and turned his head back. This was the problem with caring about someone. The worry. Fuck. Enough. Focused, he kept moving. Eventually, the ledge all but vanished. His whole world became concentration. The next foothold, the next finger grip, the way the wind blew, all senses sharpened to the extreme.

Yet, for the first time ever, while Seth knew he owned his concentration, it'd somehow come to include hers. He listened for the sound of her next foothold, her next finger grip. He even gauged how the wind might hit her opposed to him, though they worked alongside one another.

Seth was now completely aware of two people in his life.

Time got away from him but he estimated they'd been moving without a solid foot shelf for about a half an hour before he saw their destination. About thirty feet away was a cliff. He eyed the rock between them and it. Though craggy, it had some uncomfortably long sheer faces. By his estimation, not a threat to him at his height but Alana might find issue.

They kept moving. The first sheer face came up within ten feet. She could handle this one if she was careful. Seth bit his tongue from saying it. She'd hate him if he did. Stretching, he made it over smoothly. With a heavy swallow, he moved a few more feet and waited. He breathed deeply and continued to focus. If he allowed himself to get upset, his heartbeat would increase and he'd start to get nervous. Sweaty palms were a climber's worse nightmare. Slicker than rain itself, sweat was always accompanied by insecurity and self-doubt. Label yourself dead if you started thinking like that in this situation.

Alana grunted a few times, her breathing increased before she said, "Go."

She'd made it over the first sheer rock face. Seth didn't close his eyes and breathe a sigh of relief like he wanted. He went. His confidence back intact, he continued until he reached the next sheer face. It was wide enough for his arm's length if he gained air and lost grip for a swing. By any climber's standards, it was about as high-risk as things got. To add to the danger, the wind kicked up.

Not thrilled in the least he said, "You can't make this, Alana. Gotta climb up and come over the top."

Voice steady and sure she responded, "Cool. You get to the cliff then I'll move."

Nothing was 'cool' about this. But he knew that it was all about showing no weakness. Before he could overthink things, Seth eyed the rock face and memorized all the nooks and crannies. With a sure swing, he fell through the air slowly, lost contact with the rock for a split second, and then locked in. Fingers and toes sure, he kept moving until he reached the cliff and left danger behind.

Ignoring the extreme exhilaration he felt, ignoring the wicked rush, he turned and froze. The sight of her perched so high above nothing, literally sucked to the side of a mountain side, made him extremely uncomfortable.

Alana's eyes narrowed on him. "Lose the look, Seth. I don't need that crap. If you can't handle me climbing the rest of the way, get out of sight."

Seth released air through his nostrils in frustration. She was right. An incapable partner could be a climber's worst enemy, no matter the supernatural nature of their experience together. Right now it was cold hard facts and working together to ensure survival.

Nodding up the mountain face, he gave her a hard look and said, "You know how to do this. Feel your way. Don't bother falling because I won't be there to catch you."

Alana waiting a minute or two, getting a feel for the wind's patterns, before she confidently started to climb. Her lithe body and sure attitude moved her steadily up and across the sheer plane.

Almost.

Seth swore he heard it long before the first tumble of pebble fell but he'd never be sure. His magic was non-existent. Everything that happened in those several long moments was very real and extremely petrifying.

Alana had moved so well, he'd allowed his body to relax. How could he ever have doubted she wouldn't make it? And it was nearly the moment that he thought it that the foothold she'd found crumbled.

It was nearly the moment that he thought it that an unnatural gust of wind whipped up.

Her yelp combined with his, "Nooooooo!" when her body started to fall.

Seth fell to his stomach and reached out. The tips of her fingers touched his as her body plummeted past. Snarling, he leaned over as far as he could, clawing the rock. Shaking, he watched her fall, her face calmer than he would have expected, tears in her eyes.

Then she vanished beyond his sight.

Mouth bone dry, Seth stared after her. This couldn't be happening. He squeezed his eyes shut. The pain was so intense. The wind died down instantly. Seth hung that way over the ledge with his eyes closed. He should have never taken her this way. There had to have been another way.

But he knew there wasn't.

Pulling back slightly, he leaned his face against the rock and opened his eyes. The necklace she'd worn hung precariously on the rock in front of him, the black rose swinging still from the violent rip off her neck.

"Beware the black rose. It will rip from you your very center. It will take from you your heart." Seth gulped at the words... at the memory. "You'll know very soon. And when you do, your life won't be worth living."

Seth clenched his teeth and stared at the rose. Rolling on his back, he erased it from his vision and laughed. Laughed like a crazy man. Putting his hands over his face, he screamed and screamed... and screamed.

He'd done this all wrong. Leathan had done it all

right but Seth had done it all wrong. Devin had found a way but Seth had pushed everything to the edge and didn't. Why couldn't he be more like his cousins? Why did he find his girl then have her scale a fucking mountain?

Live on the edge. Find excitement. And never settle for one girl!

That'd been his motto.

His life.

"She fell. You didn't. What about her body?"

Seth stared at the sky. Calum? "Are you there? Can you help? What do you mean?"

Only dead silence met his question. Of course it did. The damned warlock was inside him and either spoke or took over his soul when he wanted. Seth frowned. What about her body? He slowly sat up. There's no way she would've lived through such a fall. Nearly frantic, he flipped over and stared down the rock face again. He assumed there was nothing but sheer drop after. But... what if there wasn't?

Seth looked at the swinging necklace then down. What if?

Scrambling, he jumped to his feet and started running down the path that led off the backside of the cliff. Half the mad rush down the winding path, he slid, the other half, caught himself on branches. Nothing mattered. He felt no pain. Could she have somehow survived? Seemed impossible, truly absolutely impossible. About forty-five minutes later he was stomping through the area she should have landed and while he was petrified he'd find a body, he kept searching. Everything remained dead around him. The forest was black and quiet and every move he made felt like slow motion.

Somewhere. She had to be somewhere. Trying to remain calm, he scanned the blackened forest. All that existed far and wide were dark trunks and mountain. Shaking his head he trudged on, stopping at the spot he knew she should've fallen. No question about it. Inch by inch, he trolled the area. She had to be here. He scuffed aside the leaves looking for her.

Dead leaves.

Seth looked up. More dead leaves.

They were still attached to their limbs to the point it made looking up the mountain face impossible. Stepping back further and further he realized that there were thousands and thousands of leaves still hanging on. Even here, where all was dead, the trees wouldn't let go. With a keen eye, he kept looking up. Could it be? He dared not hope.

Scanning the skyline, Seth circled the area. He was just about to head further down the mountain when something caught his attention. A darker clump of needles at the top of a particularly high pine slumped lazily, low.

Too low.

His heart began to thump heavily in his chest. His palms started to sweat. Seth shook his head and paced, his gaze focused not above but below. Calm down. It was time to thrill-seek. This had nothing to do with Alana, everything to do with the next ride. Because hell if that lump of dark leaves wasn't high. With every step he rolled his shoulders and nodded, let the energy start to fill him.

Nothing mattered but reaching his goal.

Nothing mattered but seeing if he could conquer the tree.

When he stopped pacing, his blood was roiling.

The Tudor Revival

Excited. Time to go!

After a quick stretch he started climbing. The good thing about pines? Their branches started fairly low. The bad thing? They pricked like a sonofabitch. He enjoyed it more when she was climbing with him. Seth ignored the sting and worked his way up the tree. For the first time ever, it occurred to pray to someone other than himself. If there was a God, let him have her be there. The thought of hoping Calum or Adlin would help didn't matter. Seth needed something much bigger than all of this.

Nearly to the top, he moved aside a bunch of black leaves and stopped.

There she was.

Alana!

Not splattered and broken on the forest floor like she should be but whole and draped over a wide swath of amazing sturdy pine branches. Everything in him urged him to crawl out and grab her immediately, confirm whether or not she was dead. But experience won out. Seth sat back on his perch and remained calm. With narrowed eyes he studying the branches that she lay upon. They weren't overly strong, but they'd been strong enough.

He called on his magic. Hoped.

Nothing happened.

With a growl, he continued to study her location. Retrieving her from the limb would obviously put them at risk. That didn't matter. He'd die for her in an instant. Leaning forward, he braced his hands on her limb and carefully pushed down. It didn't give much. It had strength. Unlike many of the branches that'd fallen, it wanted to live.

He got that.

Should he call to her? But what if she awoke confused and flailed? She'd fall straight down. Seth shook his head. The best thing was to go to her.

The tree had her cradled and that gave him endless hope. If her head hadn't hit the rock going down then maybe.... Seth didn't see blood on her head but he also didn't see signs of life. No need to further analyze or look down. If he was going to save her, it was now. Straddling the branch he began sidling out. The branch bent, but not that much. Within a foot of her he stopped and said, "Alana, can you hear me?"

Nothing.

He moved a fraction more. The branch held. He said again, "Alana, can you hear me?"

About to touch her he stopped when her lips moved and a faint whisper sounded. "Seth?"

"Shhhh," he whispered and wrapped his fist gently around her wrist. "Stay still, okay?"

Only because she was who she was, a seasoned thrill-seeker, did Alana make no sudden movements. Somehow she knew. Groggy, but alert, she slowly turned her head and looked at him. To see her golden eyes once more almost made Seth lose his focus.

"Where am I?" she half whispered, half croaked.

"About eighty feet up in a Pine so don't move. How do you feel?"

Alana blinked and worked at a grin. "Like we're back on that mountain face, living on the edge."

"Good. Think that way." Seth squeezed her wrist in reassurance. "Now tell me the truth. Any broken bones? Can you feel your feet?"

"Yeah." She looked up at the thin layer of branches between her and the sky. "Feel bruised, not broken."

He could only hope. "Good. Take a few. Acclimate yourself."

"I don't want to." She didn't move an inch. "What I really want is to be on the freaking ground."

Seth nodded. "I know. Don't worry, I'll get you there."

Alana chewed her lips momentarily and said, "How exactly do you plan to do that?"

"By reminding you how you got here."

"Oh yeah, talk fast."

Though his eyes remained locked with hers he glanced up briefly. "You fell thousands of feet after scaling a mountain face without safety equipment and you're still alive. Now you're stuck in a tree." Seth looked down briefly then met her eyes with a cock to his brow and a grin on his lips. "You intend to fall to your death now? Gonna let a tree kick your ass when a mountain couldn't?"

Seth looked away when a tear slipped free from her eye. She wouldn't want him to see it. He kept his eyes glued to everything else.

"Stop it," she said softly.

Innocent, he looked at her. "What?"

"Stop waiting." Golden eyes flared and she wiggled her fingers. "Tell me what you think I should do because I have a pretty good idea what I should but would rather you got off this branch before I do."

Seth leaned forward, winked and squeezed her wrist tighter. "You go, I go. Only you can make the next move, Alana. If you can't, say the word. I'll get you down."

But they both knew he couldn't without killing them both. She turned her head slowly both ways and looked down, studying her surroundings. A long silence passed before she said, "This isn't so bad. You're being wicked dramatic. Back up, get off the branch."

Seth didn't move. From where he perched he could save her if the nest of branches gave way. If he let go of her wrist, that'd be it...possibly.

Her eyes met his. All tears were gone. "Get off the damned branch, Seth. Let me do this."

Listening to what other people wanted wasn't his strong point. Typically, it was better if he stayed and saved. Seth knew nature though. He knew she did too. It was only that faith in her that made him slowly release her. If she made one wrong move, she'd plummet to her death and he intended to follow.

"Trust me. I won't let you down," she whispered.

Seth hated that she had to reassure him. He hated how weak he felt. But he got off the branch and said, "Alright. Come on then."

Alana nodded and grinned. "Here we go!"

Seth watched with something between horror and awe as she arched back and flipped over backwards. She neatly fell on the next branch, looked up and rolled her eyes. "Did you really think I didn't know how to get out of this tree?"

Awe hell. Quick, he raced down the tree after her. And she moved fast. By the time he reached bottom she lay on a bed of dried, blackened leaves laughing so hard you'd think she'd been listening to comedy all day.

Anger, so much anger, rose to the surface. Enraged, he jumped at her. Before he could, Alana was up, shaking her head. Still, she howled with laughter. "No, Seth, no. Don't be mad." She made a motion in the air as though she turned a knob. "Dial down the warlock!"

Either she was releasing stress or had gone insane. He had her backed against the tree so fast that she should have appeared mortified, afraid, but she didn't. She stopped laughing. Even through his rage he heard her whisper, "Let it go. I'm not afraid of the real you, Seth. You won't hurt me. Never could. I'm alive. Right where you wanted me. See, you don't kill, you save."

Her hands threaded through his hair, her lips skirted his. "Feel me. See, I'm alive, not dead. It's okay, you're not a killer. Not really evil, just intense."

Unable to control himself, he wrapped his arms around her, held on tight and buried his face in her neck. She smelled of herbs and flowers, a fresh combination of basil and Lilac. Her body was warm and alive and next to his. "You're alive," he whispered.

"And you're good."

Seth held onto her as long as he could, less concerned with what she was saying but more so with the fact she hadn't died. He hadn't led her to death and she wasn't there. Why was she telling him he was good?

"Because you are, Seth. I'd know. I deal in death."

He ran his hands lightly over her arms and looked with concern at her legs. "Are you okay? I see lots of scratches on you."

"I'm fine."

Slowly he pulled away and looked at Alana. Her eyes had shifted color, her expression soft and expectant.

"Alana?"

She shook her head no and said, "I'm Anna now."

Seth felt his limbs weaken even as he backed away. His wrist band turned white. "Anna?"

"Calum?"

Seth felt himself fall away.

"Yes, lass, I'm here, Seth's gone."

She flew into his arms. "Too long. I'm sorry. I never meant it to be this way."

Calum held on tight and whispered, "What happened? How did you get here?"

"Drowned," she whispered. "Then I was here with you…somehow, in another body."

"Why not just say so? Why possess another and not let me know you had?"

Anna pulled back, her face so clearly seen in Alana's. "I wish I knew. I'm sorry."

"Our time is short. We don't belong here." Calum held her tighter.

"You thought I was someone else," she murmured.

"Yes," he said.

"Did you follow what happened to me after you left Scotland, Calum? Did you ever look back?"

Calum ground his teeth and cursed to himself. "I did not. For you. I had to keep you and the little one safe. The coven sent the creatures…"

Anna buried her face in his neck and whispered, "You never looked back then."

Calum held her arms and pulled away. "Had I our descendants would have died. What we had would've vanished."

Hurt blazed in her eyes. Anna met his gaze and

cried in anguish, "But it did anyway!"

With a sharp shake of his head, Calum looked into the forest to gather his thoughts. He'd done all of this to protect his love, Anna. He'd done all of this to protect his descendant's. He'd done all of this because he'd made a terrible mistake when he turned to dark magic!

Crawling back inside, he let Seth loose.

And Seth didn't like it. The wrist band turned black.

"What?" Alana shook her head. "What just happened?"

Seth fell back against a tree and shook his head, watching as Alana stumbled then stopped. She gripped her head. "What just happened?"

"Calum," he cursed and tried to push away from the tree but he was too weak. "Calum and Anna."

Still holding her head like a mad woman, Alana turned back to him. "Too much. Give me a mountain face any day of the week when compared to being possessed. Get her out of my head, Seth."

With a deep breath, he shrugged off the remnants of Calum and went to her. Taking her cheeks in his hands, he said, "Soon. It'll be over. I promise."

"How," she whimpered but gathered herself. "How can you promise my thoughts will be mine again? How can you promise we'll live through this?"

Seth yanked her body against his hard and cradled her head on his chest. "Because death is mine and I own the end of this shit-hole situation." He kissed the top of her head. "And no matter what happens, we'll get through this. I'll get you through this."

While he'd hoped her arms would come around him, Seth wasn't too shocked when Alana pulled away and nodded into the woods. "We need to face that house. We need to get this over with."

Frustrated, he wanted to tell her that he was here for her. He wanted to tell her how he felt about her. But what was the point? What stood between him and a life with this woman was too large to grasp. Best to keep an eye on the target and realize he'd be saying goodbye to everyone because hell if he'd let the reaper take any of them.

As they started to walk down the mountain, Alana shook her head and softly said, "I can't help but wonder about something."

"What's that?"

"If Anna possessed Grace and raised me as her own... what happened to my mom's soul?"

CHAPTER FIFTEEN

Alana ignored the aches in her muscles as they walked. Between the extreme work out involved in staying on the mountain face, then the fall onto the Pine, she was hurting. Nothing crucial or life-threatening but more painful than she'd like to admit. Seth hadn't really given her an answer to her question about her mom. He'd basically just tried to reassure her that they'd figure everything out and it'd all be okay.

Doubtful.

But she appreciated how hard he was trying. Seth had changed for the better. While she'd always known he was an inherently nice guy, he'd never been much good at showing it. Nope. Seth had been self-absorbed and oftentimes careless with others feelings. What's worse, he'd liked who he was. And so had she... somewhat. Because he'd always had other favorable attributes and now they seemed to be taking up a permanent residence in his personality.

Alana would never forget the look on his face when she slid down that mountain. Perhaps it would have made more sense to focus on the fact she was falling to her death but she hadn't. No. His expression had transfixed her. The fear, horror and denial.

The love.

In that single moment she'd seen clearly how strongly he felt about her. It'd gone far beyond simple friendship. Strangely, she'd felt less afraid as she slid. It almost felt as if it took that extreme situation to make them both realize how deeply their emotions had progressed.

When she slid over the side and lost sight of him, well that was a different story. Then she flailed in defiance. Not because she was falling to what would be a nasty death but because she was leaving him. No feeling had ever hurt more.

Seth stopped abruptly. "It's changed."

Alana had been so lost in thought she didn't realize that they'd arrived at the cemetery. It had changed. Back to normal for the most part. Frowning, she said, "This is what it looks like in the twenty-first century."

Yet they were clearly not in the twenty-first century. Everything around them remained dead.

"Really?" Seth crouched in front of a stone. "But the black rose is still here."

"Right, the black rose." She felt her neck. The necklace was gone.

Seth stood and urged her to come over. "I think I understand the point of the black rose now." He cupped the side of her neck and she shivered with awareness, not only because of his slight touch but because of the intense look in his eyes. "When you fell, it ripped off and caught on a rock right in front of me. The things I'd been told that I'd feel in regards to it all made sense. When you fell I did feel like my center had been ripped out. It was as if my heart had fallen off that cliff with you. In that moment, life sure as hell wasn't worth living."

How many times had she wished he'd say something like this to her? It almost felt surreal looking up into his face and hearing the words. Had they really come so far or was it all part of the freaky situation they were in? No matter. Alana was sick of doubting and wondering. Standing on her toes, she kissed him. A sweet but caring kiss. The last thing she wanted to do was incite too much passion and end up having sex in a cemetery!

Seth kissed her then pulled away, his eyes dark and intense. He started to say something but stopped and shook his head. Instead, he turned and crouched. "Did you see this?"

Alana worked to catch her breath. Everything about him left her breathless. But now wasn't the time for romance. She tucked her hair behind her ears and crouched beside him. Her mother's stone was here again. A fact she chose not to dwell on. But that wasn't what he was staring at so intently. Fixated, he continued to stare at the stone with the black rose on it.

"I thought we'd figured out the mystery of the black rose," she said.

"We did." Seth continued to study it. "But what if there was more to the message? Think about it. The necklace served its purpose but why the headstone? It makes no sense."

"I don't even know who the family member is," she remarked. "So you might be on to something."

Seth ran his fingers over the black rose and murmured, "But what?"

"Well, what do they have in common besides being black roses?"

He shook his head slowly. "Nothing."

"Hmm." Interested in the mystery, Alana said. "Then maybe it's a matter of relating the two beyond that. What did the necklace do for you? Who made the necklace? Why was it around my neck?"

"So that I'd realize how much-" Seth paused and looked at her. "The necklace clarified my feelings. I don't know who made the necklace but I know it was around your neck to send me a message about how I felt."

Alana nodded slowly. "Which meant that the black rose is a symbol sent by someone who wants to help you."

Seth's brow quirked slightly. "I like the way you think."

She shrugged. "You always did." With a wink she said, "Until I started overthinking, of course."

Chuckling, his attention returned to the stone. "Then there's a reason for this." Expression grimmer, he said, "And death is always around the corner."

A chill ran through her and every hair on her body stood up. Alana looked around. Nothing. Then, as if something straight out of a movie, candles began to flicker to life around them and the headstone. Seth continued to study the rose. He couldn't see them!

"Seth," she whispered.

He scraped the rose stem with his thumb nail. "Yeah?"

"Something's happening."

His gaze shot to hers and she nodded slowly. "Don't move."

"You sure?"

"Positive."

One by one, candles ignited until they were completely surrounded. She started to shake and Seth's arm came around her. "Is it the reaper?"

"I don't know. Don't think so."

As the strange eerie lights illuminated everything, forms began to appear. They stood beyond the candles creating an outer circle. "There are ghosts here. Still can't see them."

"Ghosts?" Seth looked around. "I see nothing."

Voices started to meld with the transparent bodies. "They're chanting something." Alana squeezed his arm in excitement. "It's Leathan… and Devin! Wait, I hear the girls too!"

Seth smiled. "Hell yeah! About time. What are they chanting. Tell me. Be very specific."

Alana closed her eyes and listened closely. "Ultima Being…no no, that's not right." Their chants grew louder, clearer. "Bellum! Ultima Bellum!"

"Final war," he whispered and frowned. "Sounds more intense than a mere battle, huh?"

Eyes round, she nodded. "Yep. Why are they chanting it?"

"Because." He stood and pulled her up. "Hold my hand, concentrate on them, chant the words and bring them closer."

"Seriously?"

Eyes dead flat, Seth looked at her. "Do it. Now. Don't be afraid."

"Okay," she said softly then, "Okay," with more conviction.

Together, with voices strong, they started to chant ultima bellum over and over. Seth turned and took her other hand so that they faced one another holding both hands. Alana focused on the words and tried to remain strong. Seth closed his eyes. The air turned frigid, colder and wind started to blow. The otherworldly candles flickered briefly but remained steady. This was dark magic surrounding her. Alana knew it without question. This was their magic, Calum, Seth, Leathan and Devin's. She could feel all four of them in it.

Somehow she became part of it, almost as if she controlled it.

And as she felt she could finally see.

Four of them, close by, a tight circle around them holding hands. She knew they could see her as well. As she chanted, Alana looked at each carefully. First Leathan, then Devin, Dakota and Isabel. Everyone chanted, their voices growing stronger. The wind grew harsher but didn't seem to move the trees. The air cooled to the point she could see it billow from their mouths.

All of them. The air. The same air!

Alana started to chant louder, stronger. Something intense was happening. Seth kept his eyes on her, watching her expression closely, his voice growing louder alongside hers. Leathan's features became more and more clear. As did the others'. With a tight squeeze of reassurance on Seth's hands, she continued to chant ultima bellum.

The trees fell away until it was only the six of them and the stone. Nothing else existed. The air thinned. It became harder to breathe. The candle flames shrunk low. All stilled. Only their unified voices remained. Seth's eyes widened but he continued. He nodded at her. He could hear them! Perhaps see them?

"Ultima Bellum. Ultima Bellum. Ultima Bellum."

Then it felt like the pressure changed. Her ears popped. Stars flickered in her vision. Alana closed her eyes and continued to chant. Pop. Pop. She opened her eyes. The candles roared up. Seth pulled away and spun.

"Shit! Say you're really there!"

Alana put her hand over her mouth and shook her head when Seth, Devin and Leathan group hugged. They were touching each other! They were here!

Isabel and Dakota were at her side smiling.

"You did it, Alana. You did it!" Isabel cried.

"What?" She wiped away a blasted tear and said, "I did what you all did!"

"Screw that," Dakota said. "You summoned the dead. Us! Even though we're alive. Somehow you got us here!"

Before she knew what hit her, Seth was hugging her fiercely and spinning her while laughing. "What can't you do?"

Though he put her down, he didn't stop hugging her. "What can't you do?" he repeated in wonder.

Alana chuckled into his shoulder. "No idea what I did. But you're making it sort of hard to breathe."

Seth smiled and pulled away. They turned to find the others staring at them oddly. A long moment passed. Leathan cleared his voice first and said, "Thank you, Alana."

She shrugged, a little uncomfortable. "No prob. Not sure what I really did."

Devin stared at their surroundings with a critical eye. "Looks like you brought the living to you versus the other way around."

Alana's heart felt like it stopped. She'd done what?

"What he means to say is you brought us all together at last." Isabel smiled warmly and frowned at Devin.

Devin's eyebrows rose in understanding and he said avidly, "Right, lassie. You got us back together. I mean who knows, we might be dead and you're the ones who are alive."

Isabel's frown deepened and she rolled her eyes.

It occurred to her that the others hadn't questioned her appearance. "Do I look like myself to you guys?"

"Of course. Why?" Leathan asked.

She and Seth looked at one another then them. "Because we don't look like ourselves to each other. Well, not entirely I guess. In fact, we look like those whom we're possessed by... sorta."

Silence.

"That's intense. Even for you, Seth," Devin finally said. "You're both possessed?"

"Did you expect anything less from my haunting?" Seth retaliated.

Devin shrugged. "Guess not." His savvy eyes skirted between Seth and Alana. "Turns out your haunting has taken us completely by surprise, cousin."

"Aye," Leathan agreed.

"For sure." Isabel smiled.

"Too cute." Dakota winked with approval.

Alana narrowed her eyes and while she looked at the group she talked to Seth. "Are they always like this?"

"Yep." Seth grinned. "And you're one of us now so get used to it."

Everyone's eyes rounded but they all managed to look elsewhere in a hurry.

"And even though we're doing our best to focus on you two, care to share where we are laddie?" Leathan asked.

Devin's eyes roamed dark. "Aye, everything's

dead here."

"A side effect of this haunting I guess," Seth said. "Death everywhere."

An uncomfortable silence followed.

"Where's Andrea?" Seth asked.

Startled, they all seemed surprised.

"She was with us." Devin frowned. "She was part of the circle."

Growling, Seth started to pace. "Where is she now then?" He scowled in the direction of the house and repeated, "Where is she?"

"She's not here," Alana said. "I have no idea how I know but I do. She's not here. I didn't see her in the circle. She's not here."

Seth's dark gaze fell on her. "Are you positive?"

"Yes, I am." Seth's gaze darkened and she nodded with what she hoped was assurance. "She's not here."

He watched her for several more moments before the tension seemed to drain from his body and he stopped pacing. "Alright. Good."

Dakota raised her hand. "Question."

"Shoot," Seth said.

"Sorry about the 'rewind' but you two said you were possessed. By who exactly?"

Alana sat on a rock and waved a loose hand at Seth. "Him by Calum, me by Anna."

All four jaws dropped.

"You're kidding, right?" Leathan said.

Seth shook his head. "Nope. Wish we were. Can you imagine Calum being inside your head then taking over your body at will?"

"Fuck, no," Devin said. Isabel frowned. "Sorry. Trying not to swear."

Leathan sighed and shook his head. "What I'm more interested in is Alana being haunted by Anna. Are we talking about Calum's wife from Scotland? Our great, great, a few times over, grandmother? The love of his life. What happened to Grace?" His eyes locked on Alana. "Your grandmother."

Alana shook her head and looked at Seth. "They're way out of the loop, eh?"

Seth grinned. "Seems so." With audience intact, he explained everything they'd learned here. As anticipated, his story dropped their jaws once more.

Isabel spoke first, her voice sad. "Are you okay, Alana? Seems you've suffered the most. I'm so sorry."

Touched, Alana nodded. "I'm okay. There's still so much mystery. To tell you the truth I'm not sure what to be sad over."

"Because you don't know what really happened to your mom," Isabel said.

Yes. Exactly! "It's okay. Really. The bigger issue is getting out of here. I'm the one who should be sorry. While I know you're all stoked to be together I'm worried I've only led you to death. Literally."

Leathan shrugged, looked around and grinned. "Wouldn't be the first time for any of us, lass."

Everyone nodded with lots of 'mm hmm's'.

"Stop worrying about your part in any of this, Alana. You're meant to be here." Seth shrugged and said, "This is all meant to be."

"He's right," Devin seconded, his smoky green eyes growing serious. "Now we focus."

"Aye." Leathan looked around. "Where's the reaper, Seth? Why are we here and it's not?"

Seth shook his head. "Wish I had all the answers

but I don't. The reaper should've been all over us by now. But like I said, in the cave it made it apparent it wanted us back at the house. Now I've got a question of my own. What's up with ultima bellum?"

"Actually, that was Adlin's suggestion," Dakota said.

"So he's been visiting you guys too?" Seth said.

"Here and there. As usual." Devin frowned. "We weren't happy about the ultima bellum thing. Seems harsh using the word war."

"Our thoughts exactly," Alana said.

"It's Adlin. He must've had his reasons. He's never led us astray. Can't imagine he would now." Dakota looked at Seth. "Any luck finding the stone?"

"Nope," Seth said. "But I'm still curious about that."

"What?" Devin asked.

"The gravestone." Seth went over and crouched once more in front of the stone with the black rose.

Alana shook her head. "You thought it meant good and it did. Your family is here. Maybe that's all there is to it."

"No," Seth said softly and brushed his hand over the rose. "I don't think so."

"What is it about that rose?" Alana joined him again. They should be heading for the house right now. They should be working as a team. The odds that they'd beat the reaper had vastly improved with the arrival of his cousins. "It's a rose on a stone," she murmured.

"Right." But he kept staring. "Rose on a stone... stone."

Seth's eyes narrowed and he kept repeating the word 'stone', his eyes growing wider. "Shit. Get back

Alana."

Scrambling sideways she watched him stand, his expression determined.

"What are you doing?"

Seth spun and kicked fast, she flinched and fell back. The side of his foot hit the rock so hard a loud crack broke through the forest and the gravestone shattered like a brick of dry clay beneath a sixty-story cement building. Coughing, she cracked open an eye to see a small, black pebble rolling slowly in her direction. It stopped at her foot.

Alana reached down and picked up the rock. It was beautiful, unique... special.

"We found it," Seth said. "The third stone in Calum's Curse."

CHAPTER SIXTEEN

Seth immediately moved to Alana and held her. Something was coming.

A loud roar echoed off the mountains and what sounded like a freight train started to scream up the mountainside. The others joined them in their little alcove of rock. They huddled together as the wind screamed over them, tearing all the blackened leaves from the trees. Pure fury bellowed far and wide. The sound of screeching wind couldn't compare with the rumble of the earth beneath.

Alana covered her ears. "I'm scared," she whispered.

Seth held her closer. "Don't be."

He knew she hadn't intended to be heard. The ground felt like it lifted several feet then fell. Angry, Seth waited as the air chilled to what felt to be just below freezing. The raging wind suddenly subsided and the ground stilled. The rage that the land had unleashed stopped as soon as it'd started.

"Fuck," Leathan muttered and moved out of their huddle first. "It's like the Victorian all over again but now it's everywhere, not just a house."

Dakota followed, obviously eager to stay close to Leathan, more to protect him than anything. "We won then. We'll win now."

Seth kept his arms around Alana. Though she trembled he saw the set of her chin. While she was afraid she was obviously also pissed. Pushing free from him, she stalked into the cemetery, the stone clenched in her fist.

"It's time to go. Now. I'm sorry." Frustrated, she looked around aimless and unseeing, determined in an odd way. "I'm going."

Seth watched her stalk away down the mountain and couldn't help but smile. Had she been rational she would've taken the time to make sure everyone was okay, to get her facts straight, but no, she wasn't rational, she was Alana. Ridiculous and relentless and live-on-the-edge. Immensely pleased despite her idiocy he stood and stretched, then grinned as he pointed down the mountain. "I'm with her."

"Hell lad," Leathan said behind him.

"Bloody Americans," Devin muttered.

But he knew they followed him. They always followed each other until time and space separated them. Seth trotted until he caught up with her. Alana looked ready for war. Or was it ultima bellum? Damn, she was his ultima bellum right now. She always had been. War, peace, love, lust, drama and all that.

The house had just come into view when she stopped suddenly and turned to face him. Everyone stopped behind them, waiting. She'd somehow made herself the leader in this paranormal pack. "I take it back. I take what I said to you back, Seth."

He crossed his arms over his chest and said, "Fine, Alana."

Alana crossed her arms as well, chin jutting out further. "The minute I saw you on that ski slope I didn't fall in love with you, I fell in lust. You were hot." Her eyes skimmed him briefly before they locked onto his eyes again. "I hate that I didn't love you on sight. In fact, I hate that I love you now but I do. You and I are a cliché. The more I got to know you the better I liked you. Then when you went and died on me and then haunted me." She shook her head. "No, when you died on me I realized how much I loved you. Then when you haunted me it was like acid on a raw wound."

Silence reigned; nobody said a word as she moved closer and glared up at him. "Then you had to go and be a friend when I was dealing with all things Grace and you chased me up and down a tree. You couldn't just leave bad enough alone. You had to make it better than good." She bit her lip and shook her head. "You had to go ahead and be you. Amazing, wonderful, fucked up, you."

He was about to respond but she shook her head sharply and held up her forefinger. "No talking. The last words get to be mine. I love you, Seth. I am in love with you. That's my emotion. I own it. I know how you feel but I don't want to own that emotion. I want nothing to do with it. Truly. Because I'm still angry that I feel this way. That I allowed myself to feel this way." Alana paused for a moment, her eyes searching his. "But I needed to actually say it. So that you would hear it. I love you."

Like the little storm trooper that she was, Alana didn't give him a chance to respond but strode across the lawn toward the house. Seth stared after her, a little dumbstruck. Not by what she'd said but by how strongly she still separated them. How much she felt the love was all hers. Not his.

Devin and Leathan walked up alongside of him and stared after her as well.

"She's a firecracker, laddie," Leathan said. "I'm impressed."

"Aye, you've found your lassie," Devin agreed. "Good luck."

He looked from cousin to cousin with nothing but a wide smile to be found. Looking skyward, he shook his head and said, "Our girls were the first battle. Time to go face death, my friends."

So they started toward the last house in Calum's curse, the Tudor Revival.

Alana was nearly there so Seth picked up the pace. The girl didn't know when to back down. Halfway across the dead lawn, he sensed rather then saw her and the house getting further away. Shaking his head, he broke into a dead run. Alana!

Wind seemed to rush up in his face, swamping him in dust and black leaves. He stumbled back and fell. Enraged, he leaped to his feet and kept running. Rocks began to sting his legs, pebbles spitted rapidly off his arms.

"Holy shit! Stop Seth!"

Arms came around him and pulled him back. Seth flailed and fought but his cousins brought him to the ground. Pinned, he watched the Tudor Revival start to turn into a black hole. Alana? Lost somewhere in that. She hadn't stopped. No, she walked right into it. What for? Why the hell would she have done that?

"She's not afraid, Seth," Leathan said. "Trust that. Let her go."

Though he flailed again, Devin and Leathan were too strong. Devin's eyes met his. "Don't look at it. Look at me. Stay with us. As a team we can fight. Separated we fail."

Seth ground his teeth and fought their strength. "You sound like a god damned super hero. Fine. We save. We fight. As a team." He snarled in Devin's face. "And fuck you by the way. If that was Isabel, you'd already be there. And you'd hate me for holding you back."

"Aye, lad," Leathan piped in, his eyes intense. "What about Calum? What would he do? What the bloody hell would my lad, Calum do?" he yelled at Seth.

He stared at his cousin's faces. They were sweating from the strain of holding him down. He shook his head. Who cared what Calum would do?

Wind screamed. The black hole grew larger.

Then his body went numb. This time he felt it when the arch warlock roared up. This time he felt Calum struggling to resurface, take control. Shaking his head, Seth said, "No! It's not about Calum. It's about me and Alana. Let me go. Let me get her. This is my moment! This is my love. Let me go." He didn't care if he drooled, spit or looked like a total wuss. Alana had always been his, from the moment he laid eyes on her. He didn't want to fight as a team. He didn't want to listen to reason.

He just wanted to get her back.

Calum's voice in his head vanished. Devin and Leathan continued to stare at him.

"Let him go," Isabel yelled.

"I agree. Let him go," Dakota echoed.

Devin and Leathan glanced at each other and Seth.

"You've put us through hell since we've known you," Devin muttered.

When Devin pulled away Leathan's pressure grew stronger. He'd always led them. Leathan knew what was best. He was the oldest. And hell if he wasn't the strongest. Magic aside, no Devin there,

Leathan could still hold him down.

"Let me go," Seth repeated.

Leathan's eyes narrowed and he leaned down, his eyes dark golden and lethal. "You and Devin are my heart, my kin, my clan." He shook his head. "Och, you've both been a pain in my arse from the get go. But you've also been my best friends. You-" He clenched the material over Seth's heart and squeezed, his pupils flaring. "Are the youngest. The life of us all. You're not only my cousin, Seth, you're like a brother. And so help me." Leathan looked away briefly and ground his jaw before his eyes locked again with Seth's. "If you die, I will find you and kill you again you little shit. I'll kill you so harshly that the reaper's first death will have seemed merciful. You got that, lad?"

Fury kept pumping through Seth's veins but he understood the love in Leathan's voice. And somehow, he understood that he needed to turn down the emotion… no, turn it off. The only way he could fight this war was if he used his brain, not his heart.

Blackness grew. The wind howled.

Leathan leaned down until they were six inches apart, eye to eye, and said, "You've always been different than us. You don't think like we do. That's your advantage. You like to live on the edge and push everyone to their limits. Do that now but do it while remembering everything you've learned since the Victorian. Pay attention and do it right. You know how."

Leathan pulled away and yanked Seth to his feet. "You know how."

Seth didn't rush in a mad fury toward the house but looked at Leathan then Devin. They looked right back, their gazes steady. Taking a deep breath he turned his attention to where the Revival had stood. It was now a huge gaping black hole of swirling cloud.

Alana couldn't be part of this. Neither could his cousins.

Nothing could stand between him and death.

Nothing ever had.

All the near-death stunts he'd done in his life rose up. He never should have survived most. Now that black void that'd wanted him every single time waited...wanted. Seth stared at it, as he had so many times before.

Funny how it suddenly looked familiar.

His monster didn't scream out. It didn't attack. No. His monster had always waited for him to go one step too far. In this case, the monster was a minion with only the purpose of its master at its disposal to feed on.

Death.

"Ironic," he muttered as he stared at what could easily be the bottom of his latest sky-diving stunt or a slide down a sheer mountain face. "Guess death was always meant to find me not the other way around."

Devin and Leathan said nothing. He hadn't expected them to.

Screw this.

He had to save her.

So Seth ran.

Every step he took felt like he was being sucked down into the ground. As if the dirt pulled him like quicksand. It was far more intense a feeling than any stunt he'd ever pulled. No matter, he kept walking. After all, there was nowhere to go but forward. The world around him started to seem dreamlike, not natural. Air grew thinner, as if he were traveling up not down. He tried to call out for Alana but it seemed his words couldn't travel far. It was almost like trying to hear one's echo in a padded cubicle, scientifically impossible.

Then everything was completely black and far too silent.

"I always did appreciate your courage."

Seth spun. Calum had walked up beside him. "So you're out of me now? When did you manage to do that?"

"I am very good at what I do," Calum said dryly.

The warlock was dressed in long black robes, the hood pulled over his head.

"What's with the outfit. You going into battle dressed like that?"

Calum's expression didn't change but remained stiff, emotionless. "How I am dressed is irrelevant."

Seth shrugged. "Whatever. Tell me where we are. Where's Alana?"

"Where she belongs."

"And where exactly is that?"

"I thought I would not like this experience but I have. It was something of a game keeping you alive for so long."

Arching a brow, Seth said, "Not following you, Calum."

"I am not, Calum."

It felt like icy daggers scratched up his spine and he took a step back. Unable to stop himself, he looked into its eyes. Every dare-devil action he'd taken in life came screaming up to the surface of those strange black eyes. But those weren't so bad. More like one huge thrill seek. What was bad were all the other memories. Emotions he'd apparently become very good at repressing. In that single moment, he remembered everyone he'd loved who had died. He remembered the true fear he'd felt when Leathan had been sucked in by the Victorian's lure. The fear he'd felt when Devin had fallen into the time-warping embrace of the Georgian. He'd been so afraid for them. Too afraid. Seth clenched his fists and kept his eyes locked with the reaper.

Oily and slick, the eyes sucked him in further, quickly replaying the moment that it knew made the biggest impact. The moment Alana slid by him on the mountain... that devastating second that she slid over the edge. No matter how much he knew for a fact that she'd survived he couldn't push past that moment. It felt like everything that'd happened after that had been a dream and the reality was that she had died.

"That is because she should have. At least part of her."

Seth snapped out of the strange spell and staggered back a few more steps. "I don't understand. A part of her?"

The reaper cocked its head, the movement strange and puppet-like. "How do you think death works, Seth?"

He worked hard to keep terror at bay. "Is that a trick question?"

"Answer."

It was impossible to believe he stood here having a calm conversation with a reaper, with death itself. Seth was trying damn hard not to focus on that. He shrugged slowly. "You die when it's time."

"Are you sure?"

"Guess so. I'd hate to think you die when it's not

your time. Honestly, I've never given it much thought at all."

"It sounds as if you have, Seth. And you have spent your whole life looking for me."

Seth swallowed hard. "That's where you're wrong. Not much interested in what you have to offer. Now you've been sent after me... to kill me and all, I sort of have no choice."

"I do not like magic in any form," the reaper said. "It disturbs the natural order of things."

Seth couldn't help his next questions. "Then why are you here? How did you fall victim to it?"

"I was trapped both by coven and warlock. And I am one of many. But not that many. Again, Seth, how do you think death works?"

He didn't want to respond. Seth wanted his own answers; the first being where was Alana. Yet—and even he knew it was an odd new addition to his personality—Seth didn't ask questions. No, he figured he'd get his answers if he humored the reaper... maybe. So he said, "According to beliefs, a reaper, or death, leads a soul to the next level of existence. Heaven or hell or whatever there is out there."

"Yes," the reaper said. "And no."

It felt a little hard to breathe. He really didn't want to know death's place beyond that.

The reaper continued. "Sometimes death helps you stay alive as well."

Better explanation than he anticipated. "Okay. That's good I think."

"It has never occurred to humanity that angels or other such entities might lead a person from one plane of existence to another. Death always gets blamed for that. The truth is death plays a much larger part in the passing of time and souls than humanity could ever realize."

Despite the blatant terror he'd felt minutes before, Seth was intrigued.

"He who is in you has been very naughty." The reaper's finger moved slightly and Calum fell out of Seth's body. The sensation was jarring and uncomfortable. His body chilled and weakened and his legs gave way. Leaning back on his hands, Seth waited for the creepy feeling to pass. Meanwhile, Calum came unsteadily to his feet.

"Did you not think I knew you were in him?" The reaper asked.

Seth stumbled to his feet and tried to regain balance. "You sonofobitch Calum. Evil, rotten piece of shit. You possessed me!"

"I was trying to protect you," Calum said.

It was strange talking to two Calum's who were dressed identically. However, his ancestor didn't wear the hood.

"With the actions of the coven and yourself, you have changed the course of history," the reaper said so softly and lethally that Seth rubbed his arms in alarm.

"Somehow I doubt that," Calum muttered. "Death, in its many versions, is not affected by the temporary loss of one of its many fingers."

The reaper's eyes didn't change, just grew blacker. "Your arrogance has always been your downfall, Calum. You and your coven have affected the order of things." He sniffed the air as if sampling it to locate someone. "That stone is mine now. As are the souls connected to it."

Seth's chest tightened.

Calum stood up straighter. "Anna and I are yours. Not Alana and Seth."

Seth eyed Calum. Really?

"So many souls misplaced by your misdeeds, Calum." Death shook its head, fury evident in the rise of its voice. "Misdeeds that touched many outside of your group of humans, your descendants," it said, disgusted. "Selfish."

"Human," Calum defended. "I am human."

"You are warlock!" Death roared, its face twisting and grim, before it snapped back to first the visage of Calum's face before it slowly transformed to nothing but a human form with blackness where a face should be.

Seth's stomach flipped.

He'd much prefer to battle an army of vampires and werewolves to the single creature that stood before him. The terror he felt was impossible to describe.

Death turned to him. "And I am tired of this game. I am not good, nor am I bad. I am nothing and everything. Until this point, I never knew emotion. I was never supposed to know emotion. It has no part in my existence with good reason."

Nausea receded. Seth watched Calum closely. The reaper was a bit too intense to watch. Its voice changed, grew deeper and more hallow. "Ultima Bellum."

Holy shit. Adlin hadn't helped bring his cousins here, the reaper had! But why wait? Why not do it right away?

Calum's eyes narrowed. "I never really trapped you at all did I?"

"Enough so," Death responded. "But never entirely. No magic could ever be strong enough."

Seth's eyes rounded. "You've been with me all along."

The reaper nodded once. "Somewhat. Sent by a foolish coven to destroy you. But the woman of this house draws death to her. She draws me close."

Seth flinched. Alana.

"If you've always had access to me, then why aren't I dead?" he said.

"You mean why are you alive?"

Seth paused. "You could have had me at any time."

"Of course. But that was not the natural order of things. And I did not particularly want you."

Calum humphed. "All of this for nothing."

"It was not for nothing," the reaper said. "Was it, Calum?"

When the reaper gave its full attention to Calum, the warlock stepped back and lowered his head.

Seth had never seen Calum appear so humbled. "No," he whispered. "It was not for nothing."

A white speck was walking toward them from far off, its point growing and growing. Seth's eyes widened. Was it the infamous white light coming for him? Calum grumbled for a split second before his expression sank beneath the black nothingness of the reaper's face, a black hole as lethal as it'd been when it swallowed the house.

Seth sighed with tentative relief when the white speck became the form of Adlin.

The wizard looked at Calum. "You thought you were in control the whole time." He shook his head and continued speaking before Calum could. "You thought you had it all figured out. But you misplaced Grace and Alana in time. You used them. They deserved more years together," Adlin growled, his eyes glowing bright blue. "Then you figured you could fool death by hiding within the forms of Seth and Alana, until the stone brought all of your descendants together to destroy it. Because after all, you'd all have to be together to even have a minimal chance at defeating death itself."

Calum's chin inched up a notch. "I did what I did to protect my family. You know that."

"You haunted a house from two angles!" Adlin roared. "You waited in the past for them to come from the future."

"What? How?" Seth asked.

Adlin cocked his head at Calum. "Tell him. You're running out of time, lad."

Calum stood straighter as though he were a teacher and Seth his pupil. "Simple enough. I trapped myself in the Tudor house with the reaper." His expression faltered briefly. "I sent Grace and Alana forward through time and used Alana to find you, Seth. She was always such a gifted child. I loved them both. It was never my intention that Grace would age... that they'd both lose time."

Seth whispered in disbelief, "How could you know that Alana would love sports, that she and I would be so alike?"

"That might have had something to do with me," Adlin allowed. "I was always determined that good would come out of all of this. You boys deserved that at the very least."

"So we're not who we really are?" Seth asked. That possibility scared him more than any of this.

"Oh no," Adlin assured. "Nothing that extreme. Just a little bit of good magic and what turned out to be a great stroke of luck. Trust me, you both were crazy before you were born." He looked at the reaper. "Isn't that right?"

"You have always had compatible spirits," death said.

Calum nodded and smiled, as though he were a child being let off the hook. "So you see, it all worked out just fine, lad. A haunting from two sides. Really very clever of me if we're all to be honest."

"You ran away from love. You ran away from Anna and your child," Adlin said. "Nothing was honest or clever about that."

"I had no choice!"

"You had a choice the minute you turned to dark magic."

"We've been over this a million times, old man," Calum grumbled.

"So we have." Adlin shook his head. "Let me ask you this, if you could do it all again would you do it differently?"

Calum paused for several moments and was about to respond but stopped. It appeared he was surprised by his own revelation. "No. No, I don't suppose I would."

"All the harm done and you wouldn't change it if you could?"

It was obvious Calum struggled internally. Pain flickered in his eyes. Eventually he shook his head. "No. I truly believed that I was helping my family. I felt I had no choice. Leaving them behind was devastating. It has hurt every day since, even in death.

But my choices allowed me to know my descendants, Leathan, Seth, Devin and even Andrea. And knowing them changed me when I didn't even know I needed changing." Calum looked hard at Adlin. "And you. It allowed me to know you better. You're not so bad for a meddling wizard."

Adlin's expression grew even more serious. "You've come to the end of your road, Calum. Do you think you achieved your ultimate goal? Have you protected your family? Seems things are a bit shady right now, lad."

Calum looked at the reaper. "Why ultima bellum? What are your intentions?"

Seth realized in that moment that there was no way that he and his cousins, even with Calum and Adlin's help, could defeat death. Closing his eyes, he shook his head. He wasn't sure if he really wanted to defeat death.

It felt important.

Necessary.

"Do you fear me now, then?" The reaper asked.

Seth opened his eyes. The reaper had been talking to him.

A hundred emotions went through him but it all came down to being honest. Even with death. He crossed his arms over his chest and shook his head slowly. "No I don't. I never have been...at least not for my sake anyways. But I do fear you for those I love. I have respect for you."

"Why?"

"Because you've earned it. Because you deserve it."

Had he really just said that? Yep. And he'd meant it. Seth took a deep breath and tried to stay calm.

The reaper remained still. "If you live, will you continue to tempt me, Seth? I have seen your face many times, always so eager."

Seth thought about it for a few seconds. "Probably the wrong answer but yes, I think I will. I'm drawn to you."

Dead silence reigned while the reaper seemed to contemplate this. Seth wouldn't be surprised if his world was snuffed out in an instant.

"Anna?" Calum whispered.

Seth watched in amazement as a young woman rushed through the darkness to Calum. Shocked, Calum wrapped his arms around her and buried his face in her hair. "Anna, my beautiful lass. You're here." He cupped her cheeks and shook his head. "I can see you. I can touch you."

Calum leaned his forehead against hers. "I am so sorry for the pain I put you through. I never meant to hurt you. Only help. I wanted to give you a good life. Instead I ruined it."

"None of it matters now," she whispered. "It's all behind us."

"There's so much I missed. Our son…"

Seth was amazed to see Calum's eyes fill with tears as he looked at Anna.

"He did well." Anna shook her head. "You left when he was so young. He didn't remember you. I died… I think, when he was older. He was a good, strong man."

"Did he… did he have the gift?"

Anna shook her head. "I don't think so. Not that I ever saw."

"Thank God," he whispered and leaned down

slowly, his kiss long and thorough.

When their kiss ended, Anna said, "It is going to be okay."

Calum's eyes fell over her shoulder to death. "I think you're right."

His eyes lingered on Seth and then Adlin before they met hers. "Are you ready to go?"

"I think we should have already been gone," she whispered.

Seth's attention turned to the reaper. It said nothing. Only waited.

Calum readjusted his top hat and held out the crook of his arm to Anna. With a small smile she tucked her arm into his and nodded. Seth watched with alarm as the reaper walked toward them, its form growing taller and wider. Darkness rose up and seemed to cover the couple in one quick swoop.

"Wait!" he cried and lunged to stop them. "What about Alana?"

Suddenly, darkness receded and he'd lunged into the foyer of the Revival. It was daylight and his cousins sat in the living room... just as he'd left them when he'd traveled back in time.

Devin narrowed his eyes. "Good question!"

Seth shook his head and slowly walked through the foyer. Everything was as it had been. Sheets covered things and dust motes floated. But death was gone. No more blackness everywhere. In fact, the house had returned. He blinked several times and said. "I'm back. We're back!" He looked around with a smile on his face. "Where's Alana?"

Leathan stood, a look of alarm on his face. "Seth, you walked into that foyer, paused for a minute then turned and came back to confront us. Alana was with you. Now she's gone."

A chill ran through him. "No. That's impossible." Seth frowned. "So much has happened. Alana and I went back and were with Grace and Calum. We were possessed."

Andrea came over to him, eyes wide and concerned. "You both just vanished. No time has passed, Seth."

"Impossible." Seth started to run from room to room and yelled, "She's got to be here somewhere. Help me look for her!"

Everyone started to scour the house. Seth ran upstairs, exploring each room. She had to be here somewhere. He'd somehow made it through this nightmare. Surely she did too. But what if she hadn't? What if the reaper had made true on his threat?

Air thinned. Breathing became impossible. He struggled for comprehension and shook his head. "Please no."

Anguished, he returned to the foyer and studied every corner, every piece of furniture. He had to be missing something!

Andrea and Isabel walked through the front door. Isabel said, "We looked everywhere outside, right to the property lines. There's no sign of her."

"I checked the basement. Nothing," Dakota said, a little breathless.

Seth leaned against the door jam and shook off Andrea's concerned touch. "It's worse than the other two houses," he whispered.

"What happened?" Leathan strode over and grasped Seth's arms. "Focus. Now's not the time for emotion. Recap, cousin, we'll figure this out."

They didn't doubt him for a second. His cousins had been down this petrifying road before. Dumbfounded he stared aimlessly. "Death. Death happened."

"The reaper hasn't made another appearance. Where is it?" Leathan asked and made Seth look him in the eye. "Tell. Us. What. Happened."

So he did, bit by bit, as well as he could through the numbness. When finished he said, "We loved each other."

Silence fell for several moments before Andrea said softly, "Oh Seth. I'm so sorry. Don't worry. We'll find her."

But a sinking sensation had taken hold. She should've returned when he did.

Devin whispered something but it was too low to hear.

"She can't be dead," Seth muttered. "She can't be."

Leathan ground his jaw in frustration. He knew exactly what Seth was going through.

"It's all here," Devin said louder.

"What's there?" Leathan growled, obviously hurting for Seth.

"In the journal," Devin said. "The next page starts it. Seth's story is here. Calum wrote it. Seth was right. A lot did happen after he vanished."

"But it'd been empty." Seth shook his head and rushed over to grab the journal. Flipping through it he read everything he'd felt, seen and experienced through his eyes… and Calum's. "Holy shit."

Flipping to the last page, he skimmed over it. Nothing existed after he returned to the foyer except some final words from Calum. "The curse has been lifted. You are safe. Goodbye, family."

Nothing was said about Alana living after he'd confronted the reaper. Nothing was said about her returning to the present with him. Calum would have written it if it had happened.

"He's gone," Seth whispered and shook his head. "He's gone. She's gone. They're all gone."

He sank down onto the couch and sat back slowly, the journal falling from his limp hand. "They're all gone."

Andrea sat next to him. "Again, I'm so sorry, Seth. I'm sure there's more to this. There's always more to these hauntings."

"No." He shook his head. "There's no more when it comes to death. And I have to respect that."

Nobody said a word until Dakota cleared her voice and said, "Seth?"

He met her eyes, emotionless. "Yeah."

"Are you out of your frigging mind!" she said. Before he could respond she stood and shook her head. "I might not have stared death in the face like you did but I met death the hard way through my parents then dealt with vampires. Vampires! Mine was a true hell." She scowled at him. "Leathan and I went through hell to find each other. So didn't Isabel and Devin for that matter. And Andrea had her fair share of heartache. But we all had one thing in common. We never gave up hope."

"Exactly," Isabel piped in. "We wanted to. Every single one of us. Calum's curse is terrible. But we never gave up. We haven't given up."

"No way," Andrea agreed.

"Never gonna happen, lad," Devin added.

"Through to the end," Leathan said. "All of us.

With you."

Seth shook his head and said through clenched teeth. "It is the end."

He stood and walked to the door where he stopped but didn't look back. "Listen, I'm sorry. I know you're trying to help."

Seth walked out the door. He didn't want to talk anymore. He didn't want to sit there while they tried to cheer him up. The air was cool and comfortable and fresh. The sun sat low in the sky slicing its rays across the lawn in such an angle that the green grass turned golden. He went to the only place he could right now.

Their rock.

Leaning against it, he stared at the Tudor Revival. It glowed. Beautiful and alive and well-tended, it looked like it had been revived. And he supposed it had. After all, it'd been as dead as a house could get earlier that day. But the truth was, it'd never seemed all that dead to him because Alana had been with him. She'd always made it seem thrilling.

He rubbed his eyes and hung his head.

"You should've let me tell you how I felt," he whispered.

Frustrated, he shook his head and pushed away from the rock. "I should have told you," he growled and started walking into the woods. "And I will."

If she had died then she should be with her family. Alana should have a place with her kin. Or at least he hoped death was that decent. One part of him dreaded where he was heading but another part was desperate...furious.

Within minutes he was at the cemetery.

Keeping his anger as a solid shield against his

tormented emotions, he started to search the stones and said, "You have to be here somewhere, Alana. I never got to tell you how I felt so you have to be here."

Where was she? Where was her headstone?

"Here," someone whispered.

Seth spun and rushed around the rock ledge sidling the cemetery. Alana?

Bedraggled but in one piece, she sat slumped against the rock. Slowly, she raised her head. "What happened? The last thing I remember we were heading back toward the house with your cousins."

She was alive and here! Somehow, by the grace of death, she was here.

"You're alive!" He fell to his knees but didn't touch her. His heart raced. If she was seriously injured, he'd hurt her more if he moved her. Instead, he started to examine her head, arms, everything. "How do you feel? Are you hurt?" He pinched her. "Are you a ghost?"

"Ouch!" Alana shifted slightly. "No, I'm fine. Just a bad headache. What happened, Seth?"

Trembling, he pulled her into his arms. "It's over. The reaper's gone. Calum and Anna are gone. It's finally all over. We made it, Alana."

Her lower lip quivered. "Really, just like that? Did Grace…somehow…"

"No, I don't think so." Seth held her tighter. "I'm so sorry."

"It's okay," she murmured. "Even if we had less time than we should have it was worth it. I'll always remember her. Oh…"

He looked where she did. A well-maintained gravestone nestled nearby. A beautiful black rose flourished at the top. Beneath it were the words, "Grace. Grandmom. Friend. She who controls the love of the black rose. May You Rest In Peace."

No years of birth or death had been provided.

So Grace had somehow helped them from beyond the grave, even beyond possession. It hadn't been all Adlin.

"I have no doubt you'll see her again," he said softly. "Someday."

A small smile flickered over her lips. "I think you're right."

Alana's expression turned grim. "I want to hear what happened. Are your cousin's okay? Is the house still standing?" She peered around, as if seeing things for the first time. "Glad to see that all the blackness and death is gone."

Seth brushed hair away from her face. "Everyone's fine. The house is standing. I'll fill you in on the details later. None of it matters right now." He cupped her cheek. "I came here to tell you something. You told me not to before and I shouldn't have listened. We almost died and you would've never known!"

"What are you talk—"

He put a finger to her mouth. "You need to know that the first time I saw you on that ski slope I fell in love. I was in love at first sight. Alana, I'm in love with you. Always have been and always will be."

Alana studied his face for several long moments before she whispered, "I know you are, Seth." She touched his cheek. "And I love you, too. Can't help myself."

It was obvious she had no recollection of telling him her feelings before she'd vanished into the house.

But she felt the same now. That's what counted. He ignored a rush of relief and added, "And you know you're my best friend."

Tears welled in her eyes and she nodded.

As crazy as Calum's curse had been, things had worked out in his favor and Seth knew better than to question it. Or doubt it. Death had been merciful.

Leaning down he kissed her, cherishing the feel of her lips against his.

Had he been forgiven? Was this a second chance? He supposed it didn't much matter. It was what it was. And he didn't intend to screw it up.

Not with her.

Not ever.

He pulled her closer and didn't let the kiss end. This time when he made love to her, and that'd be damned soon, it would mark the start of the biggest thrill of his life.

EPILOGUE

"You like to live on the edge." Alana's amber eyes twinkled. "Yet I see a parachute attached to your back."

Eyes glued to her lovely face, Seth nodded. "Yep."

"But didn't you say you had a death wish? Screw death?"

Wrapping one arm around her waist, he pulled her close until their lips were within inches. Her cinnamon hot breath mingled with his. "Nope. I clearly said death couldn't touch me but that I had a great deal of respect for it."

"Ah, interesting… and weird." She laughed between their kisses. "This is the craziest thing we've ever done, you know."

"Yep." Seth kissed her once more and asked, "You sure you're up for it?"

"Since the day I was born," she responded, her excitement building.

"The temperature can freeze your body. Lack of pressure can boil your blood."

"Right. Hence this suit I'm wearing. But thanks for the reminder."

Seth stared into her eyes, amazed that they'd been given a life together. He understood more now than ever how much he should cherish it versus defying it. Death would come when it was time. There was no way around that. But it didn't want you to stop living. Seth knew now that he'd never escaped death. In his own way he'd been right all along, death came in accordance with everyone's time.

It didn't make him sad or angry, it just made him live better than he ever had.

Because he truly valued his time now.

Which by no means meant that he intended to keep his feet safely on the ground.

Far below, his family waited for them. It was time to take the plunge.

Seth kissed Alana one more time then pulled what was essentially a space suit over her head. "You'll take off yours when I pull off mine. When it's safe. That'll be at about—"

Alana nodded and waved away his next words impatiently.

"We're the first couple to skydive from an altitude that is considered outer space," he reminded and adjusted the small oxygen tank hitched to her side. "You remember what I said about speed, pressure and dizziness?"

Alana nodded and mouthed, "Supersonic spacesuit. Here's hoping we don't pass out first."

"Or get hit by a plane." He winked. "Remember, no air before sixty-three thousand feet. After that, air's still pretty useless. Best to trust dependable air at about nine thousand feet. But that's a long ways down."

She nodded and smiled.

"You understand that you have to fall a certain way from this altitude, like we talked about? Thirty-five degree angle at first. I'll be right behind you."

Alana shook her head, rolled her eyes and mouthed. "Don't pull this crap, Seth. Let's just do it."

With a wry grin he nodded and pulled on his

helmet. Before he had a chance to preach more, she hit the button that opened the hatch and jumped. Seth smiled wide. His kind of girl. With an internal 'whoop' he jumped after her.

He could have sworn that moments before he leaped, he saw Adlin standing there grinning.

Maybe he did. Maybe he didn't. Either way, nothing mattered once he started to fall.

YouTube viewers far and wide watched the scene unfold live. It was intense, fast and live-on-the-edge stuff. Seth and Alana were the second and third person to ever make the jump. It was a twenty-three mile plunge from the edge of outer space. They'd be traveling at about seven hundred and sixty miles per hour. Might even break the sound barrier.

It was a wild and crazy jump.

They were looking death right in the eye.

The wind roared. The camera view flickered then went dead for several moments.

Had they made it? Would they live?

Suddenly, the camera flickered on.

The last thing viewers saw were two parachutes popping open about three thousand feet above Earth. They were black with big bold, white letters.

Hers said, "Just."

His said, "Married."

THE END

Dear Reader,

I hope you enjoyed my Calum's Curse Trilogy. The characters in this series kept me guessing. Amazing and unique, they certainly had their own tales to tell. If this book was your first introduction to the series, be sure to pick up Leathan and Devin's stories, *The Victorian Lure* (Calum's Curse: Ardetha Vampyre) and *The Georgian Embrace* (Calum's Curse: Acerbus Lycan). But I don't intend it to end here. Expect more exploits from The Worldwide Paranormal Society in the future.

Meanwhile, I recently re-released *Darkest Memory* (Forsaken Brethren Series- Book One). This series focuses on a family of vampires who break all the rules for love and become shunned by their fellow vampires.

Did you enjoy getting to know wizard Adlin in this book? Follow him through *The MacLomain Series* as head shaman to the medieval MacLomain clan. Then go back further in time to when he fell in love as a young man in *Highland Defiance*, a tale from (The MacLomain Series- Early Years) coming this autumn.

Best Regards Always,
Sky

ABOUT THE AUTHOR

Sky is the best-selling author of seven novels and several novellas. A New Englander born and bred, Sky was raised hearing stories of folklore, myth and legend. When combined with a love for nature, romance and time-travel, elements from the stories of her youth found release in her books. Readers have described her work as "Refreshing" and "Unforgettable."

Purington loves to hear from readers and can be contacted at Sky@SkyPurington.com. Interested in keeping up with Sky's latest news and releases? Visit Sky's Website, www.skypurington.com to download her free App on iTunes and Android.

Visit Sky at www.SkyPurington.com
Twitter @SkyPurington

Made in the USA
Lexington, KY
19 January 2013